*Your step.
by step guide
to changing the
world!*

Robi. x

SOUTHERN
CROSS

ROBIN RYDE

Situation Press
LONDON

Published by Situation Press
www.situationpress.com

Southern Cross, Robin Ryde
First edition, 2016

A CIP catalogue record for this book is available
from the British Library

ISBN 978-0-9930190-2-9

Typeset by Chandler Book Design

Printed and bound in the UK by
4edge Limited

Artwork/Cover Design by
Dominic Thackray

READ LOUD

Situation Press
LONDON

I'd like to give thanks to a small number of people that have helped to improve this book through their generous counsel, their provocations and merciless testing of the material. A very big thank you to Penny Rimbaud, Debbie Hantusch, Mark Nelson, Tom Howell, Marilyn Tyler, Jill Hume, Jude Smith, Greg Bull and Neil Barns.

Special thanks go to Dominic Thackray for his cover design, and to Lisa Sofianos as editor and believer.

Dedicated to Jackson and Frankie.

CONTENTS

1

The South China Sea

The water rises in the captain's cabin. It is here where a small handful of hopefuls are congregated. It is no safer here than anywhere else on the ship but the surroundings - the ornate wooden desk, the floating leather stool, and the bookcase, complete with Shakespeare's finest work, create a false sense of order and security. Surely the heavens would not destroy this oasis of refinement? The ship rears up. It is vertical. It seems impossible. Almost one thousand tonnes lifted clean in the air. The fickle body of water immediately changing its direction sucks everything with it. The congregation is scattered. All but three of the group are flushed out of the cabin. The ship has dispensed with them efficiently and without fuss. Ejected from the chamber. The ship slams back to a horizontal position. The three remaining passengers grab at each other, indicating, without a word, that the next time the ship moves that they will hold on to each other for dear life. It is a couple. A Chinese couple in their thirties wearing plain unadorned clothes. Paying passengers, travelling across the globe to London having spent the sum total of their savings for the pleasure of doing so. They are but half of their party - their children consumed by the first advance of the storm. And the child between them, a Western girl, no more than twelve years old. She is wearing a gown. Her waist is pinched with a dress that suggests unfeasibly wide hips. She has a pleated bodice. Her hair is knotted and curled. She is wearing square-toe slippers with elaborate lacing that trails up her ankles. She is dressed as if she expects to attend a dance.

The night passes and the storm subsides. The three unlikely survivors hold onto one another. Saving the child has become the only enduring ambition for the couple. Everything has been taken from them; their livelihood, their belongings, their own family. But not this. The child will survive. This is their solemn commitment. They lie face down on what is left of a deck beneath them inspecting the polished surface and the nails holding the deck together. The heads of the nails are smooth. And the wood, still perfect in places. Shiny. New looking. Ready to receive a thousand more footsteps, were it not for the smashed and serrated edges that mark its separation from the rest of the ship. This deck stands between them and death. Less than a foot thick, but enough to hold back the ocean's appetite.

Rather than sinking cleanly to the seabed, taking with it all of its contents, the clipper has instead been torn into pieces. The sea has slashed and mauled and part-devoured the vessel. Now sated the ravaging storm has returned to its sleep. Shards of wood ripped from the body of the ship, float on the surface of the water, absent-mindedly jabbing into one another. The ship's bell, complete with its mounting, has survived. It rocks from side-to-side, occasionally ringing out. A sad, half-hearted clang. A clang that is empty and without message. As the sun rises the extent of the desolation is revealed. From a distance it looks like tiny screwed up pieces of paper have been scattered across the sea. The Tea Clipper can no longer be thought of as a single entity. No longer an it. Instead a deconstructed ship. Flakes of wood catch the early morning light.

A part of the hull knocks into the couple and the frightened girl. The girl puts her hand out to nudge away what has drifted towards her. Under her fingers she feels the cold raised surface of some words. It is a nameplate. Bronze mounted on wood. It is the ship's name. The ship may not have lived on, but its name has. The *Southern Cross* – one of the fastest clippers of its time, having embarked on its maiden voyage. Bound for England. Now dissected, and transporting three unlikely survivors across the South China Sea.

The debris from the clipper rises and falls in smooth rhythmic movements. It is hard to imagine what had occurred the previous evening. Over a hundred and twenty people had perished in the storm. The captain, the crew, the passengers, the young girl's parents, the Chinese couple's children. No one left, other than the three survivors that cling together on their fragment of deck, their legs and arms entwined. They are like one being; a single mass of bodies. Inseparable. It has been a couple of hours since the waters have calmed. The sun is higher in the sky now and the temperature has been steadily inching up in degrees throughout the morning. It is a new day. Time forever pushing forwards. After the long night, the sense of relief that the three had initially felt is beginning to be substituted for something different - a creeping realisation. Having escaped one trial, they recognise that they face another – one that is unfolding in front of them. Drifting hundreds of miles from land they are lost. Without food. Without water. Without any means of drawing attention to their position. They squeeze and cuddle into one another. The father strokes his wife's brow while she in turn strokes the girl's. They are too exhausted and too shell-shocked to craft a plan for survival. And even if they could, it would be difficult to imagine what it might comprise.

Occasionally an item of clothing or a broken piece of furniture from the ship bobs past. This helps to sustain the group. They drag it towards them with a loose piece of wood to see if it might be useful. A dress provides extra protection from the sun. A ladies fan sails by at one point and although it is sodden, the young girl stretches it out on the deck to dry it. The mood changes when a bloated and disfigured body bumps against the accidental raft. The body hangs around well beyond its welcome and the father gently pushes it away with his foot. Sometimes it is not so easy and it takes a few shoves to uncouple a body from their makeshift raft. The women turn their eyes away until it is gone. A far too real sign of what the future may hold for them.

The wreckage has started to thin out and the visits from random objects reduce in frequency. This lowers the spirit of the group. They miss the company it offers. Although the clipper had been torn apart and it no longer resembled a ship, they find it comforting to know that they aren't alone in this vast space.

It has been a while since their last visitation from the sea. And so it takes them by surprise when a solid object knocks into the floating deck. A confident thud, announcing its arrival. The three slowly lift their heads to see what the noise has brought. It is another body, this time stretched out on top of a small piece of broken mast and sail. It is the body of a tall man who is lying face down. His rounded spectacles have lost their shape but remain fixed to his face. The mother and the girl return to their nest leaving the husband to deal with the body. As he leans back to kick the wooden mast, his state of exhaustion causes him to overshoot and he narrowly misses hurling himself into the water. He regains his balance and has another go. Again, he misjudges the movement and this time kicks the man straight to the bridge of his nose. It produces a crack of cartilage. He shrieks and leaps back. The person lying face down that they assumed was dead, let out a muffled yelp as the foot strikes his face. He is alive. He'd survived the storm and had been unconscious for what must have been hours. The violent, sharp stab to his face had brought him around. The father drags the man's body onto the larger piece of floating raft, where he is greeted by cracked smiles from the two women and a confusing combination of apologies and embraces from the father. Three people facing certain death, have now become four, and although no other circumstances have changed, there is a rebirth of optimism.

The new passenger is named Hjarand and as he clutches his nose the four of them piece together sentences using Mandarin, the Queen's English and a Scandinavian accented English. It is a conversational mess but seemingly no less enjoyable for it. They each try to explain, for the first time, who they are and what they were doing on the ship.

The girl, named Victoria, is the daughter of the Ship's captain, a moderately wealthy and respected seaman. He had sailed numerous clipper ships across the trade routes between China and Europe, as well as to America. In fact, he had gained a limited degree of fame from his successes in the Great Tea Clipper races of the time. This, the Southern Cross, was due to be his final voyage taking his family back home. Victoria was returning to England, having lived with her family in Shantou in Southern China for almost three years. She had been brought up within a tiny, close-knit European community, rarely coming into contact with the locals, and for Victoria mainly in the company of other women. She had however picked up a little Mandarin during her time there, which oiled the conversation on the raft.

The Chinese couple were named Yo Yo (the husband) and Pandi (the wife). They were not wealthy by any stretch of the imagination, rather they afforded their expensive passage to London through disciplined saving from the day of the marriage some seven years ago. Both Yo Yo and Pandi were school teachers with a fascination with England and the life it seemed to offer. It wasn't that they imagined a better life, or one of greater wealth or security, after all England was no richer than China, but they believed in seeing the world, and in educating their children beyond books. Yo Yo and Pandi's explanations came to an abrupt end as they mentioned their children. The silence was painful and so Hjarand stepped in.

Hjarand was born in Oslo, and was in his late twenties. It was clear that he had travelled. There was something worldly about him. He explained that he was an academic, involved in the study of human behaviour. He was on board at the invitation of the Captain. This is what he said. Victoria looked a little puzzled as she wasn't aware of any such invitation on the part of her father. Her father had always spoken to her as if she was much older than her years, and this is the kind of thing he would have mentioned. Hjarand had a confident way about him, so she let it pass for the time being. The initial burst of conversation died down as a cool and welcome breeze bathed the group. They closed their eyes drinking in the air. In the distance a clang could be heard. The ship's bell, perhaps now a mile or so away, too had been revived by the wind. After a short reprieve the blazing heat returned offering a reminder of their predicament.

2

Circular Quay

If my hair feels like it's getting too long it affects my mood. I start to feel depressed. But when it is cut, as soon as I cut it, my mood is lifted. I feel lighter. I feel abler to think clearly. It's like a reverse Samson. Y'know, the story about the strength of Samson residing in his long curly hair. Well it's the opposite for me.

I travel a lot on planes and for some reason I find it hard to read on planes, so I watch films. And lots of them. On a flight from London to Sydney I might watch six films in a row. The combined experience of watching so many films and being trapped in a metal tube for twenty-four hours makes me very emotional. I wipe the tears from my eyes at thirty-seven thousand feet, and laugh out loud. I must look very strange. I find the whole experience very surreal. They bring you boiling hot white towels. They encourage you to buy expensive things from a magazine. Window shutters have to be opened, then they have to be closed. Safety briefings always assume a crash into the sea, even though most of the flight is above land. The Cabin Crew simultaneously treat you like you are royalty and like you are a source of great annoyance. They smile. And grimace. And mother you. And ignore you. The system has to be restarted. This seat doesn't recline. My knives are blunt. We're in a holding pattern. Can you break wind under this blanket? Would you like a chocolate? Oh, it's dark chocolate, no thanks. Oh shit turbulence! Seat belt signs on. Fuck! Did you feel that drop? Oh fuck. My teeth are clenched. My stomach is twisted. My drink's going to be all over my lap in a second. I want a pee. I'm not allowed to pee. I really want to pee.

It's okay now, the seat belt signs have been extinguished. I'm walking to the toilet in my socks. They've become stretched and droopy at the end. I have feet like an Oompa Loompa. Back in my seat again. Feeling sleepy. My eyes become hot and heavy. Then all of a sudden someone's shaking my hand. His name is Russell. He has a tie and a tie clip and a winged badge. With wings on it. He's like the Captain but he's not. He's pretending. He's got nothing to say to me but we're still talking. "Yes, London. Yes, from the UK. Sadly, for business. Yes, I'll try and get some time to travel" (I won't). Neither of us want this conversation. He smiles. I smile. We smile. He's gone as I try to recline my chair. It's stuck. I think there's a fork stuck down the side. It's not happening. I'm switching to the music channel. It's shit. Its adult orientated rock. Soft rock. It's so mediocre it hurts. It really does upset me. Best not start crying again.

My grandfather was a coal miner. He was brilliant at the game of Draughts. He drank hot tea out of a clear glass cup. He was called Arthur. My grandmother was

*called Ada. Arthur and Ada. She worked in a factory in the
Midlands and had a broad Mansfield accent. I would visit
them with my parents every other weekend. Once we were
hosting a French student as part of a school exchange. He
was called Pascal. That was his French name. Ada greeted
him by prowling around him like a panther until she said
"Are you alreet mi duck?" He said nothing. "Gerin back
kitchen and al get you some tea. We've got a nice bit of
am". Jambon!*

I'm standing in a hotel reception. I smell of plane.
Almost a day sitting in the same seat alternating between
being too hot and too cold, and I stink of plane. It's not
quite time to check into the room. It could be a couple
of hours. I'm grumpy. The queue is really long. I can
smell myself. Wifi had better be free. They screw you
these bastards. They do. There are a series of Pandas
behind reception that are in some way an emblem for the
hotel. It's not clear why. Some are naked and some are
dressed in waistcoats and shorts. Some have hats. Some
have a badge with the name of the hotel on. Someone must
buy this shit. Kids. Probably kids hassling their parents.

I'm in my room now; they let me through after all. I
decide whether it feels right. I always do this. It's a question
I pose to myself. It does feel alright. The TV is fuck-off
big. There is mini bar. There is shower. There is in-room
dining. Something is written about towels and ecology
on a pyramid shaped card. Something about vanity kits.
There is thin plastic dry cleaning bag. I'm on my back. My
shoes are off exposing my swollen ankles. I'm in a better
mood now. The window looks out onto a badly composed
landscape. It's a 'city view'. In inverted comments. But
it's also a back of buildings view. A frowning external air

con system frames one corner of the view. Half a balcony pokes into the frame. I watch TV and fall asleep.

At school, teachers make it up. All of it. The rules, the lessons, the discipline, the whole shooting match. To a child it is utterly ridiculous, isn't it? Why poetry? Why glaciers? Why Bunsen burners? Why French? Why Abyssinia? Why Bromide? Why ropes? Why Kill Mocking Birds? Why the Guiro? Why? And it's the presumption that taking away your time, so much of your time, every day, is ok. The bare-faced cheek of it all. School children should form Unions and get radical.

Meetings. I have a lot of these to do. They're like timed conversations. All of them taking sixty minutes. The routine goes like this:

1. Pull up my agenda for the visit.

2. Go on the internet to learn about who I'm talking to.

3. Map where they are in relation to me.

4. Find them.

5. Meet them.

6. And leave. All smiles and promises.

Like checking in to a hotel, or a flight, this also involves visiting a reception and explaining who I am. "Robin Mann. Yes, M A N N. Yes, I might need a pass but we might just go out for coffee." 'Going out for coffee' is the language of semiotics. If I said "going out for cake" or "going out for lemon and lime bitters" that would arouse suspicion. Why would a grown man want to announce having cake and lemon and lime bitters at nine thirty in

the morning? Going out for coffee is acceptable code for
all of the above without having to say any of the above
and sounding like you are on the road to diabetes. The
person I meet has a name that has two words. I don't pay
attention to names usually. It's only out of a vague sense
of professionalism that I look like I'm interested in the
words that make up their name. We go out and I return
the pass that the receptionist has just given me. Everyone
smiles. This apparently is mildly amusing.

"Can I get you a coffee?" he kindly asks. I ask if I could
have a slice of cake and lemon and lime bitters? But I don't
just say it like that, I'm not an imbecile. I say, something
like "I know this is going to sound strange but because of
the jet lag I really feel like a slice of cake and some lemon
and lime bitters, would that be okay?" And that makes it
okay. He says "Yes, of course that's okay" and smiles. It's
hard work isn't it, trying to render things as normal? A
Sociologist called Harvey Sacks once wrote about this.
Doing being ordinary he called it, and that's what it is.

We talk about work. Every conversation has its own
mood and pace. Like all conversations it is all constructed
in the moment. It isn't easy however. There is so much
going on. There are the pleasantries and the process of
just saying agreeable things; at least initially. Then there's
the 'this is what I do' stuff which always seems to start
too far down the track. In this case I've already heard
three acronyms I don't understand while I'm writing the
date at the top of the page in my notebook. Then as he's
speaking, a woman arrives at the coffee shop dragging a
large suitcase behind her. This makes a lot of noise and
seems incongruous. My attention returns to the man
talking and I start writing his name at the head of the page

but forget how to spell his surname. So I just write his first name. I don't feel too bad though for not remembering who he is as I notice that he has a pad too and he has my name at the top and he's spelt my first name incorrectly, as Robyn. With a y. In Australia, most people spell my name wrong. It's only got five letters and there are well known figures like Robin Hood who have their name spelt like mine. It shouldn't be that hard to get it right. But it clearly is.

The conversation ends at 10:25. We've both had enough. We're both experienced meeting attenders. This is just another meeting. I'd rather be SCUBA diving and he'd rather be errr...actually I've got no idea. I've met this man for an hour and I don't have the faintest idea what he really cares about. I might never see him again and all I will remember is that he spelt my name wrong and I ate cake. He'll probably remember that I couldn't spell his second name and I seemed distracted. He gives me his business card. I don't carry mine these days so I say I'll send a line across by email. We squeeze each other's hands and he's off.

From the outside it looks like people have it all sorted out. People seem to know what they're doing, what matters, and where they're headed. I haven't got the slightest idea. Not a clue. It's as incomprehensible to me now as it was twenty years ago. And I've only lived this life once. This is my very first time. And I'm pretty sure this is my last too. And so I'm not going to pretend it's all perfectly normal. It's not. It's all very strange.

The sun is going down on day one. The chatter of the day slips away leaving a kind of calm. No one has claims on my time now. I can do anything I want. A walk in

the night air might help with the jet lag. I'm alone in a
city of four million people. No one knows me or cares
about me. This is a privilege. I walk towards the quay.
There are some homeless people sitting on the ground. I
walk past. I want to sit down and talk with them. Some
have small nap sacks. One has a dog with him. There is a
woman with a faraway look on her face. I slow down my
pace so that I can give one young lad twenty bucks. He
is very pleased. I am pleased. I ask him what his name
is. He says Robin. "Robin with a y?" I say. He says "No,
with an 'i'." I chuckle to myself. I don't tell him my name
as that would make things weird.   I say something like
have a nice evening. This sounds dumb. I make it sound
like he's about to go for dinner with the family. His skin is
pale and bleached in places. He doesn't look well. Maybe
that doesn't matter though for the moment. He is happier
than he was a few minutes ago. I walk on.

It's three am and I'm back in my hotel. And I'm wide
awake. I can't sleep. In fact, I feel like I need to run. Jet
lag doing its thing. I close my eyes. They ping open like
a roller blind. I walk around the room. My legs move
quickly. They have a mission it seems. I put my contact
lenses in. And I get dressed. I don't know why. I find
myself brushing my teeth. I wash my face and pull out my
hair to make a shape I like. The hotel is deathly quiet. Not
even the usual trolleys being wheeled outside the room, or
the lifts making their ting noise. I peek through the heavy
curtains. It's black outside. There are no cars moving. I
can't quite see the quay from my window but I can guess
where it is. Without seeming to have any influence over
my own thoughts, I decide to go out for a walk. A night
walk. Or is it a morning walk?

I leave the front of the hotel while the security guard is sleeping with his head on the desk. I cross the road diagonally. No pedestrian crossing needed. No cars anywhere to be seen. I feel lighter. Less weighed down by the obligations that the city imposes on me by day. The shop fronts are mostly dark, with the occasional neon sign switched on. Capitalism has gone to sleep. I would have to walk a long way to find a store that could sell me something right now. I have beaten the Capitalist system just by waking up while it slept. The light has changed since I peeked from my hotel window. It is still black but it now has a glow; the promise of morning. I feel excited. I am a foreigner here and yet the city is mine now. I feel horny too. How strange.

The water at the quay is simply beautiful. The boats are sleeping and as they do so they rise and fall gently as the sea breathes in and out. The surface of the water reminds me of copper that has been beaten with a soft headed hammer. Tiny reflective indentations appear on the surface. The sea is stippled. The morning sun, still not fully with us, has started to offer a hint of its presence. I do something that is a little bit weird. No one can see me so I figure that it's okay to lie on the floor on my back. I want to touch all of the ground. I shut my eyes for a second. I breathe out and hear my breath escaping. I feel like the world and I are close now; like longstanding friends. We know each other. During the day the world is taken over. It is used by everyone. The mining companies dig into it and remove minerals. The corporates erect giant buildings on its surface. The advertisers bellow brand names from billboards and hoardings. Millions of people pound their feet on its surface as they are pulled to work each morning. I don't feel close to this world. I walk the length of the quay. A few distant noises rise then fall away. The light has shifted once again. Now it is silvery, creating a kind of hyper reality. The normally dull plains of the cityscape are lifted and made dynamic. Still and moving. Resolutely in motion.

On the way back to the hotel I walk past the same row of homeless people that I saw earlier in the day. Robin with an 'i' is not there. His rug is still there, but he isn't. I wonder where he has gone. I search for options in my head but there is nothing there. I have no idea. Where would I even begin in working this out? The lady that I noticed before is sitting in a semi-upright position with her eyes half closed. The angle of her body and her clear interest in me makes it seem like she's awaiting my return. She squints her eyes at me sizing up my intentions. We both look at each other quizzically. A Mexican standoff occurs in the gloaming, only the haunting sound of a guitar is missing. It continues. "What are you looking at?" She speaks, but her lips don't seem to move. I'm confused. I look confused. She shuffles and tilts her body toward the pillar next to her. "What are you looking at sunshine?" It happens again. Her lips remain shut. My heart stutters a little and then starts to speed up. I feel locked in her gaze. I say something that sounds very Hugh Grant – "I'm sorry, did you just say something?" Then there is silence. The lady shuts her eyes as if our psychic conversation has ended. I have been dismissed. I turn around to see if anyone has witnessed this event. There is no one there. At least no one that is awake.

I remain standing with stillness all around me. My feet are buzzing from the walk. My eyes starting to feel hot again. I look to where Robin with an 'i' was and his space remains empty. I think for a moment. I look down at my clothes. I look back at Robin's space. My brain is thinking, making a decision. I take a step forward towards the rug. I check if the world has changed with my movement. Does it have a view on what I'm about to do? It remains silent. I lean forward and pause. My eyes search around. My ears are on duty. Then, placing first my hands on the rug and swiveling my bum, my body comes to rest on the rug, Robin's rug. My back is pressed against the wall. I am three or so metres from the now sleeping lady. I am part of the row of rough sleepers. I look out onto the city from my piece of pavement. I have no idea why I have just done this but it seems right. I close my eyes and drift into sleep.

3

ACAB

First the sun wakes me, and then a boot to the foot. "Move it friend," the policeman says in a bored voice. "On your feet. Shift yourself. Come on!" I blink to see the silhouetted shape of the officer. There is no one else left in the row of rough sleepers. I am a row of one. A full stop. I screw up my rug in my hand and try to stand. My legs have been crunched up for the last few hours and as I get up I fall as if in slow motion back against the wall. "Come on you drunken bastard." The policeman is sounding less bored now and more irritated. I must look a little odd sleeping rough while wearing four hundred dollar jeans. They don't seem to notice. I haven't been particularly slow in returning to a standing position but out of the blue the policeman kicks me right in the back. A firm, skilled, jarring boot to the spine. A yelp comes from my mouth, "for fuck's sake!" follows immediately. I'm expecting another blow to the body but it doesn't come. The police are walking away. I am doubled over. This is the briefest form of harassment I can imagine.

With my rug in hand I brace myself against the wall and pull my body upright. Like a boat leaving the harbour I push away from the wall and start walking. Away from the pavement and back to my hotel. My clockwork limbs loosen up as I pass the shops that are starting to open. I reach my hotel and nonchalantly breeze through the automatic glass doors. I reach into my pocket and wave my card key purposefully. Anyone watching me would know I'm just a regular guest. A regular rough sleeping guest. With a rug. Smelling this time not of plane but of the streets.

Into the room. Into the shower. Onto the bed. TV on. Fuck, its *Top Gear* or the News. Hobson's Choice. Later on today I have some more meetings. I think about these briefly and then, curled up on top of the bed, I slip again into sleep.

"What's the name sir?" The smart woman at reception asks. "MANN, Robin Mann." I sign in the book. My pass number is 042. I'm asked in the register which company I'm from. I write *ABZ*. This isn't the name of my company but I don't feel like telling the truth. You could say I am somewhat disengaged from my work and from the rigmarole that accompanies it. "If you could just wait here sir". I wait here. There are three banks of lifts. And four lifts in each bank. After a few minutes the smart woman asks me to go to the reception on floor twenty-two. I find the correct bank of lifts and I am greeted by a display. I have to enter my floor on the display and then it tells me which lift to get. I don't like this. I feel managed. I am told to go to lift D. It arrives. I get in and as a reflex I look to find the button to push inside the lift. There aren't any. They aren't needed. This decision has already been made and the lift knows about it.

I go to the reception on the twenty second floor and I'm asked by a smartly dressed woman for my name. "MANN, Robin Mann," I say. I'm asked to fill in the visitor book. I write that my company is called *Kafka Ltd*. That isn't true either, but it keeps me amused. I'm not given a pass this time. I'm asked to wait. The person I'm meeting will be with me shortly. I sit down on an uncomfortable but stylish sofa. "Do you want a drink?" I'm asked. "No thanks." Other people arrive at the reception and do the same as I did. I bet their meetings are sixty minutes long too.

After a short while, a different smartly dressed lady comes up to me and introduces herself. I assume she is an Executive Assistant to the person I'm meeting. I shake her hand, smile and instantly forget her name. We walk out of the reception towards the bank of lifts. We're on the move again. "How are things? Busy?" I say. "It's mayhem at the moment" she replies. I nod knowingly and wait for an explanation. She says something about year-end. Or it could be we're near the end. We arrive on floor twenty-five and after leaving the lift I am shown into a room. It's bland and corporate as fuck. I've been in scores of rooms practically identical to this. "Would you like a drink?" I'm asked. I shake my head "We'll be just a minute. Please take a seat." I take a seat. I'm spoilt for choice. There are twelve in here. I take a pad and pen out of my bag. Through the door walks my rendezvous. His name is Bob. He smiles a lot. I smile back. He's a nice man. I can tell. He asks me if I'd like a drink. Despite my two prior refusals, he does it so nicely I say "Yes, a coffee please, milk, no sugar." He calls after his EA. She hears his request and disappears along the corridor. We talk. I drink the coffee when it arrives. We finish talking on the hour.

We shake hands and part ways. He gives me his card. I thank him and say I'll send him an email to make the connection. I leave the building.

I have three more meetings that day. Each one like the last. At five pm I leave the last office block and head for the hotel. I'm tired. I get into my room. It is clean. The maid has folded my pants and placed them on the bed - like a cat that's caught a mouse and leaves it on their owner's chair as an offering. The toilet paper in the bathroom has been shaped into a point. The air con is fiercely refreshing the room. The sun shines through the blinds creating a beautifully lit square on my bed. I change into some jeans and a T-shirt. I double lock the door and do a kind of *Fosbury Flop* onto the bed. I'm safe now. No one can touch me. The TV drones away in the background as I struggle to keep my eyes open. A blissful feeling comes over me. I surrender and disappear into sleep.

My sleep brings a dream. I have cobbled together characters from the TV to populate my dream. Ross from Friends is wearing a basque and I am talking to him like an old friend. We're on a boat together and the motion of the boat is causing Ross to fall backwards and forwards. He is wearing high heels and as the boat moves he clatters around like a baby calf. I am finding the conversation boring and I tell him. He fades away and next I am on the shore and I hear Spanish guitars being played. There is a reception in front of me but the lady behind it isn't smart. She is dressed scruffily. She asks me for my name but her lips don't move. She scares me. Her look is vacant. She shouts at me. Her lips remain shut. I wake up. I am disorientated. It takes me a few seconds to remember where I am. The memory of the homeless woman is still with me.

It's ten pm and I am ravenous with hunger. I call down to In-room dining. I'm now on the nighttime menu. It's a limited range. It's a rubbish range. I'm too hungry to argue. I order Tomato Pasta and garlic bread. The thought of it depresses me. Twenty minutes later there is a knock at the door. And when I open it there is a pretty young woman in a waistcoat standing there. She has a trolley and a wooden tray on top. My food is hidden underneath a metal dome. "Would you like it on the table?" "Yes, over there." I point. She looks nervous at being in my room. She puts the tray down. I sign a piece of paper. There is a five dollars' tray charge. What she is doing now costs me five dollars. I don't even get to keep the tray. She smiles before almost breaking into a run to exit the room. I shovel the food into my face. No one is watching. My dream lingers in my mind like the steam from my pasta. I re-cover the now empty plate with the silver dome. I relax into the chair and slowly slump down into it. My eyelashes become heavy. My eyes sore. I see in colour and then nothing.

It's three am and my internal alarm rings. Fuck it! I'm wide awake. The transition from sleep to wakefulness has arrived abruptly and without compromise. Without thinking I brush my teeth and get dressed. My legs are fizzing with energy. They've got to move. I know what I'm going to do. There is a part of last night's experience that remains unresolved. I pick up Robin with an 'i's rug from the back of the chair and head out of the hotel past the sleeping security guard. Once again walking in the city at this time of the morning is a joy. For a while I walk down the middle of the road, just because I can. I spring into the air to hear the muffled noise as my feet hit the ground. My eyes scan the scene. A coffee shop. Dry Cleaners. Phone Repair shop. Tourist shop. Jewelry shop. 7-11. Grocery store. Travel Agents. Department store. Tobacco store. Mobile Phone store. Massage Parlour. Cafe. Every one of them black and asleep. Not open for business. I hear some noises. Cars. In the distance. I pass a line of taxis. One has its light on but there is no one in the driver's seat. I can see the keys in the ignition. I drape my hand across the door handle, like I'm touching the surface of the water; just to see what it feels like. I continue on my journey.

I'm nearing the quay. I can faintly hear the water lapping against the underside of the boats. I turn ninety degrees and make my way towards the site where I first saw the rough sleepers. I can just make out a few bodies on the ground. I find myself arranging the rug around my shoulders and slowing down the pace. Now I'm ambling towards the undulating bodyscape. I count four shapes. All are still. There is a body that is slightly more erect than the others. It is shored up by a pillar. It looks like the woman I saw yesterday. Her eyes are closed. There is an empty space next to her on the other side of the pillar. It's about to happen again. I feel nervous. I softly step next to the pillar, my feet making no sound, and I sink to the ground making a final flump noise as I come to rest. I'm here again. Home from home. I look out from the pavement to the city. I'm in the picture and looking out of the picture.

Without moving my head, my eyes glance to my left, giving a suspicious quality to my enquiry. I verify that it is the same woman. I hear myself speaking. "Are you awake?" I'm reminded of when I used to sleep in the same room as my two brothers. We would whisper into the dark.

"Are you awake? Are you awake?" "Of course I'm awake." Comes the reply. Her accent is less Australian than I expect, more British if anything. I didn't get the chance to see if her lips moved. I twist my body and look directly at her. Her face is pretty, and more delicate than I remembered. She reaches into a small grey woolen purse the size of a mouse. She fishes out half a roll up and places it in her lips. With the other hand she flicks a lighter and the cigarette glows. All in one smooth motion. Exhaled smoke billows in my direction.

"What's your name?" I hear myself say with a slight crackle in my voice. "Depends." She says calmly and with a smile. "What are you after?" I'm transfixed by her mouth. Checking that all the words line up with the movement of her lips. They do. Nothing to see here. I haven't answered her question. I wonder why I am here. I start to question my own motives. My attention drifts back to the woman. She looks strange. Something doesn't quite add up about her. Hard to put my finger on what it is. The more I look the less she seems like someone that would be a rough sleeper. She has a natural confidence and lightness about her. Her eyes look bright and her posture is straight in the way that a ballet dancer's might be. Then I hear the words "Are you looking for someone?" And it happens again. She does it again. What I've been waiting for. I hear what she is saying, but her lips are motionless. This seems even more absurd now that I am concentrating on it. I feel disassociated and a little too tired to craft a cunning way to say what's on my mind, so I say exactly what occurs to me, "Why don't your lips move when you talk? Are you sure you're feeling alright?" She shoots back with a smile. Lips in sync this time. I wonder if this is the jet lag playing tricks on me. It seems the most likely explanation. She grips my hand. It is cool and smooth. My instinct is to pull it back. I don't like being touched by people at the best of times, particularly in more recent years, but I let it stay in her grip. "Perhaps I can help you." She says looking directly in my eyes and raising me to my feet, the palms of her hands now under my elbows. I clutch my rug, my comfort blanket, and I'm led away from the quay. "Victoria" she says. "Victoria. That's my name."

I always wanted a motorbike. I can't tell you how much I wanted a motorbike. It was like an addiction, a desperate need to own one. I was fourteen at the time. The thought of it filled me with such excitement. I didn't know how to ride one. I'd had a go on a friend's moped once; one without manual gears; a twist and go. It wasn't the same though. I'd never actually ridden a motorbike. I'm not even sure if I knew what it was that I wanted but it was such a powerful desire. To this day, some thirty years later, I can still find that feeling, that place of yearning, within me. I can transport myself instantly back thirty years just by summoning this memory.

We are walking, or more like Victoria is skipping, up the road and I am being pulled along with her. It is still the early hours of the morning and edging towards that silvery light. I have no idea what I'm doing. This is the one thing about which I am clear. Victoria is no longer holding my hand but we are walking together like we are friends. She is leading and I am following. We head up in the direction of my hotel. "Where are we going?" I ask? "Don't worry, I'll explain everything shortly" she says. "Do you have a car?" I am confused. "Why would I have a car?" I say. Surely she can hear that I'm English and I couldn't look more like someone that doesn't live here. "A lot of people do she says." "I don't live here" I say with a hint of irritation in my voice. "I know. But you can get a car right?" she replies immediately. "Why do we need a car?" I reply. Victoria ignores my question. "Can you get one though?" My mind goes back to the driverless taxi I passed on the way down, the one with the lights on. I turn to Victoria to speak. Her eyes dart across my face. "Well, let's go then" she directs. It must be the heat, or the time of the morning, or something, but I comply, now leading as Victoria follows. We pass the darkened shops. The sounds from our footsteps echo off the buildings. The warmth of the night keeps our pace in check. We turn a corner and I start to wonder whether any of this makes any sense. I have meetings in the morning. I have a report to complete by Friday. I have two Skype calls to the UK tomorrow evening. And I am wandering around in the early hours of the morning with a homeless person contemplating stealing a car. It feels unreal. Dreamlike. But the situation, Victoria, the otherworldliness of the situation, speaks to a corner of my psyche, a place that aches for life and excitement. A part of me long since decommissioned.

I approach the parked taxi from the driver's side, using the wing mirrors to see if the driver is there. The seat still looks empty. My heart beats a little faster as I step alongside the car and stand next to the driver's door, peering inside. The window is down and I can clearly see the keys in the ignition. I can see a pendant of the Hindu deity Ganesh hanging from the rear view mirror. The gear stick has an orchid cast in glass at the end of it. I like this. The back of the driver's seat has hundreds of tiny wooden beads covering it. I've always wondered if these were more comfortable than a regular seat. There is a lot of electronic payment equipment in the foot well. A Credit Card machine. A Cabcharge machine. A radio handset. How does this person even fit in there? I muse to myself. I am becoming distracted. My subconscious is leading me away from my next move.

Before I have even considered my next source of prevarication Victoria has slid into the passenger seat. I whisper loudly. "What the fuck?" She whispers in return like she is joining me in a whispering game "Get in and drive." Clear and simple. "Get in and drive." She says. I pull on the handle of the door. No one is around to hear this. I am in the seat. My whole body is charged with energy. I'm about to steal this car. Is this the excitement I've been looking for? I can't afford to turn the key and for it to stall or for a car alarm to go off so I check the equipment in front of me. Steering wheel. Gear stick. Dashboard. Pedals. Handbrake. Indicator paddle. I am orientated. It slowly dawns on me that this is the same make as my car at home. It's a Lexus. I recognise the radio. The positions of the instruments all seem familiar. This has suddenly become a lot easier. My fear levels have returned to below critical levels. I pause for a second to gather my thoughts and then I twist the key. The engine fires up, a positive comforting sound of strength. Victoria yelps. She's excited. Seamlessly I depress the clutch, slip the gear stick into first, push the gas pedal and we're off. I look in the rear view mirror as we swing into the road. No one is disturbed. No one follows. We're on the move. I'm stealing a taxi. What the fuck am I doing? Victoria takes her shoes off and puts a filthy pair of feet on the console on front of the passenger street. She smiles at me proudly. I feel like I am lucid dreaming.

She directs me towards the tunnel that stretches under the water. She does it with such certainty and self-assuredness that I do what she asks without question. For the first time since I left the hotel I see other moving vehicles and I sense some discomfort within me. The world had been placed on hold and I'd been briefly liberated from the mania of the day, but the more movement and life I see around me the more real the situation is becoming. Then, Victoria starts to speak at length. This is the most I have ever heard her speak since we met and the contents of what she has to say leaves me dumbstruck.

"Robin, I want you to listen to what I'm about to say."

This is how it starts. Like she is addressing an audience. I wonder if she has done this before.

"What I'm about to tell you will sound ridiculous. You will find it hard to believe, but I want you to listen to me. To hear all that I have to say before you make any conclusions."

I remain silent. I think she wants me to agree to the terms of the conversation, that I have to wait and perhaps suspend disbelief until she gets to the punchline. Having already stolen a car for her I don't feel inclined to do anything of the sort. My silence indicates that I will choose to believe whatever I want to and when I want to. I always find that talking tough is easier when you do it in your head.

"First of all, I'm not from the streets. It's true that for a long while now I have moved from place to place and slept here and there, but I am not a homeless person. Not in the sense you understand it."

Unaware that I'm doing it, and undoing all my good intentions, I notice that I am nodding in agreement. Victoria points at the road indicating a turn to the right. I follow her instructions.

"The truth is that I have a gift, a gift of sorts." Victoria hesitates. I feel her eyes on me.

"I want to show you something. For you to see what I mean."

Victoria has said enough to set a few alarm bells ringing. My instinct is that she has some mental health issues. Even in my somewhat addled, jetlagged, state of mind, I can discern that much. There is probably a name for what she has - some kind of delusion. Perhaps this is a psychotic episode. I am starting to regret being so easily led and so keen to reconnect to a part of myself that had been lost for years. The problem is that I am now stuck in a car with someone that needs help and may even be dangerous. "What a mess!" I think to myself.

I start my response.

"Victoria. I'm going to be straight with you. I think this is a bad idea. I really do. I can tell that you mean well, and I'm sure you're a great person." I feel like I'm reading from a how-to-disarm-a-psychopath book. "But, I honestly think we should be getting back now." I accompany my words with an earnest look and a conciliatory nod of the head.

I continue driving and await a response. She indicates with her hand that I should turn left towards the tunnel. I feel tense. I don't want to be trapped underground with her. Underground and underwater. This would be a bad plan. To buy time and to keep things calm I do as she says and turn left towards the incline that leads to the tunnel.

"I know what you're thinking Robin. I honestly do. I'm not crazy. But think about it. Just for a second. What is there to lose? Your meetings tomorrow aren't going anywhere. Your nice hotel room with your giant TV isn't going to disappear. Your deadlines will still need to be completed. Your flight back to the UK at the end of the month will still be waiting for you"

How did she know about my room? About my work? I suppose she could have guessed that I might be staying in a hotel. And one with a big TV. Nothing too mysterious about that. I suppose.

I keep silent waiting to hear what she'll say next.

"You don't think our meeting was coincidence do you? Don't you think it's just a little bit strange that you, a businessman, of sorts, with a perfectly nice place to stay, decided to leave your hotel at three O' Clock in the morning to sleep on the streets. Next to me. And twice?" She had a point. I wasn't coming out of this looking very good. It didn't scan well. Perhaps I am the one having an episode?

We enter the tunnel and pass what look like some enormous jet engines that feed air along the tunnel. It reminds me of my flight over. The clean, white, hot towels smelling of lemon. I look at Victoria's dirty feet on the dash. I look at the dirty rug that I stole from the other Robin. With an 'i'. Yesterday's meeting with Bob enters my mind.

"Pull over. Here. Past those cones. There. Now!" She commands.

I wouldn't have seen it if it hadn't been pointed out but there is a kind of layby in the tunnel. It makes sense really, I suppose. Cars break down in tunnels sometimes and need to go somewhere without bringing the entire tunnel to a standstill. It's just that I didn't expect it. Not least because it leads behind a wall. It's properly hidden out of view. I abruptly turn into the hidden layby and the car stops with a jolt.

"We need to walk from here," Victoria says.

I'm still planning on getting out of this situation I just haven't worked out how yet. I wonder whether this might be a sting of some sort where I get mugged or worse by some of Victoria's accomplices. But it strikes me as a rather elaborate way to rob someone.

The car door groans as Victoria starts to push it open. Her feet swing round in unison and with her hands pressed against the side of the passenger seat she rises gracefully out of the car. I am unable to move. My body remains locked in place in the driver's seat. I see Victoria through the windscreen striding slowly but confidently forward. My eyes fall on her arse. Her hips swing left and right. I find myself for the first time thinking of her in a sexual way. I surprise myself a little not least because this was the last thing I thought would be on my mind. She stops, her back still toward me. I struggle to organise my thoughts. To put them in order. I'm not sure if it is because I feel an attraction to Victoria or because I've decided that there is no real threat, but I find myself pulling the door lever and sliding out of the car. Our shoulders touch as I stand beside her.

When I was twelve years old I went to the Isle of Wight with my school. The Isle of Wight, a small Island off the south coast of England, is the perfect place for a school trip. It is like a nursery itself. It has places where there are giant plastic dinosaurs. And caravan sites.

And pirate-based amusement parks. And petting zoos. And record fairs. I first went there over thirty years ago and I can remember aspects of it like it happened yesterday. I remember the layout of the bedrooms. The two bunk beds in my room and my three friends who were there with me. I remember the multi-coloured sands. The cable car ride. The gaudy seat covers of the school coach. My history teacher wearing corduroy trousers.

I remember receiving a letter from my parents. It was something the school had pre-arranged with the parents so the children didn't feel lonely or something. It was a strangely formal letter addressed to Master Robin Mann. It started with Dear Robin, not 'Hi' or 'Hello" but 'Dear Robin'. It had been hand written which of course at the time was pretty much the only way that letters were written. My parents had bought a new car. It was an Austin Princess in russet brown. I knew what brown was but had no idea what russet brown was. I wasn't aware you could get varieties of brown apart from dark and light. They had enclosed a picture of it clipped from a magazine. A lot of effort had gone into this briefing. It looked like a brown triangular wedge of cheese with wheels. It was undoubtedly a pleasant enough car but I couldn't muster the excitement that my parents clearly shared. "I've got a new car," I said to my friend John. He looked at the clipping and replied "Its brown". "Russet brown" I said. He looked confused. I didn't blame him.

On the final night of the school trip they held a dance. Everyone was quite excited about this, even the teachers. The boys got very sweaty, occasionally dancing, but mainly due to running around the hall from group to group. The girls seemed to know what they were doing. They knew how to dance. A particular song would come on and the girls would scream and swarm the floor. They would point and sing and twirl and dart from side-to-side. The boys would look on. As the last song was played the sense of the party coming to an end descended on us all. Back in our bedroom we giggled until we were told to keep the noise down.

The tunnel smells damp. The temperature has dropped to that of London on an autumn morning. While I haven't been drunk at any point since my arrival in Sydney, I feel like I am starting to sober up. Victoria is walking a few yards in front of me. I hear my feet scrape to a halt beneath me. Victoria mirrors me and freezes. Her back is straight. She appears to be taller since our first encounter. The invisible rope that has tethered us is under strain. She waits silently and I stare at her darkened shape. It feels like the calm before the storm. She bends forward like a school teacher scrutinising the work of a pupil. My body, seeming to echo her movement, bends enough so that I have to put my foot forward to keep my balance. Our synchronous march forward is restarted.

As we push past the grey, heavy industrial door at the far side of the hidden layby, the scene that greets me is somewhat ironic. It looks just like a mini-cab waiting room. Having just left the stolen taxi a few feet behind us, this put a smile on my face. A few worn plastic chairs are spotted around the room. There is a dirty looking table in the centre of the room complete with a Formica tabletop and numerous circular coffee stains I assume left from polystyrene cups. The artificial light buzzes above our heads. As I walk through the door following Victoria I halt once again. There are other people in there. I don't know what I expected, but the thought of other people existing in this story takes me completely by surprise. It is probably too late to turn and run, so after a momentary pause I continue walking now feeling unsure if Victoria is an enemy or my greatest ally right now.

There are two young men sat in the corner smoking cigarettes and a woman probably in her late forties sat behind a desk holding what looks like a CB radio handset. The two men are both dressed in brown leather jackets. The jackets look like something that would be worn in the early 1970s. They remind me of undercover police from the TV show Starsky and Hutch. They both have fantastically elaborate side burns. Sideboards. Side whiskers. Mutton chops. Buggers grips. The woman behind the desk has distinctive walnut brown eyes and dark skin. She has a kind of punk look to her; a red streak in her hair that is styled up with a Miss Jean Brodie look. A lick of red hair dangles across her right eye. She has dark purple lipstick and is wearing a tunic jacket that squeezes her tits together into fleshy hillocks. She looks in great shape for someone of her age, presumably in her late forties. She reaches for a cigarette from a packet with the words *Lucky Stars* written on it.

"What have we here Victoria?" the woman behind the desk says in an American accent and a surprisingly deep rasping voice. "Ladies and Gents, this is Robin, he's a friend of mine." All faces are pointing in my direction. I smile in a dimwitted manner and say nothing. "Robin, this is Georgia, Larry and Edward." I pause. I have no idea what to do. I quickly search my memory for an analogue of this situation but the cupboard is bare. I'm frankly out of my depth, and struggling to understand what has caused me to comply so consistently with Victoria on this increasingly fantastical journey. A voice comes out from within me "Who are you all?" Not my finest opening gambit but perhaps the most honest thing I can say right now. Victoria replies on behalf of the group "We are colleagues, we work together, and we're also friends." Cryptic as usual, I think. Victoria continues, "But we're not the kind of people you would meet every day". Feeling strangely affronted by this I reply pointedly "Well, I meet a lot of different people". "No" Victoria says firmly "You meet the same people every day." I start to feel angry. Victoria gently takes my arm sensing my frustration. "I'm sorry Robin. I know this sounds a little cryptic and I did say that I'd explain everything, and that's what I'd like to do." I am gently led into a side room that has two cheap leather-effect sofas in it. There is a sign on the wall, it looks like an old subway sign. The sign reads *Southern Cross*. Victoria sits me down and begins.

"We...are...Activists." She waits for a moment, choosing her words with care, "Georgia, Larry, Edward and myself are all activists." Another pause. "And in order to do our work. Work that is undertaken to make the world a better place, we make use of a particular sort of technology." Victoria is aware of how vague she is sounding. "And the technology that we use, enables us to travel great distances, at great speed." It's not coming across well and she knows it. "It's difficult to explain this without showing you, but the point is". She hesitates once again. This is a speech that is clearly causing her some difficulty. She continues. "The point is that within a few seconds I could be in a different city, a different country.

I could be in Rome, the scorching heat of Death Valley, or London, where you come from." I hadn't told her where I'd come from, although, this is the least of my worries.

She waits to see the reaction on my face. I am concentrating on wearing a blank expression so as not to give away my disbelief. "Can I have a cigarette?" I say. Victoria hands me a rolled up cigarette and lights it in a single movement. I take a monster-sized drag from it. The tip of the cigarette glows brightly and the smoke bites at my lungs. "Go on" I say, thinking that since we are already deep in the land of fantasy what harm could be done by hearing more. "We can cross to anywhere. That's what we call it 'crossing'. Literally any destination. Although, we tend to cross to known safe places that are dotted around the globe. This avoids complications, and means that we are less likely to draw attention to our activities. The safe places are either manned, like this one, or they are far enough out of the way to minimise risks. Is this making sense to you?"

I let out a huh! noise, but nothing else. "Do you have any questions?" Victoria asks, keen to ensure that I'm listening properly and taking her seriously. I'm trying but I can't keep my silence. "Yes. I do. I do have a lot of questions. There are so many really but let's start with how? How do you do this? How do you flit between countries at the blink of an eye?" I go on "And are you, Georgia, Larry and Edward tourists? Like globetrotting tourists? Is it like tourism for the time poor, is that what you do?" "It's a good question Robin" Victoria returned. "And the answer is an emphatic no. It's much more than it seems. We're trying to accomplish something much bigger. It's something that I hope you will be interested in." Oh fuck I think. This is a cult. Victoria wants to recruit me. I knew it. I didn't really.

I'm about to respond when Larry, or Edward, not sure which one is which, bursts into the room. "We've gotta move. There's a problem." There is loud banging outside the first room that we entered. It could be the Police I'm thinking. They've found the stolen taxi. That would make sense. "Is there a way out? A back door? An exit somewhere?" I say to Larry, or Edward, who knows, my voice climbing an octave. He looks at me disbelievingly. "Too fucking right," he replies. And with that Victoria grabs me by the wrist and drags me, with a surprising amount of strength, into a third room and immediately as we do I am greeted by a horrendous pain, like somebody has taken an iron bar to my guts. I feel like throwing up. Saliva streams down the inside of my mouth. I feel my eyes rolling into the back of my head. The blood in my temple is throbbing and causing my entire vision to shake with it.

And then nothing. I see nothing. I hear nothing. I sense nothing at all. I'm sure that I still exist, in some sense, but without any evidence whatsoever to support this. Never has the philosophical proposition 'I think therefore I am' been so pertinent, I think.

Southern and Cross are two words that have been stencil-sprayed on the wall above my head. My sight has now returned, and then I feel it. The incredible warmth. I feel like I have woken up on a desert island. It must be at least forty degrees here. The air smells different from the dank tunnel. It smells floral. An incense smell. Victoria is still holding on to one of my hands. Larry. Or Edward. Difficult to tell. Is holding on to my other hand. Georgia is standing in front of me taking her tunic off and buttoning up her blouse incrementally covering up her breasts at each twist of a button. And the other one. The other Larry or Edward is slipping a gun into the back of his trousers. He has a gun! Why does he have a gun? Where the fuck are we? "How did you find your first crossing?" giggles Georgia. She's playing with me in my obviously confused state. I'm still thinking about the gun. "Don't you believe me?" She says. Her lips don't move. Her lips don't fucking move. They're all at it. Now finished dressing, Georgia waddles over to some white blinds against the wall. She pulls the string to the side and the slats climb towards the ceiling. As a reflex I cover my eyes. The light is blinding. I feel that my legs are bending and my body is now braced against the wall. I am standing. Outside the window I see it. There, clear as day. Unmistakable. It's a desert. A desert with sand and shimmering heat.

"We are in a southerly part of the United Arab Emirates. The closest village is called Alyhyali. This is a safe place for us. And it looks like we need one right now." My mind is slowly catching up with the reality of what has just happened. Not there yet, but the view out of the window and the sweltering heat is hard to ignore. "And before you ask, Larry, that's Larry over there" she's pointing with her nose, "carries a gun like all of us. This is normal. It's necessary." Victoria takes over from Georgia. "For the time being we need to work out how we were uncovered in the tunnel. They're getting closer all the time and we need to sort this." There is a steeliness to Victoria's voice. "You see our gift, the technological gift that we have, gets out every now and then. Whether it's a disgruntled colleague, sloppy practice or something more deliberate, people get to hear about it. And when they do, they want it for themselves. The problem is that most don't know the half of it. If they did we'd all be in real trouble. it's not just about being able to cross, as you might have guessed, we can skim the thoughts in peoples' heads. Even those they'd rather not reveal." Victoria winks at me. I blush. I didn't know I could blush at my age. "The only real limit to what we can do with these skills is your imagination" Victoria raises her eyebrows at me playfully.

Georgia sits down behind a different desk where there is another device that looks like a CB radio. "Right she says. You and Robin." She's addressing Victoria. "Cross again. We need to split up and keep moving. "Larry and Edward, I'm sorry, but I want you to go back to the tunnel. We need to establish what exposed us and who is behind it. If you have to close down the operation there, then do it. Much better to be safe than sorry." As if talking as one, Victoria takes over, "We will all rendezvous in Reykjavik at midday on Friday, the twenty fifth. And to be clear, we will be at the main safe place in the city council building. Got it? When we get there we'll take this to Jan. he'll know what to do."

4

Mr. Grimes

I report to the reception and explain who I'm here to see. I complete the registration book. My name? Robin Mann. My Company? I write Southern Cross. My host? I write his name, John Grimes. The smartly dressed receptionist asks me to take a seat. She gestures to the white designer sofa to the side of the reception. As I sit down I feel the cold hard edge of the gun barrel poking into my bruised ribs. My face is expressionless. A minute or two later Mr. Grime's Executive Assistant appears and introduces herself to me. "My name is Julie I'm John's Executive Assistant." As we travel in the lift I ask her if she's busy at the moment. "Its mayhem. It's year-end of course and he's only just returned from Istanbul." I know this. "I'm sorry we couldn't get you more time with him. Is thirty minutes going to be enough?" "Plenty" I reply with a smile. "I'm grateful for your flexibility, Julie." She likes the cut of my suit. And my aftershave. She's thinking about a dance class she's attending this evening. She hands me the earpiece. "Mr. Grime's English is good but he prefers his mother tongue". "No problem" I say as I slot it into my ear. It's barely noticeable.

After Julie leaves the meeting room Mr. Grimes arrives a couple of minutes later. He is wearing a white robe. And sandals. He has a white pendant around the chain on his neck. It's hardly visible against the colour of his robe. Some sort of traditional dress from the Northern region of Turkistan. He shuts the door behind him and asks me to take a seat. I take out the gun and shoot him in the side of the head. The gun makes a muffled noise like the sound of someone thumping a pillow. Mr. Grimes is dead as his body falls to the floor. I leave the room calmly. A minute later I am walking out the front of the building into the street. I stroll past some rough sleepers on the pavement and I am reminded of Victoria.

5

Rockaway Beach

After the obligatory blow to the gut and the nausea Victoria and I cross into what appears to be a hotel room. The stationery on the bedside table identifies the name of the hotel – *the Southern Cross*. No surprises there then! The carpet is patterned in red and blue. It's horrible. The heavy beige curtains to the room are drawn and the TV is showing a local religious channel. The accents are American, probably somewhere in the Midwest. It feels like a small town but it's difficult to tell without peeking beyond the curtains. Victoria unhooks her hand from mine. She looks tired. "How do we do that? The crossing? How do you actually make it happen?" She exposes the underside of her wrist to me. "Put your thumb on my wrist and try to feel for my pulse." I do as she suggests. I can feel her pulse, the blood throbbing under my thumb. Her wrist is thin and delicate. It is strangely comforting amid this chaos. "Can you feel it?" She asks. "What?" I say. "A small lump, the shape of a banana." I circle her wrist with my thumb. Then I find it. "Yes, I feel it. It's tiny. It's like a crescent-shaped grain of rice." "That is an implant that makes all this possible. After a while all of its technological capability, so to speak, embeds into your body. You and the technology become fused. What you can really feel there is a shell of what was. Some basic reserve capability remains in the shell, but none of the special stuff. Jan will give you yours. He'll explain to you how it works."

"What you need to know is that when you want to cross you need to focus on a destination with everything you have and you'll be taken there. It sounds simple, but it's anything but. For many people it takes them months to learn how to do this. Some never get it and a few instinctively know how to use it from the outset. To be honest we haven't worked out what seems to influence this. However, once you've got it, once you know how to trigger it, even if your image or notion of the place you want to cross to is a little inaccurate, the system makes the appropriate adjustment. You might not have been to, say, Tokyo, before but the device works it out for you based on your request. It's smarter than you. Much smarter."

"Why do you carry a gun? Why would that be necessary? And what is your role?" I blurt out three questions back to back. She stifles a yawn "I'm really tired. I need to get some rest. Can I tell you later?" "Pretty please" she asks, this time without moving her lips. She smiles sweetly and crawls over to the bed. I watch her as she sleeps. Her feet are still filthy. The tip of a gun handle is poking out the back of her jeans. I take the other bed and lying on my back I attempt to sleep. My eyes won't shut. I'm exhausted but wired. I'm back in a hotel room again. How very me.

Victoria makes a small snorting noise. She's in a deep sleep. I wonder what things she has seen in all her travels. I try to imagine the possibilities of being able to travel anywhere, at any time. Is there a maximum distance that can be travelled? Is there a limit on the number of crossings in one day? Does travel have to be on the earth? Could it be beyond the earth? The moon? Further? It blows my mind thinking about this. I mull over my earlier questions. What is the mission that Victoria, Georgia, Larry and Edward seem to be on? And who is Jan? My eyes close and I sink into sleep.

We both wake at about the same time. Eager to introduce a bit of normality to the situation I suggest that we go out for lunch. I partly suggest this also so I can verify that we are no longer in the UAE. Or Sydney for that matter. I'm still in a partial state of disbelief. We both visit the bathroom separately to freshen up a little. I can hear Victoria peeing in the toilet. I turn the volume on the TV up to drown out the noise. It's not that I don't want to hear her peeing, it's just that I imagine she would rather not think that I could hear her. Come to think of it, she probably knows this already with her ability to steal my thoughts. This might start to annoy me. She appears in my line of sight. She has changed clothes. Now she's wearing white jeans, ankle boots, a black thigh-length dress shirt. It's partly tucked into a belt. I can't see it as she faces me but I assume her gun is jammed into the back of her jeans. I guess the shirt helps to conceal its shape. "There are some spare clothes in the bathroom if you want to change. They might help you to fit in a little round these parts." She adds an unconvincing Mid-West drawl to her speech. "Oh and there is a gun and body holster in there too. Best get it while you can." "I've got no idea how to use one. Not that I plan to" I add quickly. "It's easy," she mouths. With that she pretends to draw two guns from her hips like she is in a Western. Before putting her imaginary guns back in her imaginary holster she blows imaginary smoke from the barrels. Victoria likes to tease people. Or maybe just me.

Dressed in blue jeans, a black T-shirt, a light zip jacket and pair of plain cowboy boots I walk out of the door of the motel. Our room opens straight out onto the parking lot. There are only three cars there. I don't know much about cars but they look slightly old-fashioned. The one in front of our room looks like a Cadillac of some sort. "Do you wanna drive?" Victoria asks. "Is this yours? Ours? Does it belong to us?" "Sure does honey." "Are you going to keep that atrocious accent up?" I hear myself say. "Sure am!" As I turn to approach the driver's door she kicks me square in the ass. This is done playfully but it's one hell of a kick. She giggles. I point at the side of my jacket where my gun sits. And give her a knowing look. Her face lights up with pleasure.

Travelling along the highway I see a sign for some towns that I vaguely recognise the names of. Casa Grande. Mesa. Avondale. Tucson. We must be in Arizona I conclude. There are cacti as far as the eye can see and broken glass decorating the edges of the road. We pass a sign that tells us that we are passing into a reservation. I don't catch the name of the tribe. In the distance the road shimmers. It's long and straight. After seeing nothing for twenty minutes we come upon a roadside diner. It's called *Rockaway Beach*. The name couldn't be more incongruous with the surroundings. We pull into another parking lot.

We've barely spoken since leaving the motel. A comfortable silence though. One that doesn't feel like silence.

We are shown to a booth by a lady called Mary. She is fresh faced and chipper. "How can I help you two this good morning?" It's gone twelve. I can see by the clock on the wall. This mismatch between the real time and our waitresses' greeting bothers me. This is the kind of thing that does. Victoria replies in a hammy Mid-West accent that sounds awful. "Well, thank you sweetie. We'll be having some coffee and some of your delightful pancakes this fine day." She knows she sounds absurd but it makes her enjoy it all the more.

I share with Victoria what I'm thinking. "What do you, Georgia and the gang actually do?" Victoria is ready to speak now. "Well." Victoria takes a breath as if she has a lot to say. "As you can probably imagine, our gift gives us a considerable advantage over regular people." Her lips are plump and glossy, and as she speaks small lines appear and disappear creating tiny smiles around her mouth. "The device that we have in our wrist means that we can be anywhere, anytime. For example, you and I now could travel to Macchu Pichu, The Acropolis and The Pyramids and be back before Mary brings the coffee. And in the beginning that's how many of the group, the gang as you say, treated our gift. I suppose as a plaything. Something of immeasurable power, but at least for a while as a toy. But as time went on they recognised the opportunity that had been presented to them." I was intrigued by the distinction that Victoria drew between her and the 'others' in the gang, but for the time being I let it pass. "And so, as world events would unfold we could be there. As soon as we heard about an earthquake, a meltdown at a nuclear power plant, a major flood, the hunting of elephants, we would be there to make a difference. We had and still have a unique ability to influence the outcome of some of the most horrendous events known to man. We tip off the news crews to get the word out. We re-direct aid to the places we know are in greatest need. We get people out of the way before the militia storm into the village. We make it difficult for business transactions involving nuclear weaponry. We have toppled governments. We have protected species on the verge of extinction. We have brought down human traffickers. I have been present at pretty much all of the major conflicts in the world; Iraq, Afghanistan, Palestine, Serbia, The Congo, Vietnam, Cambodia, East Timor, Kuwait, Chechnya. You name it we have been there trying to make a difference. Tourism. Or 'Inter-rail for the time-poor' as you called it, couldn't be further from the truth."

"You look pale" Victoria comments. I feel pale. Or shocked might be a better description. There is only so much that the mind can accept in one go and I think mine is reaching capacity. But I am also trying to place when the various conflicts Victoria mentioned happened. I was seven years old when the Vietnam War ended and Victoria didn't look much older than me. Another question to be added to the list.

Mary arrives with our pancakes. Fluffy buttermilk pancakes. Maple syrup. Proper maple syrup. Not maple flavoured syrup. Sugar sachets. Salt and pepper cellars. Hot Chili sauce. A stainless steel condiment holder. Low hanging table lamp. Knives and forks stacked vertically in a pot. The pot is branded. It has picture of an Indian smoking a pipe and the words Big Wigwam. Bacon smells.

Solitary customers perched at the bar. Local radio playing.
A flash from the kitchen. A burger momentarily catches
fire. We are both hungry and make light work of lunch.

Mary appears again in front of us. She's smiling. Of
course. But she looks uneasy. "Madam. There is a man
at the bar who'd like to buy you and your friend here a
drink." She tilts her head towards the far end of the bar.
Victoria and my eyes rest on the man seated on a high stool
near the cash register. We both expect him to return our
gaze, but he remains transfixed on the coffee cup in front
of him. "He says he'd like to speak to you." Mary lowers
her head towards us both in a strangely conspiratorial
way and whispers. "He sounds like he's from Europe or
something. I don't know what would bring him here.
We're miles from anywhere" Victoria is wearing the
expression she has when she's reading someone's mind.
"Mean anything to you?" I ask Victoria. Her face looks
serious. She says, "Thank you Mary, you sure have been
helpful. Tell the gentleman we'll be delighted to join
him in a minute." Mary retreats with her smile almost
intact. Victoria turns to me and in a calm and clear voice
tells me to follow her lead. "I don't know who this guy
is. I'm pretty sure it's not good news, but he may know
something. Do you have your gun?" I nod.

As we pay at the cash register the seated man swivels
around in his stool, smiles unconvincingly and introduces
himself. "My name is Jean-Paul. I wondered if you both
had a moment to discuss a business proposition." His eyes
signal towards the underside of his wrist. He's trying to
indicate that he too has an implant. That he is one of us.
With all my non-gifted mind-reading skills I'm guessing
that he is not. Aware of some reticence at least on my part

he returns with a single word "Please", gesturing towards a side room. I look to Victoria and she glides forward seemingly unperplexed. I follow as per the plan. The first room is actually a passageway that loops around to what must be the back of the diner. Behind the kitchens. We finally come to a stop in a makeshift office. There is a desk, a chair, a calendar on the wall and a kind of en-suite toilet. And not much else. As Jean-Paul shuts the door behind us two figures appear from the toilet. We are outnumbered. A thought occurs to me, but not of my own design. It is a message. From Victoria. "Stay close to me Robin. Don't forget that we can cross at any time. In the blink of an eye. Just stay close." Our hands touch.

Jean-Paul speaks. "Let's be straight. Shall we be straight? I think we should be straight." He already sounds unhinged, I muse to myself. And no doubt to Victoria too. "We all know that before my friends over here can take their guns out you will have disappeared to some other place, with your oh so special skills." He emphasises the word 'special' mockingly. "So, you can leave at any time, that we know. But what you need to understand is that we are onto you. Every safe house you have, we will shut down. Your dank cesspool in Sydney has been burned to the ground. Nothing left. Well, nothing left but this little memento." The two men stand away from the entrance to the bathroom and reveal a slumped body resting against the base of the toilet. It is a man with blood matted into his hair. It looks like he has been beaten badly. It is difficult to tell if he is still alive. I don't recognise him. Victoria does. Her hand moves away from mine. Like lightning she leaps over the desk and both men fall to their feet. Where they stood they now lie. It is seamless and happens in less than a second. There is blood. I have no idea where it has come from. Victoria has a knife in her hand. She is back standing next to me and Jean-Paul is now slumped into the chair behind us. It is like he is a man-shaped balloon that has suddenly deflated. His neck is spilling blood like black gravy. His shirt is drenched. His face looks surprised. I turn to Victoria who refuses to meet my gaze. She is now in the bathroom. "He's alive!" she exclaims with relief in her voice. "Get over here and grab Larry's wrist," she commands. I stumble over to Victoria slipping in the blood that now lies at the feet of the two men. I clumsily crash into the bathroom and reach for Victoria as I do. We begin to cross. As I begin to feel the pain in my stomach, there is an explosion at the far side of the room. Jean-Paul's body is lifted clean off the chair. The blast throws him towards us. His bloodied face is inches away from mine. Then nausea. Then nothing. We have crossed.

Our three bodies are piled on top of one another. Me, Victoria then Larry. Victoria and I slip from the pile like penguins. Larry is motionless. "He's going to need help," Victoria says with a quiver in her voice. "I will be back. Give me one hour. Don't move from here. I will be back for you. Don't worry." She kisses me firmly on the lips. And with that she and Larry are gone. For the first time I look around to see where I am. It looks just like my hotel room. The one in Sydney. I move from my stomach to my knees and I look at the bed. My pants are still folded and presented like a gift at the end of the bed. This is my hotel room. This is my room. I am back exactly where I started.

6

The Crossroads

Sat on the back seat of the bus the sunlight would flicker through the trees. And every now and then, as the bus bounced along a particularly narrow road, tree branches would scratch and poke their way into the open windows of the bus. At the age of thirteen years, travelling to Nottingham on the back of the bus with my friend was the purest form of freedom. Out of sight. Unknown to anyone in the world. This was freedom.

I awake exactly an hour after Victoria and Larry have left. I'd set the hotel alarm. I didn't want to be asleep when she returned. I didn't want to miss her. The air conditioning in the room is still belting out freezing cold air. My jeans are those that I'd changed into in the motel in Arizona. On the knees I notice patches of blood. And on the shins. My Cowboy boots have blood on them also. I look at my hands. Tiny grains of sand and dirt are lodged behind the fingernails. I feel the gun under my jacket. It is a solid hunk of metal. I take it from the body holster and roll it around in my hand. It has a black handle and silver barrel. There are words. Compact 92 Berretta 9mm Parabellum. Cold. Heavy. I can see a small safety catch. To the rear of the trigger is a button. I press it. The magazine flies out. I re-insert it. It clicks in an assuring way. Despite its uncompromising exterior and impersonal looks, it's strangely comforting to hold. It feels quite nice.

Another hour passes and no sign of Victoria. I shower and put some of my own clothes back on. It's three in the afternoon. On the far side of the room my phone pleeps. I bound across the bed to get it hoping that it's Victoria. It's not. The number is a UK number. It's the office in London. I let it ring out. I have five missed messages. I remember that I was due to have three separate meetings today. They must have been trying to track me down. I find it hard to engage with the world of work now. It seems ridiculous. It was always ridiculous but I was good at it. Night falls and I'm worried.

I'm outside the hotel walking purposefully towards the quay. I figure that Victoria might have gone back to where the rough sleepers are. I know it doesn't make any sense but it's all I can think of. The city is different at this time. Everyone is hurriedly walking somewhere. From work. To work. Talking. Gesticulating. There is a sickness to this hyper-living. There is no love here. Just furious distraction.

It takes a long time to travel such a short distance. With Victoria I could have been in the Amazon basin by now. I arrive at the site of the rough sleepers, but there is no one here. No rough sleepers. No blankets. No sign of Victoria. Nothing. I draw a blank and continue retracing my steps.

I'm in a taxi. "Sydney Harbour Tunnel please" I say to the driver. "And where do you want to go after that?"

I say something about having to inspect the electrical circuits in the tunnel. The driver doesn't believe me but with an extra hundred bucks in his hand he speeds off as I step out into the hidden layby. Cars whizz by. I approach the door. It opens with a gentle push and I tentatively bend my head around the corner. Without even looking in I can smell what has happened here. There is black soot and burn marks from floor to ceiling. The first table that I saw when I entered this room now looks like charcoal. There is very little left of the sofa in the second room apart from an acrid smell. Just like the diner in Arizona, this safe house has been obliterated. Jean-Paul was telling the truth. Remembering Larry, I start to get a shiver down my spine. This must have been the place where Larry was beaten until bloodied. Time to get out of here I think to myself. It's not long before I'm in another taxi and walking back through the doors of the hotel. Defeated. No Victoria. No way of contacting Victoria. I'm faced with Pandas. There are men dressed in suits. Luggage trolleys. People with conference badges. Lanyards. Chinese tourists. Smells from the kitchens. Chatter. Bright artificial lights. Drinks glasses are scraped along glass tables. Foreign accents. German. Japanese. Small children clutter the walk ways.

Upstairs I take out my room card. As I'm about to place it over the handle Victoria's voice enters my head "Where the fuck have you been?" She's on the other side of the door. She's in my mind and on the other side of the door. She's here! I excitedly push the door. Her face is there to match the voice. I'm so pleased to see her. We embrace with such gusto that it takes us both by surprise. I'm told that Larry is recovering but he'd been beaten badly and they'd cut out the implant from his wrist. So close to the vein he'd almost bled out. He's being well-looked after now I am assured. Victoria thought that I'd been taken away and was about to assemble a search party. She looks worried.

Victoria asks me to give her my hand. I do so. She produces a silvery syringe from her pocket. "What is it?" I ask. "It's the device." I draw my hand away from her and step backwards. It's a reflex. "It's a bit earlier than I'd planned, but they're after us now. And after you too. You've seen what they can do. It may be the only way that we can keep you safe." I don't feel good about this. Victoria gives me some space but keeps talking "Robin, you've already experienced what this allows you to do. There are no surprises for you in this." She's right of course, but being faced with the prospect of having an implant injected into my wrist, about which I know very little, makes me suddenly very nervous.

This is a crossroads, you see. Up until now, I've been making a pretty good job of opting out. A past master in the art of going through the motions. A life in suspended animation. The thing about losing someone, someone that you love, is that when you eventually drag yourself back to the world, usually doing it to appease others, the things you once did - working, going out, talking, eating and so on, not only feel pointless, but you don't feel anything at all. I've spent years telegraphing emotions on the outside – happiness, excitement, interest, concern, joy, anger, even sadness, while inside there has been nothing. It is in this moment now that, for the first time in years, I feel my emotions stirred. This phenomenally short period of time with Victoria and this frankly unbelievable series of events have started to break through the screen I've been behind. And as regards the implant that Victoria is keen for me to receive, I really don't feel like I have anything more to lose.

I turn to Victoria and nod. She presses the device against my wrist. It feels just like getting a regular injection. Frighteningly insignificant when you think about what it can do. Victoria fixes me with a stare. "That's it. You should be able to cross in just a few hours. Welcome to a very elite club!" She pronounces the last three words slowly and deliberately. A very, elite, club. I hate clubs. I hate the rules. And the obligations. And the in-group out-group thing. She leans into me, smiles and kisses me fully on the lips. Her lips taste sweet. I feel the warmth coming from her. Our bodies press together for a moment again. This time it seems like I sense her thoughts a little. Could this be the implant working? Or just our new found intimacy. Over her shoulder I can see my folded pants on the bed. This is not a good look, I think to myself.

Behind me there is a knock on the door. Thump! Thump! Victoria holds her finger to my lips in a shushing motion, and reaches behind her back to take the gun out of her jeans. The knock comes again. "Turn down service!" a lady announces. We wait. The silence lasts for a second or two before there is a shuffling of feet on the ground. The person on the other side of the door walks away. It has broken the mood inside the room and we both look slightly awkwardly at each other. Separated by a turn down service. Should be called a turn off service.

We would wander from record shop to record shop. At the time it was all about punk. The Clash. The Damned.

The Buzzcocks. Stiff Little Fingers. UK Subs. Crass.
Anti-Pasti. The Subhumans. Anti-Nowhere League.
Flux of Pink Indians. Poison Girls. Vice Squad. The
Pistols. PiL. 7 inches. 10 inches. 12 inches. Singles.
EPs. LPs. White label. Limited edition. Promo copies.
Split records with one band on one side and another on
the B-side. We'd pay for some records and nick some
if we could. The best albums would have special treats
inside. Coloured vinyl. A free poster. A song booklet.
A gatefold sleeve. They were often bought entirely on
recommendation, never having been able to hear them
before purchase. So if it turned out to be a really bad
record then you'd deliberately scratch the vinyl and take
it back to the shop the following week. They'd allow you
to exchange it for a different one. We'd take our booty,
our haul, back on the bus. The tree branches would try
and grab our records on the way home.

"How many of us are there?" This is my first question.
Victoria is sitting on the small sofa at the foot of the bed.
Not far from my folded pants. I'm monitoring my body
closely to see if I can detect any change from the implant.
Nothing to report. There is a packet of shortbread
dressed in a Tartan wrapper, on the desk a few inches
from Victoria's eyes. The mini-bar is buzzing to her left.
Before Victoria replies I hear myself say, "Would you like
some shortbread? Or a drink from a very small bottle? Or
a cup of tea?" She looks unimpressed. "Folded pants?"
She giggles and smiles broadly. It's nice to see her like
this. "Eight." The number pops out of Victoria's mouth.
She looks slightly embarrassed. "There are eight or so of
us that can cross." She gives emphasis to the word 'us'. "I
thought you'd say fifty or a hundred. Or at least more."

I say. "We used to be more Robin. It's a dangerous business. Considerably more so in recent times. I've lost my best friends here. We've all lost someone." "How?" I ask. "The people in the diner. The people that nearly killed Larry. They were paid to do what they did. They can't cross but are employed by people who can. They have a 'with us or against us' policy. Be recruited or be executed. It's that simple. Almost that simple." She smiles meaningfully. "And before you ask. About twelve. There are about twelve of them. With a few more hired thugs to boot."

I feel my eyes searching the ceiling. I'm thinking. It comes to me. I am starting to piece something together "So, was I recruited? Did you recruit me? Is that why I'm here?" Victoria replied with a quick "No!" It doesn't sound convincing. "No. Actually, you were a very lucky coincidence. We sometimes recruit from the streets. People who are 'off-grid' so to speak. We want people who have no attachments. People who won't be missed. But we also want people who share our politics. People that don't care much for corporates. People who are capable of empathy. Of deep empathy. People who might be willing to exchange their lives for one of service, as we have done. That's why I was down by the quay. We were actually looking to recruit Robin. With an 'i'. The other Robin. Remember him? The person who's rug you stole. I'd been sizing up Robin for a while and then along you came. A lucky coincidence. Certainly for me". Victoria playfully kicked my foot.

"Okay" I say as if having reached a conclusion. It feels anything but conclusive though. "Three more questions. The last three. Honest." I choose these carefully from a long list. "Why are they after us? What is their mission, beyond pursuing us? And why isn't it as simple as them wanting to recruit or execute us? What haven't you told me?" "That's four questions," Victoria notes.

"Okay". She starts. "They are after us because we represent a threat to them. They have used the gift that is now embedded in your wrist in a very different way to us. In short, to amass wealth and influence. Many of them have major investments on the stock exchange, which, as a result of their ability to be close to the action everywhere, all of the time, means they make it big. You only have to be a few minutes ahead of every other mug on the stock exchange to make money. And it gets darker than that too. While we're dragging people out of floods in Banda Aceh, they are collapsing mines in Yanacocha to cause a spike in the price of gold. And every one of them has a mucky hand in the corporate world. CEOs this, Chairmen that, Sleeping Partners, Venture Capitalists, Angel Investors, Corporate Lawyers. It makes my skin crawl thinking about it. They're careful though and work very hard not to draw too much attention to themselves. You can see why they would want us onboard or overboard. And as you have already seen, these fuckers are ruthless. If necessary, they will slaughter every last one of us as we sleep. They're evil! They didn't all start out like this, in most cases far from it, but it's certainly how they've ended up. And for your third, fourth and fifth question, well, what can I say? It's complicated."

I raise my eyebrows and tilt my head on its side awaiting further exposition. Victoria's gaze centres on mine and her eyes narrow. I feel like I'm being assessed. Like she's deciding if I'm worth hearing what she's about to say.

"I don't know what to say Robin." She pauses evaluating me once again. "They know that the gift, the technology can do more than just cross." "You mean mind reading? Mental suggestion?" I chip in. "Well, there is that. But it's not as impressive as it seems. We can only pick up the thoughts that are on the surface of peoples' minds. The stuff that's buzzing around. We can't get to deeper thoughts or for that matter the stuff that people really don't want to share. And we can't really suggest anything with any degree of predictability. We can just toss some more thoughts into the mix. If you're lucky people might run with an idea you've projected into their mind, but on the most important decisions they almost always go with what they want."

I feel like I'm being distracted. Like I'm being shaken off the scent. I come straight out with it. "So what else do they think that you can do apart from cross or read minds?" Victoria stands up. It looks like she's about to tell me. Her mouth opens. "Turn down service!" We both look at each other confused. Then we realise. The announcement is coming from behind the door. The words come again. It is a man's voice this time. This is not right. We both draw our guns. The door handle beeps. The door is swung open. The man is holding a gun. Victoria opens her legs slightly so that her knee touches mine. We are in physical contact and about to cross. The man at the door sees us both looking at him. He sees the guns pointed at him. There is an explosion. He has pulled the trigger to his gun. The bullet passes between us both and I hear the bullet smashing the window behind us. I feel a blow to my stomach. Then nausea. Then nothing. We are on a beach. "Are you okay?" Victoria asks. "Yes, fine." I say.

"Hang on. We need to move again." Victoria holds my hand. My stomach hurts again. Nausea. Nothingness. We are lying next to a stream. It smells musty. We are on the edge of a wood. I hear a gunshot. It's like it is right next to my ear. My stomach feels like it's been kicked for the third time. Nausea. And nothing. I am throwing up. Victoria has her hand on my back. "Do you feel better now?" She asks. Before I can answer she follows it up with an apology. "Sorry to do this. But…" Another blow to the stomach. More nausea. Whiteness. We have crossed once again. I feel completely shit. I must look a mess. Even Victoria looks pale. "Okay. We stop here now. We had to create some distance" She breathes out as she speaks.

It feels like we are on a boat. It's a passenger ferry of some sort. Outside through the plastic windows I can see a huge expanse of ocean. The sun shines brightly unimpeded by a single cloud in the sky. I look at the other passengers. They look Chinese and we are the only Western people on the boat. Victoria and I are draped over one another on one of those double reclining seats. Despite looking like Europeans no one seems to notice us. This kind of thing isn't unusual I'm told. Victoria explains to me that after crossing from location to location over the years she'd learned that from a psychological perspective, people will do anything to render what is out of place or extraordinary – like two people appearing out of thin air – as if it were normal; something they'd just failed to notice. Otherwise they are stuck with having to make sense of something that clearly doesn't make sense. People need narratives to understand the world and if there isn't a plausible narrative to hand for specific occurrences such as this, most will resort to more familiar explanations – *I must have missed that! I think I'm getting old! I'd better stay off the sauce!* "We should be safe now." Victoria says. She is snuggling up to me and moments away from sleep. She is asleep.

7

Madame Fontainebleau

I report to the reception and explain who I'm here to see. I complete the registration book. My name? Pascal Derrida. My Company? I write EMX. My host? I write her name, Madame Fontainebleau. The smartly dressed receptionist asks me to take a seat. She gestures to the grey designer sofa to the side of the reception. "Un moment monsieur!"

I am shown into the meeting room. Pandora Fontainebleau is seated at the head of the table. She is flanked by a man on each side. Pandora looks impeccably dressed. This is a woman of wealth and taste. She is in her early fifties. She asks me if I would like some coffee. "Du café, monsieur?" "Non, Madame" I reply politely. She likes the sound of my voice. A gentle smile settles on her face. She touches a screen in the table in front of her. The windows slowly darken until the room looks like it is dusk. One of the two men stands and approaches me with a black cane. It is a detector of some sort. "Ce est une formalité simple" Pandora tells me calmly. "Une formalité!" she repeats. I start to raise my arms. Pandora's head falls to the table accidently triggering the display device and causing the window screens to return slowly to daylight. Her throat is pumping dark purple blood out along the table towards me. It is like an oil slick. The two men lie unconscious on the floor. I wipe the knife on the curtains as I leave the meeting room. I glance behind me to see the purple blood turning red in the daylight. "Compliments de la Croix du Sud!"

8

The Temple

Tomorrow we will all rendezvous in Reykjavik. This is the plan. I will get to meet the four other people that I haven't yet met, including Jan. Enormous car tyres strapped to the side of the boat buffet against the walls of the harbour. The boat tilts then rears up. It bobbles from side to side until it comes to rest. We have arrived. The other passengers on board sound like a flock of seagulls. I cannot speak whatever language they speak – Cantonese or Mandarin. Or something else. The smells wafting over the boat are tremendous. Cooking smells. Vegetation and spices mixed with poor sanitation. It's a bold aroma. My guess is that we are somewhere off the Chinese mainland. Near Hong Kong or even Vietnam. I look for a sign to see if the boat has a name. I'm hoping for the comforting words, the Southern Cross, but they are nowhere to be seen. I suspect the Southern Cross safe places are no longer safe, and this is why Victoria has brought me here. As this thought bounces around inside my head I suddenly remember that I have an implant. I stroke it with the heel of my hand. It's there! No mistaking. A curly bit of rice lying under my skin. This means that I can cross. It means that I could, if I wanted to, cross, right now. This second. As I start to picture some locations in the world I also start to panic. Shit! I think. What if I just think of a place and pow! I'm transported there? How would I know where to come back to? I notice that I have my fingers in my ears trying to block out any thoughts. "It's okay." I hear Victoria say. "I've told you. It's smarter than you. It knows when you mean it. And it knows how to get you back here. If you want."

Welcome to Lantau island. 欢迎来到大屿山. The sign says. We're holding hands and walking together. Like we're together. Are we together? Is this what is happening? As ever Victoria appears to be leading me. We're passing through a market. Snakes in buckets. Thousand-year-old eggs. Carved Buddhas. Bronze Buddhas. Wax Buddhas. Crystal Buddhas. Small Buddhas. Big Buddhas. Standing Buddhas. Seated Buddhas calling the earth to witness. Birds in cages. Reptiles. Insects on sticks. Jewelled Buddhas. Paper Buddhas. Racks of material. Empty massage seats. Bent old women. People that look like Buddha. Monks in saffron robes. Monks in drab brown robes. Feet. Sandals. Plastic bags. Incense. Petrol fumes. Body sweat. Sun. Haze. Smoke. Victoria's hand. Victoria's thigh brushing against mine as we walk.

In my first job I had to draw pictures of systems. Not human systems. Not interesting systems. Procurement systems. Sales systems. Revenue systems. It didn't stop there though. I'd draw diagrams that mapped the movement of money through accounts. From payments received accounts to suspense accounts through to bank accounts and then back through suspense accounts. The money didn't actually move. You have to know this. Nothing actually moves. Numbers changed to represent movement and this is what makes it all possible. Some companies would conceal money within these various accounts to give the impression that their expenditure was greater than it was. Or less than it was. It depended on the intent. You could make it look like you had spent more than you actually did to reduce your tax liability. Or you could decrease your costs to increase your profit. And these were the baby slopes. There were a thousand ways to make the system work for you. I was drawing blueprints of how to move money. For me. What I enjoyed most was rendering the system maps as beautifully as I could make them. I would perform my own concealment in these plans, but of a different kind. I would spend hours crafting a tiny image of a bird. Or a snowflake. Always positioned in a place so that it wouldn't draw too much attention. With some maps, if you squinted you would see how the map would resemble the shape of a Tiger. A snake. An anarchy sign. I took care to ensure the additions were always in tune with the style of the map so that you wouldn't think anything was out of place. You looked at my maps and angels would sing. They would. I managed to create some beauty from a miserable job.

"Where are we going?" I ask, feeling too hot to care about the answer. "I have something to show you" Victoria tells me. There is no hint of innuendo here. I was expecting innuendo. It's not there. We zigzag up the side of a hill. We swap the frenzy of the market for the calm of the countryside. We pass a monk who is walking down the hill carrying a silver bowl. Straight from BBC central

casting. He smiles knowingly. I wonder what he knows.
I bet he doesn't know how we got here. He still smiles.
The events of the last few days remain at the foot of the
hill. With each footstep we're creating distance between
the recent past and the present. It seems near impossible
now that anyone could appear from the ether and pull out
a gun. What an implausible series of events I contemplate.
My hand is still gripping Victoria's – the counter argument
to my flight of fantasy. We come to rest panting at the top
of the hill. Sweat crowning our foreheads.

And there it is. The reward for our effort. It is a small
temple with a curved red tiled roof. It has ornate carvings
at each corner of the roof. There is a line of burning
incense at the entrance. A nautical-looking bell the size of
my head hangs in the porch area. It is still. It appears to
be perfectly tranquil until two Chinese children, aged six
or seven, tumble out from the temple. Each of them locks
on to each of Victoria's legs. Victoria carries on walking,
lifting each one up in turn. They bury their faces in her
legs barely concealing their smiles stretching ear to ear.
They squeak as they are carried forward. She disappears
inside. I look out towards the sea briefly then spin around
and follow Victoria's steps.

Towards the back of the temple is a living area. We
trundle through quickly. There is what appears to be
a kitchen. There are dishes and pots and pans. Some
stools. A small wooden table. A cool stone floor. A
large clock on the wall and a cheap looking calendar.
All is simply dressed. We continue walking through the
living area to a garden. The children are still wrapped
around Victoria's legs. She must be getting tired by now.
Her patience is impressive. I would have called it a day

by now. The garden is breathtakingly beautiful. Some plants are tightly manicured, while others seem wild and unruly. There are thick dark-stemmed bamboo shoots thrusting into the sky, occasionally contrasted with flecks of sunlight sneaking through leaves. There are great hunks of silvery driftwood placed carefully around the garden. The branches and leaves of what looks like a willow tree are casually draped over the exit to the kitchen. It offers a kind of curtain marking a change in mood. Patches of red and dark green grasses hint at a pathway out into the main part of the garden. Steam is rising slowly from a large pot that is squatting above a small fire at the far end of the garden. A faint aroma of burnt mushroom can be detected. The smell is both inviting and repulsive at the same time. Intoxicating. On a single wooden bench near the pot are two people, probably middle-aged, simultaneously appearing to be old and youthful. I ponder what causes this impression. It could be the clothes they are wearing. Difficult to describe. Her clothes are dark with occasional flecks of red in the collars of her shirt. The man is wearing some quite natty looking slacks, but oddly they are held up with some old rope tied around his waist. The scene seems somehow incongruous.

Thankfully for Victoria, the children have got bored and are now play fighting on the ground. She is walking towards the couple but doing so, initially at least, with her back towards them. It looks a bit weird. I pick up that Victoria is about to introduce me to the couple and indicating to me that this is something I need to pay attention to. This is important to her. I am being presented to the two people on the bench. They rise gracefully from their seat as a single unit. Lots of smiles. We are all smiling. Why are we smiling? We keep smiling.

Victoria speaks first "Robin, these are my parents." The couple look on with smiles that seem even bigger than a few moments ago. A furrow appears on my brow. "Well," Victoria clarifies, "These are the people that brought me up and are the closest to parents that I get." We're all smiling again. My cheeks hurt. I wonder who should say something. I wonder if Victoria's parents speak English. I wonder if they know about our gift. I wonder what on earth I should say. "It is an absolute pleasure to meet you" I hear the gentleman say. His English is excellent. "We have heard a lot about you." I feel at a disadvantage. Victoria and I have known each other for barely a few days so it's hard to understand how this could be. And what's more is that we've hardly been out of each other's sight. I am puzzled. Before I can respond the three are hugging each other tightly. It's a wonderful thing to behold. The tenderness between them is palpable. Victoria is kind of crushed in the centre between the couple, her cheeks pointy with happiness and her hair scrunched up in way that makes her look like she's wearing a toupee. And then the children join in by leaping onto the standing pile of bodies. I feel like I should be in there somewhere in the scrum but, while everyone else seems to know about me, I feel very much like an outsider.

I distinctly remember the school disco. I was thirteen years old and it was incredibly exciting. It was being held in the school assembly hall that by day was a dull place of formality, mumbled hymns and kids scratching their arses. But by night, with the night air blowing through, pulsating coloured lights from 'Wayne's Mobile Disco' and the sugary sounds of pop music, the place was transformed. Well-meaning parents, no doubt with positions on the Parents-Teachers Association were in control of security, and they patrolled the hallways and the toilets trying to catch out kids that were smoking or causing trouble. The older kids, some of them a few months away from leaving school altogether, had seen this all before. And if they weren't doing something illegal or against the rules it would be a matter of great embarrassment. 'Johnny D' and 'The Boss' (these were their names) were brothers a year apart in age. In fact, they were two of five brothers from the Dawson family. The two eldest brothers were in a correctional 'Borstal'. On scores of occasions they'd been arrested and warned, fined and held in custody overnight by the authorities. Mainly for petty crimes like vandalism, theft, supplying soft drugs, causing affrays, and so on. But they'd gone too far and had tried to rob the local bank. It had been a complete disaster and they'd effectively trapped themselves alone in the bank with the alarms ringing out across the town. The police could take all the time they needed and made a big show of the arrests to make sure that the two brothers would go down for their crimes. Back at the disco Johnny D and the Boss were ostentatiously smoking joints, sitting on the back of one of the lower school benches with their feet on the plate that said 'do not put feet on the bench.' It was textbook disobedience. The volunteer security had tacitly agreed to leave them alone.

I remember being sat on the floor at the back of the hall with my arm around Jenny Bones. I think she was pretty. I can't really remember. I remember feeling thrilled to be there with her. And I loved her surname. We would kiss badly for a few minutes and then stop to watch the disco.

We would be in a line of similarly engaged people all sitting in a row at the back of the room. It was like a weird club. Steve, sat along the line with a girl from two years above (this was a big thing), had a hip flask with Vodka in it. The flask was passed along the row and the boys would take a nip, pull a face and pass it along quickly. Strange to gain such pleasure from something so plainly unpleasant.

Later that evening, as I was walking out of the hall with some friends, I saw Jenny Bones sat on the bench kissing Johnny D. Our eyes met briefly. Something passed between us; a kind of strange mutual understanding. I couldn't blame her for moving up a level. If I had the looks, the maturity, the opportunity, and the wit, I would probably have done the same. I'd been one of the gang. Sat at the back of the hall with a girl. What right did I have to complain?

Victoria told me some of the story of her and her parents. As ever with Victoria, I got the sense that I wasn't being given the full picture. But it seemed that they had met while travelling from China to London. Victoria's biological parents were from a wealthy family and Victoria was being prepared for a life of comfort. Her biological parents though had died unexpectedly in a manner that Victoria didn't explain. She didn't want to get there just yet. Her inheritance it seems did not come to fruition. From riches to rags might have been her story. The Chinese couple had effectively adopted Victoria at a young age. The story didn't add up to me. It wasn't clear for example why the Chinese couple would adopt her or why they were even travelling together in the first place. But the love between the three was undeniable and something like that can't be faked.

We remained in the garden and ate what was in the pot. It was near impossible for me to identify the ingredients but it tasted wonderful. The scene felt dreamy and unreal. An oasis. A temporary pause. I kept touching my wrist. And then Victoria. And even on one occasion I deliberately burnt my thumb on the pot. All to prove to myself that it was real. That I hadn't been dreaming. Or that the jetlag or the sleep deprivation hadn't caused some delusion. That night Victoria and I slept in a makeshift hammock at the end of the garden. We were coiled together. Occasionally rocking as one of us shifted position.

9

Sanctuary

By now there was little evidence of the wreckage of the clipper, and to an observer it would be difficult to understand why there were four people floating on a tiny plot of land in the ocean. Their presence was out of place. Wrong. A fish convulsing on a sand dune.

Looking at the three original inhabitants of the floating deck, Hjarand could see that they were struggling. The initial flurry of excitement produced by a new arrival had begun to ebb. The sun was now at its highest point in the sky. For the group, the heat was everything. It filled the air. Scorched the deck. Pricked their skin. Each time that a shallow wave of cooling water lapped over the surface of the raft, they were blessed with a temporary reprieve.

Victoria sat in a half reclined position. Her back leaning into Pandi's chest. Pandi was like a coat around Victoria. Protecting her. Reminding her that she was not alone. That she hadn't been abandoned.

Victoria's lips were dry like sandpaper. Her pale skin blotched by the sun. Her eyes barely open. The shape of

almonds. She was frightened. Hjarand dragged himself
on his knees towards her. He wanted to comfort her. He
knew exactly what he could do to help, but he would need
to exercise great care. In her state, and at her young age, it
needed to be handled delicately. He smiled at her, and over
her shoulder, to Pandi also. He spoke in a reassuring voice,
carefully selecting every word as he went along. "Victoria,
when I was training to be a researcher, we learned about
how people react to traumas." This was partly true. "Do
you know what a trauma is?" Victoria shook her head
from side to side. She had no idea. "Traumas are bad
experiences. Things that shock and can frighten us. Like
what happened on the clipper." Her eyes had widened now
to take in the scene in front of her. "We also learned about
how to help people to relax in this kind of situation. It's
kind of like hypnosis. Have you heard of that?" Victoria
nodded. She recognised the word but didn't really know
what it was. "Would you like me to try and help you? It
doesn't hurt. You just have to listen to my voice." He
took her hand in his and waited for a nod of agreement.
She smiled and said "Thank you. Yes, that would be nice."
Hjarand didn't have to say a word. He suggested to her, to
Pandi and to Yo Yo that all was well. He suggested to them
that if they were to drift into sleep that by the time they
woke up they would be rescued. He helped them believe in
the idea that there was nothing to be afraid of. They might
just as well get some rest while the rescue party comes. And
with that they closed their eyes and all three slept.

Hjarand knew what he had to do. The options had
narrowed to one.

Still in a kneeling position, Hjarand stretched his arms
out in front of him making a cross out of the shape of his

body. He bowed his head and his hands came to rest on all three bodies in front of him. He closed his eyes.

The sun bore down on a raft the size of a stamp. To an observer it would be difficult to understand why an empty plot of land would be drifting in the middle of the ocean.

Victoria was vomiting into a toilet bowl while Hjarand tried to pass a glass of water to her. She lashed out, not meaning to hit him but nevertheless the back of her hand slapped him square on the nose. He winced and recoiled. She'd accidentally caught him in the exact same place that Yo Yo had booted him in less than a few hours earlier. Seeming to ignore the pain that he was in, Pandi and Yo Yo were firing questions at him. They were angry. Impatient. Despairing. Delighted. Relieved. Confused. He could only understand every fourth or fifth word, and it was in an old version of Mandarin, but he could guess at anyway what they were saying. He gazed back at them with water streaming down his eyes. The split on his nose opened up again and a paper cut thin line of dark pink blood graced his nose.

They were in a Victorian terraced house in a suburb of London. Hjarand wasn't sure which would be the best place to cross them to, but he figured that Pandi and Yo Yo had saved for years to travel to England and Victoria would feel secure in a relatively familiar city. So, London it was. Hjarand guessed that the crossing might cause this reaction in Victoria. He'd noticed in his earlier work that the side effects of crossing were more severe the less physically robust that a person was. It used a great deal of energy to cross, not to mention the cognitive and somatic disturbances that it caused. It is principally for this reason that crossing had a kind of natural limit to a maximum of twelve or so crossings in a single twenty-hour period. For a fit adult at least. For someone of Victoria's age and in the condition he found her on the raft, she would perhaps only be able to make one more crossing that day without getting into serious trouble. Yo Yo was pacing around the bathroom. It was already cramped in there and it wasn't helped by someone striding from wall to wall with no intent of going anywhere. It was a mystery where his energy had come from.

Victoria eventually took the glass of water from Hjarand and flumped back into an elegant cast iron bath. The feet of the bath resembled the claws of a Lion. The enamel outside a cool olive colour. The first words that came out of her mouth were a question. But not the question Hjarand expected. "Are you God?" Hjarand burst out laughing, and then hastily followed it up with an apology. Victoria looked embarrassed. "No my dear. No. I'm not God. I'm sorry." He didn't know what to follow this with. Victoria was the first person that he'd exposed his capabilities to and he hadn't developed a script yet. Victoria felt justified in issuing a follow up question. "How did you get us from the ocean to here? In fact, where are we now?" Victoria angled her head in an attempt to see what was beyond the bathroom doorway. Yo Yo crossed her vision three times before she drew her attention back to Hjarand. It was even starting to annoy Victoria. Hjarand was lost for words. Not only did he not have a ready-made explanation, he had no idea how to relate to a young person's mind. Yo Yo had stopped pacing, no doubt worn out by the exertion. All four of them looked like they had been stranded in the desert for a week – depleted, dried out, a glassy look to their eyes.

Silence descended on the scene. Pandi, Yo Yo and Victoria glared at Hjarand waiting for him to do something.

He looked back at the three faces closing in on him. A twelve-year-old girl that believed he was God and a Chinese couple that could barely speak English. And then him. A man displaced in every sense. A thought passed through his head. An ignoble thought. He let the thought unfold. What harm could it do? He thought to himself. He could be released from his situation in the blink of an eye. Free from the responsibility that the circumstances had brought him. This is what danced in his mind. He would become part of a vague, half remembered experience. Perhaps Victoria would imagine that an angel had saved her. She would tell people of what happened and no one would believe her. She would know it was true, but over time she would even come to doubt herself.

Then he remembered. His life had been saved by these people. His ability to cross would mean nothing if he was lying at the bottom of the ocean. And it was because of them that he was here now. A life affirming boot to the face. He owed them a debt. The greatest debt anyone could owe.

He drew a deep breath and started with the easy bit. "We're in England. We're in London. South London. I thought if I brought you here it would be easier. More recognisable. Fewer complications." He shouldn't have mentioned the word complications. It's not a good word to use as you're about to explain something. "Victoria." He said boldly. He thought that using her name would make them less like strangers. It's hard to believe an explanation for something that sounds incredible if it comes from a stranger. He considered doing it by suggestion. But changed his mind. He felt instead it was time to be direct.

As he opened his lips, he knew his words would sound implausible. More than this he knew that he would simultaneously detect the incredulity in Victoria's thoughts drifting into his. "I used to work for a company that developed a very powerful technology that allows people to travel great distances in a very short space of time. It was that technology that enabled us all to travel from the raft to here" There, he said it! He lifted his eyes from the bathroom floor and brought them to rest on Victoria. She wore an expression of curiosity. Not disbelief. Or judgment. Perhaps it was her age that caused her to remain open to the possibility that this was true. He wondered whether that was enough. Whether sharing this portion of the story would be sufficient. But he knew that it wasn't so he pressed on. "And not only that, the same technology can also be used to hear what people are thinking. And to suggest certain ideas to them. Without them knowing. To encourage them to make certain decisions. Without them realising it." When he heard himself saying this he became aware of how bad it sounded. Victoria responded without hesitation. "But you do good things with this technology don't you?" It simultaneously sounded like a question and a direction. Hjarand nodded emphatically to avoid disappointing her.

Yo Yo and Pandi were watching Victoria and Hjarand in an attempt to gauge what was going on. Hjarand had an impossible task in front of him. How was he to explain this in the language of a young person and the language of two Chinese people? He searched the ceiling with his eyes for the answer, and found the solution that had always been there. "Can I show you?" he asked Victoria. Again, without hesitation, she accepted his suggestion calmly. "Will you ask Yo Yo and Pandi for me?" Victoria did so. They held each other's hands before indicating their agreement back to Hjarand. "We will need to sleep first. To build our strength before we travel again." Hjarand instructed. "It's been eventful".

10

The Residence

It was Friday. Rendezvous day. We would cross from the humid, peaceful island of Lantau to the cold, wind-swept island of Iceland. From a temple to Council offices. From here into the next place.

Victoria had woken before me. I must have slept in. I don't have a watch but my stomach tells me that it's getting on for lunchtime. I can hear her talking intently to someone in the kitchen part of the temple. It sounds like something serious is being discussed. I assume it is one of her parents until I start to recognise the voice. An unmistakable timbre to their voice. It is Georgia. The conversation is getting tense. Like something is up. I struggle with righting myself and exiting the hammock. It's harder than it looks. My feet plapp heavily on the ground and I hobble up the garden. My legs are still half asleep and the night in the hammock has left me feeling like weights have been placed on my body in all the wrong places. I announce my arrival in the kitchen by first getting entangled in the tree leaf curtain and then, having pulled free, by overcompensating and bolting through the doorway into stools tucked under the table. The peace of the day is broken by an ear-piercing scrape. Sccccccrape!

I had fully expected to find myself facing Victoria and Georgia. In fact, I was quite looking forward to seeing Georgia now that I was kind of *one of them*. But only Victoria remains standing in the kitchen. Georgia had crossed seconds before my clumsy arrival. Victoria had a look of shock on her face. "What is it?" I ask. "It's Edward. They've got him. They're trying to get him to speak. We're pretty sure it's Ryan." "Who's Ryan?" I say. Victoria seems to ignore my question, wearing a desperate expression. My heart flickers. "Where is Edward? Where are they holding him?" I ask. Victoria shakes her head. "We're looking now. He was cornered last night in a safe place in Mozambique. They'd chased him for hours. Georgia said he'd probably crossed about ten or eleven times before he'd just run out of strength. It takes a lot to keep moving and these fuckers don't give up." I enquire delicately so as not to upset Victoria. "But, when he is feeling stronger, can't he just cross again to get out of their way? He can escape right?" She drops her head and explains in a solemn voice "Do you remember how you managed to cross with me? How that was possible?" She waits momentarily for my answer. Nothing comes. "We simply maintained physical contact. That's all it takes. All that it ever takes. So as long as one of their trackers hang onto him, it doesn't matter whether he is in London or Lima they can continue to...to." Victoria struggles to get the words out "...to torture him. And the more exhausted he is, the easier it is for them to cross him right back to where they were. They're evil. They are." A determined look comes over her face. "It's time we stopped being hunted and started taking this into our own hands. We have to put an end to this, before there are none of us left. They're slaughtering us Robin! One by one they're murdering us."

"What do you want me to do?" I hear myself say. Victoria hands me a piece of paper with scribbled words on. Writing I assume from Georgia. It has three names on it, each with an accompanying physical description and precise location directions. It is a hit list. "These details are correct and have been verified within the last hour. We have to act quickly before they move again." Added Victoria. "And you will need to do this alone. I'm going to get Edward. If Ryan is behind it, I'll have to face him. We rendezvous as planned in Reykjavik. Is that clear? Do you understand what this is?" I did. Completely. I had been given instructions of who I needed to kill, and where to find them. But this wasn't what I had signed up to. "Victoria, I am not a killer. Are you seriously suggesting that I...that I murder these people? People that I have never met?"

Victoria slips her hand in between mine. She could hear the voices in my head as well as I could. It was a fast flowing stream of thoughts. These people might have children. A family. People who depend on them. Do they really need to be killed? They might be persuaded to change their mind, to join our side. They might agree to disappear and bother us no more. I can't kill these people in cold blood. How do I even know that they have done anything wrong? All these doubts flood my head. And then I feel them starting to move in a different direction. I find myself tuning in to Victoria. To her thoughts.

Now inside her mind. The implant is doing its work. She has had the same reservations. The same fears as me. The same sadness imagining what is likely to follow. But stronger, so much stronger than this are the images that come to mind. It was like I was flicking through an old-fashioned Rolodex. All these things Victoria had witnessed; the faces of her friends that had been beaten, scores of people that had been tracked down and tortured. Executions without hesitation and without fear. Unbridled brutality. It was horrifying. And Victoria was right. This was a war. I saw this now and was in no doubt that this had to stop. But I was not a killer. I had never harmed anyone.

With a terrified look on her face Victoria speaks, deliberately and simply. "Robin, they won't stop because we ask them to. They won't be persuaded to switch sides. They have a single intent in mind and that is to remove every last person that possesses this technology. I am asking you to do this, not because I want to put you in danger, but exactly the opposite. They have already tracked down Larry and Edward. How long do you think it will be before they find Georgia, or me, or you? We are their next target. We were lucky at the hotel, and that was a close call. It may only be minutes before they locate us here. We have to act. I'm sorry Robin, but this is the only way." Victoria pulls me closer into her, pressing the paper into the palm of my hand. I feel the warmth of her breath on my forehead. As soon as our bodies are unlinked, she crosses. She is gone and I am alone.

The first name on the list is Carlos Aguila. His location is an address in Alcalá de Guadaíra, a suburb of Seville in Spain. He is described as being six feet two inches tall, with dark curly hair, Arabic features, a closely trimmed beard, and grey-blue eyes. There are a few other details appended in note form. To anyone that didn't understand our line of work they would appear unintelligible; Easily read. Suggestible. Unable to cross. Very dangerous. I place two fingers on the underside of my wrist as if taking my pulse. My thoughts settle and focus on one thing, and one thing only. The garden disappears. I double over with the crowbar-hit. My gullet fills with saliva. There is a wave of nausea. Then nothing.

I am half standing, half sitting on a wall in what appears to be a compound. It's the early hours of the morning. The silvery light of the morning has been replaced by the warm light of sunrise. I assume that this is the private residence of Carlos Aguila, although frankly I could have crossed to anywhere. There is a small fountain in the centre of the courtyard with water that is trickling out of the spout. I keep myself close to, and with my back against, the wall and follow the line around to a wooden door. No more than fifteen feet away are some sliding glass doors. I find it hard to see through the glass. They are blacked out, no doubt as a protective measure against the sun. I worry that I might be visible to someone beyond the glass doors so I feel for the handle of the door in the wall. It turns. I slip through to the other side.

I am in a driveway. There are three expensive cars lined up behind one another. The car that is furthest away is a Porsche of one kind or another. The other two look similarly sporty. Carlos must be quite high up in the organisation I presume. He may not be able to cross but this doesn't seem to have held him back. For a moment I become distracted by how cool the cars look, and I miss the fact that there are thoughts finding their way into my mind. In my mesmerised state a conversation plays out between two men. "Right...we have an unwelcome guest...Get the boys over here...If he doesn't come quietly, you know what to do...I'll see you in the store in Santa Lucia...Don't fuck this up! Carlos, you need to move quickly..." It is a mixture of real conversation mixed with private thoughts of those involved. It is clear that I have already been seen. This thought punches its way out of me. I snap out of my trance to see a tall figure stepping into the Porsche. It rolls forward initially very slowly then, once the metal gates to the compound have lifted, the car lurches forward, then speeds off. I don't have long enough to confirm that it's Carlos. But everything fits so far.

Before I can confirm who the driver is, I find myself crouching on the ground. It's an instinctive movement and my arms are clasped over my head for protection. I couldn't be a smaller shape if I tried. Carlos' employees, who probably spotted me when I first shuffled passed the fountain, are firing at me. Four or five shots ring out. I feel the noise in my chest rather than hear it. Chunks of stone that form the wall of the compound are popping out above my head. The debris smells earthy. I retreat back inside the fountain area. Still screwed up in a ball, I reach for my gun and grip it like a vice in my hand. My eyes glance at the smoky glass doors that continue to freak me out. I feel exposed. At a disadvantage. I empty two bullets into the glass without thinking. It is the first time I've fired a gun and as the glass explodes I am propelled backwards violently towards the wall. My head connects with it accompanied by a white flash. "Fuck!" I scream. The pain is excruciating. I've almost knocked myself unconscious.

The back of my head at first feels damp and then cold as the air hits it. My head must be bleeding. I feel a warm stream of blood being deposited on the nape of my neck. For a moment the only thing I can think of is that I'm going to die. I have been here for a few moments and I already feel outpaced in every sense. I am in someone elses residence. With no idea of the layout of the place. Pitted against armed and experienced gunmen. This couldn't be worse. The thought of my hotel room in Sydney comes to mind. The comfort of the King size bed. The giant TV. The mini-bar. The shortbread biscuits. The double lock on the door keeping the world out. A place of safety.

And then my thoughts become scrambled. I hear other voices through my head. I have no idea if the gunmen are talking or thinking, but I can hear them; what they plan to do. I start to see what they can see too. It's hard to describe the experience but there are moving images that appear as if in my peripheral vision. They have a different feeling to them. A different quality to my own perception that helps me differentiate who they belong to. And because of the intensity of the feeling I get from the gunmen they come through loud and clear. This is my advantage. This is how I get out of this situation.

I have a sense that someone is about to walk into the room where the glass has smashed. I scuttle towards the fountain like a bug. I am all elbows and knees. Dust being kicked up behind me. I lie flat out on the ground. I look like a dusty sack that's been kicked through soil. I am entirely obscured by the tinkling fountain. I am less than twenty feet away from the entrance to the house, but hidden from sight. The gunman darts into the room. His feet crunch and scatter the glass. He moves sporadically;

his head jerking around like a chicken pecking for grain. He is taking in the scene. Every bit of information that might help him in locating me is being absorbed. Flat on my belly, my elbows and the handle of the gun forming a tripod. I am braced this time against the ground. I feel the grit under my chin and the sticky blood on my head. Through the eyes of the gunman I see that he is taking an interest in the fountain. He is about to change his position to get a better angle on what lies behind it. I have a second at most to make my move. I gaze along the sight-line and aim for his chest. I hold my breath. My temple pulsing with blood. I feel my finger pulling on the trigger. As if he has been attacked by an invisible wrestler, his body is lifted clean off the ground and slammed back down onto the broken glass. I raise my head to get a better picture of the scene. He lets out a groan. He is still alive. I have wounded him. I hear his thoughts attempting to enter my head. They speak of fear and nothing much else. This shocks me. I want to read hatred and anger, but all I get is human fear. But then he swivels around like a compass needle looking for North. He lifts his arm as if to shoot me. I react without hesitation and pump two more bullets out of my gun. Only one hits him, but he is now still and I feel his presence drift away. I pull sharply out of his thoughts, the life now wrenched out of him fills me immediately with a sickness.

As I am about to stand up I feel a fist being plunged into my kidneys. And then again, this time harder. I gasp for air and attempt to lurch forward away from my attacker. A hand is stuffed into my collar and my assailant drags me like a refuse bag along the ground. Drag, drop, drag, drop, drag, drop. It takes me a moment to realise what is happening. I am being taken to the dead person, the person I killed, now slumped against a sofa and surrounded by glass. It's like I am being held to account for my actions. I start to regain my senses. The pain searing along my lower back helps me to return to the present. I have to get out of this. I experience the rage that the second gunman feels. He has now carried me to within a couple of feet of the dead body. I see what he sees. The top of my bloodied head. The lifeless face of his friend. Checked-out from this world. Some strength returns to my legs and I try to bring my knee up like a sprinter on the blocks of a racing track. "Ah! You want to fucking escape do you? You want to go back to your friends. No way. No fucking way." This he says out loud. He lashes out with his boot that glances my ribs. I wince as he tosses my body to the ground. Through his eyes I see him raise his hand gun to the back of my head. I feel the cold exterior of the barrel jabbed into the side of my ear shoving my face forward. "Take a good look, my friend. Take a good look at your future." My face is now a few inches from the dead gunman. I'm going to be executed. I don't want to die. I don't want to die. And then, in a flash, it occurs to me. I don't have to. If I'm not here, I can't get shot. What the fuck am I doing? I focus. I think. And then blam! Stomach punch. Nausea. Whiteout. Fountain. I cross only ten feet away. But just enough to be behind the gunman. I pick up the gun that had been knocked out of my hand with the first blow to my kidneys. He turns. I point it at him and fire a single shot into the centre of his mop of hair. The top of his head flies off. It is dramatic and final. He falls forward on top of his colleague.

I find myself running through the door towards the driveway. Carlos has perhaps been gone only four or five minutes but long enough to get me off the scent. I crane my head into the driver's window of the first car. No keys. I step towards the second car parked closer to the exit. Bingo! There are keys. Sitting there like a gift. I'm reminded of the first time I met Victoria. The stolen taxi. The tunnel under Sydney harbour. I jam the gearstick into first gear and accelerate through the open metal gates. I'm driving a fast car in search of another fast car in a town I know nothing about. I follow the long driveway out to a single track lane. There are no turnings so I know I must be going in the right direction. The single track morphs into a two-lane road and still no turnings. I attempt to tune into his thoughts but I can't find them. I assume that mind reading has a range and I'm not yet close enough. I am in fourth gear now touching one hundred and twenty kilometres an hour. I can see that it is a long road and Carlos has to be ahead. I just need to narrow the gap. But not so easy when there is a long stream of cars in the way. Then an idea dawns on me. The cars aren't in the way. They are the way.

In my second job I would help small businesses to get hold of money. It didn't matter what line of business they were in, I'd find a way to help them get a loan, avoid some tax, attract an investor, introduce a silent partner, qualify for some government funds, or whatever helped. It was an unusual role. One day I'd be bailing out a pet shop, the next I might be helping an artist fund their first big exhibition. My clients were always happy. What's not to be happy about? I was the guy that conjured cash from thin air. I'd deal with all the dull stuff –

the paperwork, the conversations with the lenders, the legal side, the transfer of funds, everything. I took great pride in delivering to my clients, and into their accounts, exactly what they wanted within four weeks of having been first asked. And this I accomplished without fail, for every one of my clients. One dubious perk of the job was that I would regularly be thanked in the form of gifts. It was with a sense of the surreal that I kept a room in my house expressly for the purpose of displaying my haul. A printer. A bottle of Champagne. A case of kitchen knives. A portrait of yours truly. China figurines. A bag of cement. A plant propagator, nestled next to a tub of 'Juicy' condoms. A scratching post for a cat. A soda stream. Shot glasses. Crystals. A pack of six mops strapped together and standing to attention. A badly stuffed smiling Ferret. And my favourite gift, a book written by one of my clients entitled 'A Guide to Raising Funds for Small Businesses.' The business owner didn't see the irony as he proudly handed over a signed edition of the book. It was actually quite good.

After a couple of years, it all came to a rather an abrupt end. As a matter of course, I would re-visit many of the businesses I'd helped. Just to see how they were getting on. Nothing more than curiosity and with no intention of finding repeat work. As I did this I would find myself having a different kind of conversation. I'd hear about how the businesses were going of course. But, I'd also get insights into the lives of my clients; why they set up a business in the first place, their hopes, their family members, the children that had left home to travel, the elderly relatives that needed care and so on. It was one particular client though that caused me to end my line of work.

She was the owner of a cleaning company. She'd send in cleaners to offices, hotels, large houses, nursing homes, and even to clean up after family members had died at home. Most of her employees were immigrants. In fact, less than a handful were originally from within the country. They'd come from Eastern Europe, South East Asia, Africa and the Middle East. To say that they were looking for a better life would be to misunderstand the motives behind their diaspora. Many of them were fleeing conflict, persecution or tragedy of one kind of another. Some had been forced to leave family members; their children, their elderly parents, in the care of others. And it was in many of these wars that my own country, and other western powers, had played a role; and in ways that I found hard to justify to myself.

The language skills of her employees were always patchy and as a result they would find it difficult to articulate their concerns, or to assert their rights when it came to expectations that were placed on them. My client would pay them as much as she was able to, and by comparison to other similar employers, she was generous. But, ultimately the wages were poor and as someone that specialised in filling stop gaps, where regular cleaners had been sick or hadn't turned up, many of her jobs involved sending women (almost all of her employees were female) into unfamiliar places, often at unusual times. Your average office worker wouldn't see the late evening or early morning shift of cleaners. Many would be up at three am to get to their place of work, or if they were on the late shift might be getting the last bus back to where they lived. It was when I dug deeper that I appreciated the situations that they encountered and the horrifying incidents that were taken as normal.

Her cleaners would tell her, and only her, about the abuse they would receive from total strangers. They'd simply be speaking in their own language on buses or in shops and the remarks would fly. Not a single week would pass without at least one employee being physically threatened or menaced, often in broad daylight. Sexual attacks were commonplace. In the two months prior to my last conversation with my client, three of her employees had been sexually assaulted, all three having occurred in their place of work. They had very little money, no understanding whatsoever of their legal rights, and limited grasp of English – all of which led them to the conclusion that they had no choice other than to accept what had happened to them without complaint. They would keep quiet, rarely telling their friends, and always too ashamed to tell their husbands or partners of what had happened to them.

On hearing all of this, and more, I too felt shame. My cavalier attitude to business contrasted sharply with the reality that many people faced; the daily lives of hardship and vulnerability. I had felt it was enough to be good at what I did, to perform well. I took pride in wowing my customers without thinking about the politics. I'd studied the subject at College. I'd written essays about it. But, I hadn't completed the translation from the page to the street. I didn't know what I would do, but I knew that I was in danger of missing the people in all of this. I was still drawing maps, as beautiful as they might have been, but forgetting that behind them real life existed. I returned to my home and dismantled my display of gifts, with the exception of the stuffed smiling ferret, of course. You've got to hold on to the surreal, it's often the only friend you have.

Confronted by the long flow of cars in front of me, I select the furthest vehicle in the distance. It is a truck. I'm going to use it to leapfrog into Carlos' Porsche, which I hope I will see better as a result of the crossing. I nudge the steering wheel so the car is on the hard shoulder. Chippings and gravel ting against the underside of the chassis. The dial on the dashboard drops to around fifty kilometers per hour. At this speed my exit shouldn't cause too much mayhem. I double-check that my gun is still fast in my holster and reach around to the back of my jeans to find the gun I took from the other security guard. Then whoosh! I am sat next to a hairy truck driver, only his eyes visible above a thick black beard. He is dressed in shorts, a vest and flip flops. He looks like a tourist that has been kidnapped to drive a truck. We stare at each other in disbelief. His marginally greater than mine. I figure that the quickest way to get compliance is to show I mean business. I pull out my gun and casually wave it at him. "Shut up and keep driving like I'm not here." He does as I ask. The truck continues to thunder along the road. As I'm about to ask him if he's seen a Porsche, I see what looks like Carlos's vehicle going over the brow of the hill. It's too far in the distance for me to be sure, so I pick another vessel to cross into. I rule out a bus and a family saloon car as options. I don't want to drag too many innocent bystanders into this.

My body starts to feel heavy. The effects of having crossed twice in relatively quick succession are taking their toll. I know there is no time to waste though so I re-double my efforts. A silver convertible muscle car comes into view. It has single man's mid-life-crisis-purchase written all over it. There couldn't be a better candidate.

I focus. Stomach thump. Sickness. Nothingness. And then I'm in the passenger seat next to a short man dressed in slacks, a polo shirt and shades. He freaks out and grabs for my gun. The car swerves into the oncoming stream of traffic and then back again narrowly avoiding a head on collision. I wrench the gun from his hands and yell at him. "Get your fucking hands back on the wheel!" He does so. He's wearing driving gloves. I dislike him already. He's now good as gold though. Eyes on the road. Tan gloves wrapped tightly around the wheel. I spy ahead and immediately see the Porsche. We are less than two hundred metres apart. "This is it." I say to myself. My head is buzzing. I can't tell if it is Carlos' thoughts seeping in to my mind, or whether it's the adrenalin. I brace myself and then I'm propelled into the Porsche. On arrival my knees slam into the curved dashboard and immediately aware of my presence, Carlos steps on the brakes. My face is catapulted into the windscreen, which dents creating a glass spiders web. Carlos has brought the car to a stop on a patch of scrub twenty or thirty metres from the main road with a lake alongside it.

The sun is shining directly in my eyes and in the confusion I feel Carlos' hand grip my wrist, shaking the gun clean out of it. Once again I feel out classed. I have taken the advantage of the element of surprise and somehow turned it against myself. Carlos raises his elbow and jabs it repeatedly in my cheek. Five or six rapid blows to the face. I'm blinded. Carlos is climbing on top of me now, the fingers of his left hand clawing at my eyes, and his right hand around my back. He's reaching for the other gun. I force my back against the passenger door in an attempt to block him. It works for a second, but then he tries a different method. Instead of trying to rip my eyes out he grabs a fist-sized lump of hair and yanks my head against the passenger window.

The first wrench at my hair smashes the glass, and with the second, my head goes through the window. My head is at a ninety-degree angle to my torso and the gun at my back is exposed. Carlos grabs it and flicks it up to my throat. He's about to blow my head off. A throttled gargle comes from my neck. I focus and as we cross I attempt to turn my head away from the barrel. We are in the lake, horizontal and partially underwater, in less than a metre of muddy, slimy water. It's all I could think of. But it's bought me a momentary reprieve. Without the car door to hold me in position, I am free to make my escape. I realise that I can't out fight Carlos so, with the paltry amount of energy that is left within me, I cross back to the car, snatch at my gun in the foot well, turn back on myself, and from the broken Porsche window unload every bullet I have into Carlos. His body dances as the bullets plunge into him.

11

Greenwich

I needed a rest. I really needed to sleep. I checked the time on the dashboard of the car. It was not even nine am. Although the car had come to rest out of view of the drivers on the main road, it was only a matter of time before I'd be noticed. Explaining the dead body in the shallows of the lake wouldn't be easy. I knew I had to cross, if only to put myself in a less precarious location. I fingered my pocket, fished out the crumpled piece of paper in it and stared at it. It gives me the details of the next two people on the list. At this point I don't feel any remorse about the people that I've killed. It is different, I imagine, when you're not doing it in self-defence, but for the two men in the residence and Carlos, a second's hesitation and I would have been lying in the lake, or with my face mashed into the broken glass. I feel less comfortable though about what may follow.

The next person on the list is named Stefan Baden in Hamburg. The location is an office block. He is described as being tall, gaunt and bony faced, with dark eyes and an awkward gait. It is a strangely scant description but I assumed that it would do the job. It is followed by a few notes. Smart. Tricky. Can read. Can cross. Oh fuck! I think. My eyes jump to the last name on the list which is Sandeep. That's it, just a first name. He is in London. The words read – Short, round, bearded, and mouthy. The descriptions are getting worse. How am I supposed to use the description of unpleasantness to find someone? The location is an apartment near Greenwich. Skills – not fully known. Great! I think. Fucking great!

My body aches and everything above my neck feels either cut or bruised. I flip down the vanity mirror from the sunblind. The person gawping back at me looks like they've been given a good kicking. My face looks like a scarecrow's. Caked mud in different shades of dryness. Clumps of hair missing. One eye noticeably bigger than the other. Clothes at a jaunty angle. Clotted blood on my ear lobe. What looks like a bloodied sea urchin crowning my head. There are three main areas of extreme soreness; my throat, my kidneys and the back of my head. The pain bounces between the three of them like a pinball. The tiredness returns like a wave crashing onto the beach. I need to cross. I hold in my mind the one place that only I know of. A place where, if for only a few minutes, I would find sanctuary. With some considerable effort involved, I focus and then cross.

My parents were in the main cottage. I was in the caravan. It was the summer and we were holidaying on the North East coast of England. We'd come to the farm on a few occasions over the years and as a holiday it worked. It was a compromise of sorts. I had little interest in farms, and less interest in the freezing wind that rampaged across the North Sea biting underdressed holidaymakers. But I had the caravan. All to myself. Complete with mini-kitchen, mini-sofa, mini-dishwasher, mini-bed and acres of pale brown plastic, masquerading as wood. My parents would have the cottage all to themselves and the illusion of being childfree.

The back of my head hurts, so I lie on my side. The leaves in the trees flutter and the long grass quivers as the wind approaches. Through the window of the caravan I can see the countryside unfolding in front of me. Distant sheep, hedgerows and farm buildings decorate the hills like a Jackson Pollock painting. A bird sings making a comical noise as if blowing a kazoo. I notice that I am holding myself. Creating my own comfort. I am already feeling more relaxed. I instruct my brain not to fall asleep. I'm allowing myself a managed doze. Through half closed eyes I follow the line of the cast iron guttering on the cottage, then downwards to the doorway, and finally my eyes rest on the boot scraper.

My parents would skip out of the door to the cottage to pick me up on the way to a sight. A castle. Steam museum. Garlic Farm. Chilli farm. Orchid Farm. Dairy farm. Farm museum. Museum of farm equipment. Country pub. Amusement arcades. As we drove from place to place my parents would snap and snarl blaming each other for having missed turnings or for travelling on the right road but in the wrong direction. My two older brothers had long since left home, so it was just the three of us. Just the three of us, trapped in the same car together. The best bit of every trip was returning to the caravan. The car tyres would crunch along the gravel. The wet grass would lash my ankles as I ran through the field, and as I wrapped my fingers around the caravan door handle I'd immediately feel free. I'd spring onto the mini-sofa and get out a book. A novel. Or a wildlife book. A guide to the birds of England. I'd spy through the window trying to identify birds against the profiles. What a wondrous place.

There is a Greenfinch outside of the window. I spot it immediately. Its posture is regal. Upright. Head held high. I can see one black glassy eye. The pistachio colour covering most of its body is broken only by a silvery blue stripe along the wing and a yellow marker pen stroke. It remains motionless as the breeze occasionally reveals the downy under feathers. Fine and fluffy like a bantam chick's. The shutters of my half closed eyes start to open. I need to stay here a bit longer. My body is numb. It has no intention of moving. My state is meditative. Awake. Conscious. Aware. But still. I inform myself that I will need to clean myself up at some point.

I look down to my hands and watch the grime and soil that has been rubbed in. There are stains of blood in the webbing between my fingers. I can't tell if it's mine. My stomach starts to turn. I feel clammy. My heartbeat quickens. The reality of having killed someone, three people in fact, returns to me, and this time I'm feeling less at peace with it. Christ, what have I done? I hear myself thinking. Whilst it was life or death, I nevertheless, pulled the trigger. I ended their lives. And without knowing a thing about these people beyond our encounter. On the instructions of Georgia too. Of Victoria too. All of this, on the word of Victoria. I felt doubly uncomfortable. Surprising myself, I started to permit some questions to formulate. What did I really know of Victoria? Are the names listed on the paper really a threat? Do they need to be killed? I can feel the blood pulsing through my neck. A tiny but poisonous thought enters me. Have I been used?

I find myself rehearsing a counter-argument that halts the sick feeling in my stomach. I am going back to basics. The ability to cross and hijack peoples' thoughts is real. The terrorising and execution of operatives by the competition is real. The man in the hotel in Sydney, who shot at us first, was real. Carlos and his heavily armed security guards didn't think twice about unloading their arsenal on me. I retrace my steps a little to recall the conversations between the security guards as I first crossed into the compound. "It shouldn't be too difficult to take this fucker out." Those were the words that I tuned into. I was the "fucker" that was going to be taken out. This makes me feel better. It's funny how quickly existential angst flees the crime scene when self-preservation and a smattering of menace is involved. I have reconciled for now the horror I feel about the deaths of the three men. The bird has disappeared. It has been replaced by another bird. In the exact same position. As if it had never existed. The new bird is a Robin. Redbreast on show. Puffed out like it is about to blow out some birthday candles.

In summer the hedges, trees and fields would be full with chattering birds. My favourite birdcall would be the Wood Pigeon. It sounded like a Cuckoo, but slightly deeper in tone. It was a sound I could easily imitate. I would reply to the sound the Wood Pigeon made imagining that we were in some kind of dialogue, which of course in a limited way, we were. As I watched the scene develop outside the window I would jot down my sightings on a pad. A score sheet. I'd sometimes turn the tally into a hand drawn graph. I would also sketch the birds that sat there long enough. My favourite was a Pied Wagtail. It had very graphic markings. Easy to draw. Bold black and white shapes. As it pecks, its tail sits at the same angle as a tick – a cheeky kind of look. Robins too would perch on the branches. Erithacus Rubecula. That was the Latin name for them. They don't live very long. Most Robins don't make it to their first birthday. And they are highly territorial. Very aggressive. In the bird world, very dangerous.

I breathe on the glass and trace the shape of the Robin. I rub on the glass so that the redness of its breast shines through. I scratch the corner of my eyelid and when I return my attention to the Robin it has gone. Vanished.

I wash my hands, neck and face in the mini-sink. The water is stone cold, but it helps to wake me up. I dry myself turning the towel brown. I have another go at cleaning myself tugging this time at the bloody sea urchin on my head. It takes some cleaning and I dry off using a second towel. It remains more or less white. The peace of the caravan has come to a natural end. I know it is time to cross. I check the gun in my holster. Everything is in place. I pull the paper out from my pocket. I decide to visit the apartment in Greenwich first, somehow this seems like an easier prospect. My heart jumps a little, like a car stalling. I'm starting to remember what I need to do and my body is responding. I focus and brace myself.

I am in a penthouse apartment. I am crouched between a bicycle and a framed picture of some graffiti propped up against the wall. I have made myself small. I scan the room. It is enormous and divided into two levels. I can faintly hear a sizzling sound on the lower level and at the other end of the room. I assume it is a kitchen area and someone is cooking. At this end of the room, on the higher level, there are packing boxes, perhaps ten or twelve of them. It looks like the owner has only just moved in. There are a couple of stylish armchairs, a large silver computer on a desk, some original art on the walls and a vinyl record collection of what must be three hundred records. There is a sturdy looking bannister that I quietly use to pull myself up to full height to gain a clearer view. The top of my head and my eyes are visible above it. Because of the angle I can only see the bottom half of the kitchen area. There is a pair of legs and a derriere in view. The legs are short and the arse round so I assume that they could belong to Sandeep. Fits the description. I briefly close my eyes to attract some of his thoughts. There is nothing going on. Either nothing to read or something preventing them from coming through.

I'm left with a choice. I could take a shot now. Wound or kill him where he stands. While he's making breakfast. I don't need to think this through. I know I can't do it. Everything is too calm. Too ordinary. Before, I was fighting for my life. But now there is no threat. Right now, he is no more a bad person than I am. Perhaps a better person than I.

"Raise your hands and turn around slowly. Really. Fuck-ing. Slow!" This is what I hear coming out of my mouth. I sound like I'm imitating a cop on TV. Sandeep turns and faces me, but only from the waist down. "Closer to me you fucking idiot!" Holding a gun gives you a lot of courage. Perhaps too much. He steps forward a few paces and I can see clearly that it's him. "Stop there. Right there!" He does. I know what I have to do. It's the only reason why I'm here. I grip the handle of the gun and get ready. And then he speaks. "Before you pull the trigger". He pauses. He's got my attention. "You do of course realise that, like you, I can cross?" I didn't. "You do realise that before the bullet can leave the chamber of your gun, I can be in Tahiti. Or behind you. Or even, say, at…the rendezvous point with your friends." How does he know this? I think to myself. Taking a risk, I try to reassert my advantage. "If you can cross", I pause for effect, "Then. Be my guest. Go right ahead!" I goad him. "What are you waiting for?" I try to wear a nonchalant expression on my face. He remains fixed to the ground and offers a challenge back to me. "Well, it looks like you've called my bluff. I'm still here. So if you're sure it's me that you want. And if you're sure that you have nothing to learn from me about what this whole fucking war is really about, then I suggest you go right ahead and shoot. You'll either kill me or fire your gun into thin air. Whichever you do, you don't get to find out." I hesitate. Sandeep spots it. He turns his back on me and slowly returns to the kitchen hob. The gall of it. "Omelette?" he asks. I feel like my gun has been filled with sawdust.

With the gun still trained on him I sit on the step separating the two levels. I watch him carefully as he flips the omelette and slides it onto a plate. He fills up the silence. "The organisation is not the kind of operation you think it is. There are fewer than a dozen of us left and we've been falling in numbers ever since that psychopath Georgia started drawing up lists of people to be executed. Helped enormously of course by recruiting suggestible people like you to do their work. They spin a line about us being out to get them. They tell people like you that we are responsible for human trafficking, arms dealing, manipulating the stock market, torturing kittens, the whole shebang. I'm sure you've had the speech about this. They'd have you believe we're monsters. Corporate pigs screwing the world over. How lame. How fucking obvious! But of course it's different for each recruit. With their special powers, their mind reading and so on, they can concoct the perfect story that works best for each recruit. They know what buttons to press. For one person we're terrorists, for another we're the Illuminati. And for someone like you it's probably politics. Yeah. The Commanders of the Capitalist Military Industrial Complex pulling a fast one on the little people. That would work for you wouldn't it? And you with a background in corporate life. How does that work? The sickening feeling you have about all of it. Your sense of shame about having been one of them. Put that all together and they have all they need to pull the strings."

I hate every word that comes out of his mouth. But I am mesmerised. He presses on. "Oh and I forgot. The sucker punch. The attractive, enigmatic woman. Lady Victoria. Pulling you in with her fantastical stories of her poor, humble Chinese parents. And the flirtation. You'd fall for that right? A man travelling the world alone, desperately in need of some company. A deep personal loss in your past somewhere. Try to find some way to feel something, anything? You and scores of others too."

He was right about my life. He was right about my politics. And he was right about the effect that Victoria had on me. But these were second order issues. I want to know. I need to know. Had I really been played? I edge towards asking him.

"So what do you do then? Enlighten me about the virtues of your organisation?" I wave the gun at him as if to order a response. I desperately need to hang on to the illusion that I am in charge.

"Well. We're not Saints. Let me be honest. The gift that we share. The same gift that you have does create some opportunities. Why wouldn't we use it? If you run a few businesses like I do, you need help right? You probably know this better than most. I ship cargo from Africa and the Middle East. There are times when I need to see what's happening on the ground. When a well-timed face-to-face conversation can avoid a problem. When the right document needs to be put in the hands of the authorities. It's not illegal what we do. Just trying to get the job done. For example, do you know how many of my vessels that pirates tried to hijack last year?" I didn't know or care. "Four! That's how many. We can lose millions if that happens. So we nip problems in the bud. We see them coming and take evasive action. We instruct a ship to change course. The pirates go away. We save money and lives. Being able to cross just smooths the way. And let's be honest in the next few decades this will become a near redundant skill anyway. With improvements in air travel, in tracking, in virtual communication it will be next to useless. And as for the 'organisation' as you call it, it isn't an organisation. It's no more than a small collection of people who want to protect themselves and stop the technology, the secret, getting out. Can you imagine what would happen if this got into the wrong hands? Rogue states? Tyrannical leaders? Psychopaths? In fact, you don't need to imagine do you? You've already met them. In fact, it would seem that you've already joined them."

I am getting annoyed with this. Sandeep has made me doubt a lot. Or at least he's given expression to some of my deeper suspicions. He is persuasive alright, but it doesn't add up. He is trying much too hard. The multi-million pound penthouse apartment along the Thames. The original art on the walls. This is a smart guy. So much more than someone that was simply smoothing the way of business. This isn't the kind of person that would fail to see the immeasurable possibilities that the technology offers. Christ! Exactly the opposite. He must think I'm stupid.

I stand up. He sees this and his body stiffens. I don't know if I can do this, but what happens next makes it much easier. He starts to swivel his body reaching for something that is out of my sight, a gun I assume. I lift the Berretta and grit my teeth. I aim, close my eyes and blast him with it twice. The bullets scream into the brick wall behind the cooker. My eyes open as the gun snap back towards me. Sandeep is nowhere to be seen. The omelette lies on the plate untouched and coated with a fine layer of orange brick dust. I panic thinking that Sandeep might appear behind me at any time. I wrestle with the paper in my pocket. Read the next location, and depart instantly.

12

The Cinema

Jan and Victoria are locked in deep discussion. They are sitting at a table outside a coffee shop called *Reykjavik Roasters*. It is a trendy hangout packed with bearded hipsters and cool looking office workers. There is crunchy white snow all around them, and there is a subzero freshness in the air. Jan and Victoria are dressed in almost identical black padded jackets and snow boots. Jan pulls on a rolled up cigarette. He takes in a glug of smoke and breathes it out like a dragon. Their heads are close together. They speak as if they've known each other for years. They are physically comfortable around one another, although there is no suggestion of intimacy.

It's a busy area of Reykjavik. I've been here before, on business, and while it was a good few years ago it's not the kind of place you forget in a hurry. Locals and tourists intermingle, passing each other as if in slow motion. The snow invites care and deliberation in the way that people move. Even though it's mid-morning, it's only been light for less than thirty minutes. There might only be few more hours of sunlight before the dark claims the city again. It's easy to understand how tales of elves and hidden people grow up in these conditions. The stark volcanic landscape surrounding the city serves up all manner of strange effects. All kinds of eerie manifestations. Steam rises from cracks in the ground. Houses smile from the undergrowth. Thick sodden clods of moss protrude from the fields of lava like the heads of giants. The Northern Lights project a quivering green blanket onto the night skies. This is a land of magic.

Jan has classic Scandinavian features. He is tall, slim and blonde haired. He is in his early fifties but has a youthful way about him. He is wearing a pair of John Lennon style round glasses and a thin strip of leather is tied around his neck. It was probably a bootlace or strap of some sort. He seems very alert. His eyes flicker from side to side every couple of minutes taking in the scene around him. He looks like a man that is expecting to be discovered at any time by some unknown foe.

I am seated inside a different coffee shop across the square. It has an Icelandic name, something like Purkurr. There are people crisscrossing between us, and this provides cover for me. But also the window I am looking through has four or five horizontal lines of etched glass. Even if Victoria did look directly at where I was sitting she would, at best, see about ten per cent of my face, and certainly not enough to identify me. And to be honest I'd struggle to recognise myself after the morning I'd had. Jan I assume doesn't know what I look like. My only worry is that they might be able to detect my thoughts. I listen out intently for theirs but nothing. With this many people in the vicinity it's extremely difficult to strip out where they are coming from anyway. As with crossing it takes focus. You filter out everything apart from the target, whether it's a destination or someone's thoughts. And then you expand it, the idea of it, in your mind, until there is nothing else. It fills you up. And then it's accompanied by a surge of energy. More of a pulse that comes from the wrist, from the implant.

When I left the apartment in London, I'd intended to cross to Hamburg, in fact I almost did, but Sandeep's words had stuck with me. He had said enough for me to question the provenance of Victoria's story. He was not a good guy, this I was convinced of, but, I still didn't know if he'd just read my thoughts and used them against me, or whether buried in the bullshit and the deception there was some truth. And so in an instant I changed my destination and here I am – corporate drudge, turned globetrotter, turned cold weather detective.

As the lady wiping down my table lifts the sugar bottle she reveals a tattoo on her arm. It is a snake coiled around a cross. I follow the tattoo up her arm, and then jump to her shoulder and to her face. She has delicate, almost boyish features and an elfin nose. It's like the Icelandic tourist board has handpicked her. She's in her early twenties replete with smooth skin and a spritely glint in her eyes. In stark contrast she is looking at someone in his forties who appears not to have slept for days. I have bruises on my cheeks, a swollen eye and messed up hair.

The tattoo takes my attention again. "Where did the idea come from?" I say. She follows my line of sight to her arm. "Oh!" she exclaims. "What the tattoo? Well, umm, I designed it myself. Do you like it?" I didn't like it at all. "Yes. I like it a lot." I lie. She smiles. She doesn't

believe me. "Is it a comment on religion or something?"
I enquire. She looks puzzled. I elaborate. "I was just
thinking that with the cross you might be saying something
about religion." She looks even more puzzled. "I just mean
that, sometimes, a snake can be a symbol of deception.
And maybe because the snake is..." "It's not a snake!" She
interrupts. "It's not a snake." She repeats. "It's a Feminist
symbol. I've adapted it with some indigenous markings.
But it's a Feminist symbol. It's not a snake." I'd got the
message. I make a play out of squinting at the tattoo and
feigning an epiphany. "Right! oh, yeah! Completely. Of
course. That's so obvious now I look at it. I think it was
the angle. That is great. That is such a nice piece of work."
"Prick!" She thinks, her anger masking her sadness.

I'd made her feel crappy, and followed it up with a
clumsy and implausible explanation. So I try something a
little different. Something I haven't done before. I attempt
to plant an idea in her mind. Before she has left the table
I take the opportunity to suggest an alternative turn of
events to her. I invite her to believe that I actually recognise
her tattoo immediately as being a Feminist symbol, along
with the indigenous markings on it. And with it I suggest,
in a general, rather than specific sense, that we've been
having a good conversation. I replace my rather too
obvious disdain for the tattoo with genuine curiosity and
admiration. I project these thoughts in her mind and wait
to see what happens. And with this, the expression on her
face changes. Her body tilts towards me and she returns
a sparkling smile to me. "Thank you. Thank you very
much. It's been nice talking", she adds without a hint of
disbelief. She fondly squeezes my shoulder as she moves
to clean the next table. How interesting I think to myself.

Jan and Victoria appear to be arguing. Victoria is pointing at Jan like she's admonishing him. He offers no reaction. She expressively pushes the chair back from the table and is walking away as quickly as the snow permits. I can't watch both at the same time, and although I could partly solve this problem by crossing between their locations, I figure that I've only got a few more leaps left in me today. So as I see Jan starting to scoop a bag up from his feet, and swing it over his shoulder, I too rise from my chair to follow him. On the way out I hear a farewell call from the tattooed lady. "Thank you! See you again!" Momentarily, perhaps just for a second, I entertain the idea of giving up everything I now know about crossing and the darker side of it. The whole thing. I glimpse a picture of myself having an uncomplicated conversation with the tattooed woman. Just sitting down and talking about the banal features of daily life. But the image disappears rapidly. It's difficult to un-know. In anticipation of the temperature beyond the cozy coffee shop I deftly unhook a coat that is hanging outside of the toilets. It fits me perfectly and after taking three strides I am out in the street.

I maintain the greatest possible distance that I can from Jan. I know that at the slightest sign that he suspects that I am here, I will have to cross. I can't afford to meet Jan in these circumstances. He is making his way down towards the harbour, every few minutes glancing over his shoulder, or pausing to retrieve a roll up from his jacket pocket. He acts like a marked man, and perhaps this is exactly what he is. The organisation probably want him dead more than anyone else. Victoria never really explained who he was but she seemed to suggest he was the person in charge.

"When we get there." Victoria said about meeting Jan at the rendezvous. "He'll know what to do." That's what she said.

I still enjoy the benefit of the camouflage offered by the streams of people cutting in and out of one another. I am one of the pack. Jan's pace has started to quicken and I wonder what has caused this. Perhaps he thinks he's been spotted by someone and he's testing his theory out - checking to see whether it flushes them out. I break from the crowd to avoiding losing him altogether. I am still one of twenty or thirty similarly clothed people so at little risk of being seen. He holds on to a railing so as not to slip on the ice, then uses it to help switch direction towards a narrower street. Rather than follow his route exactly I dip along a parallel road. The two roads, his and mine, are about fifteen metres apart, connected by regular cut-through passageways. Every couple of minutes he appears, side-on, at the end of a passage. I remain undetected. He waits at an intersection, smoking this time. Cars file by bumper to bumper. The slush has started to pile up where the pavement meets the road. The flow jams for a second and a gap between two lines of cars opens up right in front of Jan. The seas have parted perfectly and he takes the opportunity to slip through. He is striding forward now about as fast as a walk can carry someone, particularly in these conditions. I know I won't be able to keep up for much longer without blowing my cover so I take another short cut. There is a chance I might miss him completely this way, but the alternative would be worse.

I anticipate that within a few minutes he will come into view a couple of streets away. I take up my position and lean against a post in front of a wool shop. With my foot

I absent-mindedly trace the shape of a snake coiled around a cross in the snow. Or is it a Feminist symbol? With my foot at an angle I jab away at the layer of ice beneath the snow. It isn't my finest work. There are a handful of people milling nearby. I am pleased they are there to take any attention away from me. As I am counting down in my head from sixty seconds to zero, I notice that someone is talking to me. This is very inconvenient. It is a lady's voice. She is jabbering away before I've even met her gaze. "I'm sorry sir, but do you know the directions to the Hal Grims Churcher?" These are three words I've never heard before. She has another go at the pronunciation. "Or it might be the Hattle Krims Keeeey Erca." She's clutching a palm-sized travel guide that I fear she is going to show me at some point. "It's a church. The big church. It's Lutheran. Do you know how to get there?" The lady moves a little closer to me. She is inspecting me. It must be the bruises on my face that peak her interest. She backs off a little, but aware that it was her who had approached me, she feels obliged to wait for an answer. I really could do without this distraction.

I start to reply when I sense a presence at my back. I carry on talking, deliberately spinning out what I'm saying to give the impression that I'm part of the group. The tourist is no doubt taken aback by my helpfulness and sudden interest in her sightseeing conundrum. The person behind me shifts position. I see them in the reflection of the glass. It is Jan. His profile is unmistakable. He's clearly altered his route. And here he is now, a few feet away. A shiver runs down my spine. But, he's clearly not noticed me. I briefly break into his thoughts. I want to check whether he has rumbled me. It takes a few seconds and then I'm in, wading around his mind, or at least in the shallows of his thoughts-in-motion. He hasn't clocked who I am. He hasn't even registered that I'm here. He's far too preoccupied. I keep talking, quietly enough to appear as background noise. I've already confidently made up most of an elaborate route to a sight I've never heard of, so I may as well finish the job. I finish my long, embroidered sentence just in time to see Jan stepping into the wide entrance to a cinema across the road.

I am about to step into the road when I freeze on the spot. I can't believe what's in front of me. Across the road, now also passing through the doors of the cinema is Sandeep. Bold as fucking brass. It was a short time ago when I last saw him and his features are scored into my memory. It's definitely him. A terrifying thought enters my mind. A reality that breaks through from my unconscious. I start to fear that I may have in fact have brought him here. Back in London when he ransacked my thoughts I might just have handed him the coordinates of Jan's whereabouts. I grope for my gun under my jacket and find it. I pull it out and then, remembering I am in a capital city in daylight, I plunge my hand and the gun in the outer pocket of my second, warmer jacket. It's marginally easier to use like this and better concealed. Slipping. Staggering. Waving my arm in the air for balance. I dash across to the cinema.

There is a set of stairs in the reception area. They are lit up with spotlights on the risers between each step. They near blind anyone walking off the street. I calculate that I may only have seconds before Sandeep catches up with Jan and grabs him. For someone as important to the organisation as Jan I assume that they will want to cross him to somewhere where he can be interrogated. Failing that though Sandeep might just execute him here in front of everyone. This time, I'm not going to miss. I run up the stairs. I can no longer see either Jan or Sandeep. I think about yelling out to warn Jan but it might just force Sandeep's hand. There is an array of stalls in the way - selling different snacks. Popcorn. Fizzy drinks. Ice Creams. Donuts. Pretzels. There are a surprising number of people here. There must be thirty or so people hanging around. It's not even midday. Haven't they got better things to do? I am frantically trying to work out where the hell Jan and Sandeep are. They must have walked straight through to the screens themselves, although there is a queue at the ticket sentry box processing people, and no sign of them there. My heart is pumping. I can feel panic rising in my chest. I can see beyond the sentry box to some toilets. After that the corridor leads to the screens. This is going to be my quickest route. It causes me immense pain to do this, as I'm still utterly exhausted from the last time I crossed, but I summon all the energy I have and focus. Stomach pain. Nausea. Whiteout.

I am standing with my back to the wall in the darkened passageway beyond the toilets. There is carpet beneath my feet and I can hear faint, muffled booms from beyond the heavy screen doors. I feel dizzy. My heart feels as if it's being squeezed. The dimmed purple lights in the hallway flicker like a stroboscope. I've slid down the wall and I am now sitting on the floor desperately trying to regain some energy. I start to appreciate how Edward must have felt after crossing so many times to escape his captors. I'm reminded of why I'm here. Before I'm ready, I force myself to my feet and search the faces of the people in front of me. If I can just find Jan and warn him, he can cross us out of here to a safe place. All I've got to do is get to him. I stagger forward like a drunk, using the wall as a crutch. The people making their way to their movies give me a wide berth staring quizzically at me. I'm feeling worse now. I think I'm going to collapse. My mouth is hanging open and my head is nodding. And then he's there. I see Jan. He's there. Pushing against the door to the screen. The dramatic sounds of the movie wash over him and out into the hallway. And next to him. Not behind him. Not being pursued by him, but alongside him, is Sandeep. I don't understand. I tug desperately at the gun in my pocket but it remains fast. My vision closes to a letterbox view. I stumble backwards and crash into a display stand. The sounds from the film drown out my descent. I lie unconscious on the ground.

13

The Cliff Tops

For my third job, I worked in Television. I thought it would be perfect for me. It would be an avenue for my creative impulses. A way that I could say something of importance to the world. Right up my street, I told myself. I took a 'career break' after my small business support role. I had become disillusioned, more actually with myself than the job. With the spare time that this gave me I found myself applying for a filmmaking course. I spent nine months going to college every day with kids ten years younger than me. It wasn't as thrilling as I had expected.

Fellow students would ask me why I had decided to study filmmaking and I would make up a different reason each time. A sixteen year old gothic-looking girl, dressed entirely in black, and wearing black lipstick, asked me. I told her that I was interested in the deeper desires that lived within people. A hidden side of people that I wanted to capture. A kid that looked like every member of Sonic Youth merged into one, asked me. Independent. Alternative. Music. Documentaries. That's what I said.

A geeky-looking kid, resplendent in high-waisted jeans, Hitchcock T-shirt fully tucked into his jeans, and a retro digital watch, asked me. By this point I'd given up on the pretense. I said, "I want to make films like Hitchcock did. Just like the Hitchcock on your T-shirt. Or failing that, something, a bit more digital in a retro way. If you know what I mean." He nodded. The truth of it is that I had no idea why I studied filmmaking. I really didn't. And people prefer to believe a story than hear the truth.

At the end of the course, literally the last day of study, I saw an advert in the newspaper for a Second Assistant Director with the BBC. These positions are like gold so I threw in my application without expecting anything. I was invited to an interview 2 weeks later. I turned up and answered a bunch of their questions. A week later I was offered the job. Apparently they liked my passion for filmmaking. I was tempted to write back and seriously question their assessment processes but self-interest got the better of me.

Literally one week after that I was in Osaka, Japan helping to film a documentary about Love Hotels. My role involved supporting the First Assistant Director whose role in turn was to support the Director. This was a rather top heavy arrangement for a project of this size but it transpired that it was a bit of a scam. For reasons that seemed to be related to ego, the Director had convinced Head Office that there were some complex cultural sensitivities that needed to be navigated, and that this needed more hands to the pump than usual, hence the Second Assistant Director. It goes without saying that the documentary didn't need this level of personnel, but who was I to argue?

We spent 2 weeks trying to coax embarrassed couples into allowing us to film them. Jatin, The Head of Production, had repeatedly failed to win over unsuspecting hotel guests and confident in the knowledge that the project didn't actually require a Second Assistant Director, he felt justified in making this my responsibility. This was a skill set that I hadn't been taught at College. It didn't go well, so we resorted to paying actors and actresses to pretend they were genuine couples in search of passion. But because this still conferred upon the individuals involved a degree of public shame, it came at a high price. As we imported more paid actors to the documentary, the owners of the particular Love Hotel that the production team had negotiated access with, started to get cold feet. They became suspicious of the motives behind the project and before the end of the first week they pulled out. We couldn't face returning to the UK having spent a fortune without having something to show for it.

So we used our own hotel rooms, dressed them in erotic imagery and liberally spread a few dildos around. We filmed naturalistic scenes of our paid actors as if they were the real deal. We took the external shots of the original Love Hotel and cut them together to suggest, without actually saying so, that the outside of the hotel matched the inside. When it came to the intimate confessional interview scenes where couples would reveal their fascinatingly quirky desires, or their cute fetishes, it didn't matter what they said. We'd make it all up in the subtitles. We made sure the background talk in Japanese was hard enough to hear in case a viewer capable of speaking Japanese could rumble us at some point. When we returned to the UK the documentary was put on hold *due to legal reasons. As far as I am aware it remains in the can to this day.*

Victoria is stroking my forehead with the palm of her hand. It is smooth and cool. I can't think of anything nicer to wake up to. I am lying on my back with my hands on my chest like an otter. Victoria is scanning my face with her eyes. She looks worried. "You've been out for a couple of hours. How are you feeling?" I frown, screw my eyes and tilt my head to indicate that I am trying work out an answer. I'm no longer in the cinema. I can't tell where I am. There is bright, natural light streaming in to the room from a long window. I assume we are no longer in Reykjavik. I can hear birds crying, whistling wind and nothing much else. It is calm here. "We're in Cornwall." Victoria says. "You can see the ocean from the window, it's beautiful. The cliffs are spectacular. I thought you would like it here. It's one of our last remaining safe places."

I strain my ears to hear waves hitting on rocks. As the foamy water is pressed through the holes in the rocks it makes a noise like air being released from a balloon. A salivary hiss then follows as the water is reclaimed by the ocean. My eyes wander the ceiling of the room sweeping for the source of more noises. The woo woo of the wind laps around the underside of the roof hinting at how high we must be. I imagine the view. Or perhaps it is the view in Victoria's mind that I see.

I stay horizontal for a short while. I am being given a rest from the mayhem so I am going to make use of it. Victoria tenderly brushes the hair away from my forehead. "How did you find me?" I ask Victoria. She looks sheepish and starts to explain. "I'm sorry, but I followed you. I needed to know what you were up to and whether the organisation had got to you. Y'know, they'll do pretty much anything to bring us down, including turning you into a weapon." It transpires that Victoria had seen me in the coffee shop when she was in Reykjavik Roasters. In her words - "You were really fucking obvious about it!" And so when I started tracking Jan she got suspicious. I have the image in my mind of Jan being stalked by me from about twenty metres distance, and then Victoria creeping around corners another twenty metres back. It had all the makings of a farce. "You look good in spy mode" Victoria says with a gleeful look in her face. Victoria is never too far away from making a joke.

She returns to her account. "I followed you for a while right up until you were accosted by that annoying tourist. I was impressed by your directions. They're probably at the airport by now. But when I saw you careering after Jan into the cinema with your arms waving and your gun barely concealed, I thought the worst." She held my eyes in her gaze perhaps still not entirely sure that I wasn't after Jan. "When I caught up with you, I thought you'd been attacked. You were tumbling back into a group of school kids. Popcorn and ice creams were flying. The display stand smashed into pieces. And there was you with cuts and bruises all over you, and the strangest expression on your face. You looked like you'd lost your mind. The cinema staff were really alarmed and threatened to call the authorities, so I pretended I was a doctor and asked for a quiet room to tend to you. With a bit of suggestion, I managed to get you out of there. As soon as we were left alone I popped your trousers off and checked you out properly." Big smile from Victoria. Never far away.

Always inappropriate. She finishes the story. "I left you alone for a short while. You were still unconscious at the time. I looked for Jan, but he was nowhere to be seen. We're usually pretty well attuned but I couldn't find him or pick up on his thoughts anywhere. So I returned to your sick bay and crossed us here."

I listen carefully, not allowing the banter to cloud my judgment. "And what about Sandeep?" I asked in a steady monotone. No emotion or insinuation in my voice. I just wanted a straight answer. "Who?" She replies. It was my turn to fix her with a gaze. "You didn't see Sandeep?" I ask slowly and deliberately. Victoria appears shocked. "You mean he was there? In Reykjavik?" I feel uneasy. I can't tell whether her surprise is genuine or not. It looks real, but that's never a guarantee. "Tell me again." There is no hint of humour in her question. "Robin. Tell me. Where was Sandeep?" I summon the picture to mind for her to see for herself; Jan and Sandeep walking into the cinema screen. The doors opening as they both pass through. Shoulders almost touching. They were together. Sandeep wasn't behind Jan; he was with him! Victoria's impatience had caused her to grab my thoughts before I had given voice to them. "This is true? You're not trying to fuck with me?" Victoria is frightened. She is wearing it on her face. But her fear quickly morphs into confusion. She fumbles with her words trying to get out a coherent sentence. "Why would?...What is Sandeep?... What are Jan and Sandeep doing together?...What were they doing together?" She is oscillating between believing and denying the images she has poached from my mind. She slips back to denial – "I didn't see Sandeep anywhere, and I was following you right from the coffee shop to cinema. I didn't see him once." It was a wasted effort on her part as the picture of the two entering the screen returns to her. "Fuck!" She exclaims. "Fuck!" She repeats. "That can't be right."

"But wasn't Sandeep on your list?" Victoria is still trying to piece together the puzzle. She unconsciously steps away from me shifting the angle of her head so she is side on to me. I can only see one of her eyes. Some suspicion accompanies her movement. "Yeah. He is on the list. And I did visit him. He had quite a lot to say actually." Sandeep's words came to mind. We are stood a few feet away from each other, but it feels like we were on opposite sides of the room. The atmosphere is tense.

Victoria sits down on the sofa in an effort to calm the mood. "Tell me. What did Sandeep tell you?" I hesitate, not knowing how to phrase my answer. I decide just to start talking. "He said that you, Jan, Georgia and the rest had been lying to me. That you had been murdering them for years." I emphasise the *you* and *them*. "Sandeep said that you use recruits, like me, and feed them bullshit stories to do your work. You say that they're human traffickers, or drug dealers, or terrorists or whatever it takes to turn people against them. And that none of it is true." I stopped short of all that I wanted to say. "Did he say anything else?" Victoria knew very well that there was more. I sit down in an armchair. "Do you have a cigarette?" I ask, "I could really do with a cigarette right now?" Victoria unhelpfully shrugs her shoulders. "Spit it out Robin. Get it off your chest." I didn't need to say it as Victoria was already poised to read my thoughts, and these particular thoughts were writ large in my mind. But she wants to hear me say it out loud. So I do. "Sandeep said that you were using me. That your affection for me was your way of hooking me in, like you'd done with others. He said you'd probably introduce me to your Chinese parents too!" Victoria's face softens. She leaves the sofa and kneels in front of me. She puts her hand on my knee. "He's reading your mind. I'd always suspected that he had the ability but never knew for certain. He knew exactly what to say to you. He just took every one of your doubts and your fears and used them against you. You can tell this is happening when what you hear is uncannily like what you're thinking; using the same words that you would use, the same phrases and even the same images. And it's how he must have known about our rendezvous in Reykjavik. The guy's very good. And clearly more dangerous than we thought. The problem is, we don't know where he is now."

And with that Victoria's face turns ashen.

14

The Hillside

You can smell the fumes down at the port. The mountainside is dotted with plumes of smoke. Seven or more grey columns rising into the air at different stages of their life cycle. Bells ring out seeming to answer one another. From the shore it looks like there might have been a rather precise and yet random airstrike, although what the targets could be is a mystery. There is little in the thick carpet of foliage that could warrant such aggression. Little more than deep green bushes, tree canopies, flowers, bamboos, orchids, pitcher plants, bushes. An attack on nature would be a better description.

But buried in the greenery are in fact tiny buildings. Solitary spiritual outposts flanked on all sides by the wild. Places that you would have to trek to. Not on the path to anywhere else.

On this day, the motivation for a small group of travellers to visit each of these places in turn is not for worship. Far from it.

Victoria grips my arm. It's not in order to cross, as we've already arrived. She's signaling a sense of dread that is expanding within her. We are standing at the foot of the path leading to the temple. She heeded my words, before we burst into this humid place, not to run into the heart of a trap. So we slowly creep up the path, at points almost crawling on our hands and knees. The head-sized bell at the entrance to this temple is not ringing, but there is smoke trailing up into the sky. It is coming from behind the temple, from what looks like the garden. Of the handful of sites that have been ransacked it seems that this is the most recent. Victoria can't help but quicken her pace. Now she is sprinting up the path. My foot loses its purchase and I slide backwards. Realising that I can't catch her up I pull the gun from my body holster and swing around to the right of the entrance. I figure that if Victoria is to be captured as she enters the temple then my advantage will come from holding on to an element of surprise. Before I know it I am waist deep in thick undergrowth. I lash out at bushes and tree branches managing to maintain some momentum. The closer I get to the garden the more that smoke starts to block my view. I cough like I'm laughing, exposing my position to anyone that is interested. I make a break to get through the vegetation and rip through the final natural barriers into the calm, tame garden.

It is exactly as I remembered it, although this time there is not an elderly couple seated on a bench. Nor are there children play fighting on the grass. I hear Victoria moving through the temple at high speed. She is knocking objects over as she strides in and out of rooms. Her desperation mounting. I still can't quite see the source of the smoke. It is thicker towards the back of the temple where the garden meets the foliage, so I lift my feet and walk quickly in that direction. Part of me doesn't want to see what might lie behind the corner. I rub my eyes as the smoke muddies my view. I breathe in suddenly taking in a lungful of smoky air and another cough explodes out of me. I feel lightheaded. As a reflex I turn my head away from the direction I'm walking in and before I know it I have tripped and fallen head first into the tiled exterior of the temple, and then bounced onto a wooden door that belongs to an outhouse. I slump on the ground completely disorientated. The smoke is all around me and I can barely see twelve inches in front of me. I call out to Victoria partly so she can locate me, but mainly to check that she is okay.

I hear nothing back from beyond the smoke. I remain on the floor for a moment, my plan being to jump to my feet as soon as I pinpoint the best direction to move in. And then I pause. There is a scratching sound. It startles me at first not least because I can't identify what it is or where it is coming from. When I was young I used to keep rabbits in a wooden hutch and they would regularly scrabble their claws on the walls to keep their claws from growing too long. This noise was an exact match. Perhaps the children kept rabbits, I think to myself. It happens again. I am finding it harder to breath so I pinpoint the position of the sound as best I can, commit it to memory, and then crawl back to where I started in the garden where the smoke is thinner.

As soon as I get out I see Victoria. She is bent over with her head in her hands. She is sobbing. She has been through the whole building and no one is there. With my

hands on each of her shoulders I gently move her away
from the smoke and towards the bench to sit her down.
Her body stiffens and she resists initially, the adrenalin
still pumping through her. "They're not here there's no
one here nothing at all." She exclaims in one exhaled
breath. I realise I still have my gun in my hand. I put it
away and sit down with her, having to apply some gentle
force to get her knees to bend. "Is it possible that they've
gone somewhere? To the market? To the harbour?" I
was running out of suggestions. "No. No. I don't think
so. They'd be here. The stove is still on in the kitchen."
Panic is rising again in her voice. "Stay here and let me
check it out again, you might have missed something.
Just stay here right?" I look to Victoria to see if she's
understood. She nods reluctantly and I straighten up to
search the temple.

I systematically move through the rooms. I'm not
entirely sure what I'm expecting. The parents and the
children would surely have revealed themselves by now
if they were here. I don't feel good about my chances.
I sweep the kitchen, nothing here. Then the sparsely
furnished main temple. Nothing here. Then the children's
room. Two beds, some cupboards, a stool and nothing else.
The parent's bedroom, pristine and everything in its place.
Except the owners. The final room is a larder. Long and
thin. On entering it I can see that it is empty apart from
a few food items on the shelves. At the far end is a small
open window that must be closest to the smoke. The thick
fumes are bubbling up and flowing over into the larder.
The smoke seems heavy. It looks like a scene from a low
budget horror movie. I look curiously at the room half
remembering something. It comes to mind. The wooden

door to the entrance of the outhouse. The scrabbling noise. Where was that? Where is that? It must be close because we are next to the source of the smoke. I step out of the kitchen door and, pulling my shirt up over my nose, take a sharp left, tracing the same route as I took earlier. Out of the corner of my eye I see that Victoria is no longer on the bench. I push forward against the duvet of smoke.

I repeat the exact same mistake as before falling first into the tiled exterior of the temple, and then bouncing onto the wooden door. At least I've found it. I sink to the ground where the smoke is less thick. I press my ear against the door where the scrabbling noise came from. "Is there anyone there?" I hear myself say. My voice sounds weak. I reach my hand up to the handle and shake the door. It remains still. I splutter and wheeze with the effort. It is quickly getting too difficult to breathe, so I project my voice like I am on stage. "Is there anyone there?" No audible reply comes, but I start to hear thoughts. They are garbled. I sharpen my attention. Then there is scratching again. Quieter this time. Less distinct. But undoubtedly there. I can barely see in front of me and have probably twenty or thirty seconds remaining before the air is unbreathable. I shout. "Stand back from the door. Stand back, I'm going to kick it. Do you understand?" I'm coughing as I finish the warning. Nothing comes back. I have no choice but to continue. The first boot of my foot does nothing. I have never kicked a door open before and have no idea where you direct your blow. To the hinges? To the handle? Dead centre of the door? I propel my foot out again. Nothing. I take a few steps back and run at it, this time I throw my right shoulder to the side opposite to the hinges. A blistering pain reverberates through half of my body. It's useless.

When I was ten years old a girl in my class in school trapped me in her garage. She invited me back to her house one day. I didn't know her very well, but it was such a self-assured invitation I found myself agreeing. Before we had left the school gates she was holding my hand. As I let my hand get held I tried to work out if I'd missed something in our rather tenuous friendship. Perhaps I'd signaled a fascination with her? I hadn't. Perhaps I'd been looking at her a lot. Pretty sure I hadn't. So I let myself be led by the hand to her house. She lived on the other side of the town. It was technically a town, a small one, although I've never been entirely clear about what technicalities are taken into consideration when naming somewhere a town. It reminds me of the story of the famous baseball umpire Bill Klem who was harried by an exasperated batter demanding whether the ball was a strike or not. Klem responded, "Sonny, it ain't nothin til I call it". Someone had probably just decided one day to call it a town and no one saw any reason to disagree.

Her bedroom made me feel immediately uncomfortable. Pinks and whites. Fluffy objects. Soft toys. Funny looking shoes. Cute stuff. Frilled curtains. Little things. Lots of little things. Arranged items. Tidiness. A diary. Flimsy clothes. Hairbrushes. Photographs of friends. Little pots. I would go as far as saying that there was not a single item in her room that would be found in mine. It was like going to a foreign land. I shuddered to think what other horrifying sights there might be in the house. And what happens if some of her girlfriends arrive? It was at this point that I started to appreciate that I needed to escape. It was like an epiphany. I had thought about my options. I could make up an excuse, like I was feeling ill, but I was sure that she'd whip out a miniature nurse's outfit and try and smother me back into health. I could pretend that I'd forgotten that I needed to be somewhere, but I was sure that she would outwit me on matters of timing, or by asking difficult questions that I couldn't answer. Or I could just make a break for it. Option three was a better fit with my capabilities. I could run. Running I could do.

And so when my new best, soon to be worst, friend, turned her back to take another object from her cupboard to show me, I scarpered like a greyhound out of her door. Not having noticed the layout of her house as I first entered I quickly got lost in a maze of rooms, and as the panic rose within me, I spotted an external door and burst through it to freedom. Unfortunately, it was the door to the garage and no sooner had I recognised this I heard the key being turned in the lock. I had been locked in. Actually trapped. This was my first incarceration, certainly at the hands of a ten-year-old girl. After the initial drama of me shouting, threatening and then begging to be released, I accepted my imprisonment, and curled up into an empty dog's basket in the corner. I was there for what seemed like a couple of hours, although in reality it was probably twenty minutes. I was rescued by the girl's mother to whom the girl had confessed her crime. Apparently this wasn't the first time this had happened. It was a thing she did.

I leapt out from the smoke, arms flailing. I had decided to prize the door open instead of knocking it down. My eyes scoured the garden for something to use. I saw it. Where the cooking pot had been when I first came here there was metal poker, lying on the grass, no doubt used to stoke the fire. It was narrow and pointed at one end. It was perfect. Victoria had returned and was now standing in front of me. "What is it? What is it?" she spits out. I don't have time to explain. I side step her and rush back to the outhouse, finding my way immediately to the door. I furiously jammed the poker into the gap between the door and the frame. I wedge it in and lever with all the strength I have. It is starting to move so with one last forceful dig of the poker, the door cracks. The metal lock shatters and the door swings open. They are there, at knee height. The two children curled into a single ball. They had been protected from the smoke fumes by the locked door and appear unharmed. But they are petrified. They don't move. They don't even look up.

Victoria storms in after me and without hesitation scoops them both up in her arms. She struggles a little so I support her and the children as we exit the smoke. The children, recognising Victoria, wrap their arms around her neck, whimpering. Victoria's eyes are streaming with two dirty stripes appearing down her cheeks. Reunited, the three sob and wail.

We are all in the kitchen, and in between tearful outbursts Victoria explains what the children have said. Over the course of less than an hour the fires had been started one by one at each of the temples nearby. The noise from the bells had built to a crescendo and from their house they could see lines of people down at the harbour gazing back up to the hillside. The children had been standing in the garden trying to work out what was going on, when two Western people – a man and a woman - had climbed through the bushes into the garden as if coming down from the mountain. The children had screamed and fled to their parents who were speaking intensely with one another in the main temple itself. The parents had told them not to worry, but that they should hide in the outbuilding until they had spoken to them. When they heard shouting and what sounded like items being thrown to the floor in the kitchen, they became frightened and locked themselves in the building. The door to the outhouse had all this time been locked from the inside. I absent-mindedly rubbed my shoulder in a self-soothing way.

Victoria told the children not to worry about their parents as she knew exactly where to find them. She didn't of course but this had the desired effect. We walked the children down to a friend of the family's house and left them in good care. Back at the temple, we put out the burning embers of the fire that had clearly been started as a signal to Victoria – a message that the organisation meant business. My suspicions about Victoria had disappeared. In seeking to terrorise Victoria, this had cemented my position on which side to be. "We've got to find them." Victoria says. "We will." I say.

15

His Highness Sheikh Abdulla Al Khalif

His highness was a trillionaire, and still not yet forty years old. He had ice white teeth, smooth flawless skin, and a finely trimmed beard. He had a small horizontal scar at the base of his nose that many believed had been put there deliberately to compensate for his certain lack of ruggedness. His wealth had initially come from the family's oil, and when that started to dry up he had diversified into genetic engineering and space transportation. The growth of Asia had experienced another resurgence which at the time had been dubbed the second Asian century. Its growth hadn't just been economic but geographical too, turning it into the world's leading power by a long distance. The 'stan' countries (Pakistan, Afghanistan, Turkmenistan, Kazakhstan and so on) had been absorbed into China, officially Grand China. As poorer nations by comparison occupying considerable areas of land mass, they were the perfect location for China's physical expansion. For a couple of decades, and out of pragmatism, they had retained their original names but after a while they were simply treated as regions of China. Perhaps with the exception of India, the cushion between China and the Middle East had all but been removed. Grand China and the Middle East were neighbours and trade relations were very strong if a little tense.

As Grand China's wealth and influence grew so did its interest in human perfection. It had more or less solved many of the big challenges around alternative energy supply, the infrastructure difficulties associated with such a large area, maintaining a balance between the fifty million population ultra-cities and the hundreds of thousands of rural idylls that were carefully protected and regulated. Successes had been in shorter supply in the fields of genetic modification - life extension, brain tuning, attractiveness optimisations, gender remodeling, emotion stabilisation, muscle augmentation, human energy management etc. This was a business growth area, as was space travel. Voyages to the moon to establish the feasibility of population re-housing had been encouraging. As a part of a multi-nation experiment, over ten thousand people had been relocated to the moon for a period of twenty-four months. This had proved the feasibility of off-earth living to all but the most extreme critics. The space transportation company owned by the Sheikh had been developing shuttles that could each carry around five hundred passengers. The journey would take fewer than three hours.

I'd been given my instructions to remove the Sheikh and that's what I was there to do. He was a leading figure in the organisation, which might be reason enough. But he had prosecuted his business interests with particular disregard for human life and dignity. He had negotiated unofficial deals with the Chinese that had enabled him to test his company's modifications on live human subjects, and not just in the hundreds, but in the thousands. And to avoid people hearing about this, he'd arranged for the subjects of these experiments to be disappeared. To be exterminated. Nothing left of them. Entire villages had been wiped out, and even place names removed from the digital maps. And no one knew about this, not a soul. He was ostensibly a model businessman, a man of the highest ethical standards. It was his company that would help solve the population crisis by facilitating the off-earth living projects. He was the man that would elevate the human condition, ridding it of its short brutishness. He was the man that, without knowing it, would ultimately create the invention that would secure his downfall.

I report to the reception and explain who I'm here to see. I am asked a series of questions. My name? John. That's all I say to the receptionist. He checks on a glass panel in front of him. "Do you have another name?" I chuckle. If only he knew the half of it. I might be under Anthony John I say. "Ah, I see you here Mr. John. I'm very sorry. This is entirely my mistake. I was thinking John was your given name. And your company?" I explain that I'm with the Foundation. This is the name the organisation sometimes gives itself. Other names have included Globe House and Rajvosa. They've changed over time. I'm taken to the lift and my escort travels with me to the next reception on the thirty third floor. There is a stunning view of downtown Manama from up here. It is a crystal clear day. Not a cloud in sight, and only limited pollution for this time of year in Bahrain. I go through the usual rigmarole. It's boring. The word Foundation is the magic key though. The receptionist knows that people who have come in the past and used this word, have been important. The receptionist didn't know what it signified, but it did mean that I wasn't someone just off the streets. Another irony. I lead her to believe I have an appointment, and she believes.

I'm shown into a meeting room. It has expensive handmade carpet on the floor, and three or four tan leather sofas. There is a low table at about shin height between the sofas. A smartly dressed woman is about to ask me if I would like a drink. I say no thank you before she speaks. She finds this interaction slightly strange but walks off anyway. I sense the arrival of His Highness Sheikh Abdulla. He is walking slowly along the corridor. His sandals gently stroke the tile floor as he walks. He is alone which slightly surprises me. I expected security. He enters the room and I change position to greet him. Close up he has a very pleasant face. He smiles broadly and holds his arms out so that we can hug. He smells of perfume. He has an appealing way about him. I catch a reflection of myself in a gold-framed mirror. I am wearing a slim, dark suit, and a white pressed shirt. Silver cufflinks protrude from my sleeves. I have some faint bruises to my cheek which I suggest to His Highness is simply dark skin pigmentation. He is thinking about horses. He has a ranch nearby and he will soon be taking the helicopter parked on the roof of the building there. If I didn't know better, I'd think this was a terribly decent chap. He's not. I'm tempted to dig deeper into his mind, to reveal how he feels when he orders the removal of his experimental subjects. This isn't necessary. My exercise here is damage limitation. His life in exchange for thousands more.

Before we start the pleasantries I speak "Do you want to know a secret about the Foundation?" The Sheikh looks uneasy. He wishes he'd brought security now. I continue. "It has been responsible for some of the greatest misery that the world has ever seen. It has bought and sold people like meat. It has tortured and brutalised without compunction. It has poisoned the water we drink. It has brought this planet to its knees. And all of this. Every bit of this, just so that narcissistic fucks like you can live pampered, frivolous lives. Everything that you have inherited, and everything that you have built, has come to be through the destruction of everything I hold dear." As the Sheikh is about to yell for help I place a thought in his mind. A thought that tells him that if he speaks he will be killed. His lips close. "But that isn't the secret is it?" Despite his fear he still wants an answer. "The secret is that the Foundation created its own end. It hasn't come yet, but it's just a matter of time. And the supreme irony in all of this. And I know you'll smile when you hear this. It certainly tickles me. The irony is that it's you and your filthy company that brought me to your front door." I hold my wrist on my left arm up to his face, to show him what I mean. And with the other hand I drive a knife into his neck. I feel sickened by my own actions, but it is necessary. As the security guards arrive, I vanish.

16

GenCo Storm Rooms

GenCo's Storm Rooms were split between Xi'an and the Redland region of the Off-Earth settlement. GenCo, one of the wealthiest companies in the worlds, employed well over two million people, mostly educationalists, sales and tech maintenance people. Fewer than five thousand employees worked in the Storm Rooms, which, in essence were research laboratories. Of that, perhaps only one thousand worked off-earth.

The company was divided into four business units. By far the largest was the Desirability division. It accounted for around three quarters of the company's revenue and dealt with an array of customer requirements related to improving physical attractiveness. This was addressed in a variety of ways from technologies that simulated the appearance of youthfulness, synthesized hormones that guaranteed weight control, gland implants that altered body scent, injections to alter follicle and skin colouration, voice manipulating tinctures and so on. It also included composite, and more expensive, treatments that helped to convey particular qualities such as likeability, gravitas and intelligence, as chosen by the customer. You didn't even have to be likeable or intelligent or whatever it was, you just had to suggest it. What it amounted to was a business that specialised in perception manipulation.

Interestingly, the company discovered over time that it needed to rely less and less on physical signs to engender desired responses, and instead used hidden carriers of suggestion such as modified pheromones and touch-transmitted hormones. It meant that people could effectively direct other people to think in particular ways. Providing they had the money to purchase the relevant shot or implant they could literally change other people's minds.

The other three divisions of GenCo had been created in response to the requirements of GenCo's sister company, Al Hab, which had for many years led the way in passenger space travel. The Al Hab space vehicles had been the first to be capable of covering distances of five hundred thousand miles, which they had done to service the Off-earth settlements on the Moon. But within half a century the Al Hab vehicles had made successful voyages to Venus and Mars, achievable within less than a few days. For many the step changes in innovation that the company achieved seemed unstoppable. However, the weaknesses in the system that were being revealed were related not to the technological capabilities of the vehicles they had developed but the physical limitations of the passengers. And so it was for these reasons that Al Hab's sister company built its remaining divisions around the human challenges of rapid transitions, cognitive disturbances and the physical consequences of travelling through anti-gravity passageways.

Jan walked boldly through the laboratory. He had been summoned by his boss to attend a meeting in the demonstration room. His confident demeanour belied nervousness about his unexpected involvement in the discussion. He entered the room at pace, his long legs carrying him faster than he had imagined. He looked like a man that expected bad news which, on this occasion, he was about to receive. He had been one of GenCo's star performers, leading the largest research team in the unit. A much revered scientist by training, he had been responsible for a small number of truly significant technical breakthroughs, and had displayed a flair for the business, both within the main Desirability division where he had spent a few years, and in the three smaller functions, where he had spent most of his career. For some years now he had become visibly disillusioned with the work programme - something that his boss, Badi al Zaman, had become increasingly aware of. Badi al Zaman, was barely twenty years old when he took up the position. He was a relative of the Al-Khalif dynasty, and he knew where his interests lay.

Unsurprisingly for a room of senior GenCo employees, the gathering was handsomely presented. There were four men seated at a table chatting and drinking from small glasses. White teeth. Smooth skin. Youthful physiques. Beautifully, and wholly artificially, manicured beards. Lustrous hair. Comforting scents. And a likeable presence to each and every one of them. Although not to Jan. "Sit down please Hjarand." Badi instructed. Jan remained standing and leaned against the glass wall. "Thanks, but I spend too long sitting down these days." They were ten minutes in before Jan appreciated that he was there to be dismissed. It was a somewhat humiliating experience to be sacked by a group of people, rather than one, not least because the case for his dismissal wasn't at all clear to him. They spoke of a 'release period' that would involve Jan working on some smaller research projects until his contract would be closed and he would be returned to Earth. They mentioned four months. Quite a slow release Jan pondered. One of the men in the room named Arturo would supervise him during this period. He was thanked in a perfunctory reluctant tone, and then the meeting ended abruptly, and before he could even lodge a complaint or question the decision. The group then dispersed. By the time Jan had returned to his desk his working documents had been removed and the access codes embedded in his wrist revoked.

He'd known that the axe would fall sooner or later. He also knew that if they had the faintest idea what he'd really been working on they'd sack him again, and then bury his body on the uninhabited lands of the moon. They were a powerful employer that didn't take kindly to their technological advantage being compromised. Jan had spent the last year designing programs to keep the fierce GenCo security systems at bay long enough to sneak out the files he needed.

Jan had experienced an awakening during his tenure with GenCo. In the early days, when he'd been a high flier, he'd been let into the inner circle of the executive, accompanying Board members on important visits, and even being drawn in to the social circle of the Al Hab and GenCo elite. Jan was naturally, rather than artificially, likeable. He was something of a strategist too; able to move easily from discussing wormholes to how GenCo could expand into new markets. He was humble, and instilled confidence in those around him. The senior guys liked him. And as a result he was entrusted with information that would have been appropriate for someone that was loyal to the organisation, but not for someone that had in fact decided that the company needed to be destroyed.

It was no surprise to anyone least of all Jan that the owners of GenCo and Al Hab were wealthy and powerful. Nor was it news that the company had a history of unethical conduct spanning decades that had included slave labour and human experimentation. The company had been nothing short of brutal in its scramble to lead the space travel race. And the national and global authorities had turned a blind eye believing that the crisis of population expansion, that had inspired the off-earth settlements, warranted a bold and ambitious response. The realisation that GenCo, Al Hab and the family they belonged to, owned most of the wealth on earth was however a major problem for Jan. What they effectively had was a controlling share in the affairs of every inhabitant on the earth and the moon. It meant that they governed the media, shaped the political landscape, had a firm hand in the allocation of resources and so on. And the public did not understand this level of control. Everyone knew that the Al Khalif family were powerful, but not to this order of magnitude. This had been enough to politicise Jan, but this was a fraction of the story.

What Jan's engagement with the company's most senior players had revealed was simply terrifying. In fact, when he first discovered what was going on he denied it for a long time, even with the evidence there in front of his eyes. It was a reality he wasn't prepared to face, and by this time of course, he had built some close relations with many of the individuals at the top. If he was honest, he had, despite his misgivings about them, developed a liking for many of the key people. He had been on the path to becoming one of them.

It transpired that alongside its efforts to support the off-earth diaspora, the company had been working on schemes to make some major in-roads into the problems on earth. These were issues that needed to be dealt with and so it might have been of some comfort to know that the Al Khalif dynasty were on the case. But his discoveries shook him to the core. The organisation had been developing plans to bring about de-population on a massive scale. The global one-child policies of the last century had been violently resisted, and for the dynasty more radical measures were required. And so they conducted a series of experiments that included the deliberate introduction of lethal viruses to densely populated areas, climate engineering to trigger flooding and tsunamis, and they seeded and supplied the means for armed conflict. It was important that de-population methods used were invisible and didn't attract suspicion of any kind. If they had a whiff of design to them, the consequences would be catastrophic for the organisation. If attention was attracted, the organisation would activate sleeper agents that it had placed in strategically important positions, each one of them kitted up with GenCo's suggestion implants. The very same technology that, to his shame, Jan had helped to develop. Following his discovery Jan had spent much of his working day scrolling through historical records searching for major natural disasters, and looking for the unseen hand of the corporation. Fifty thousand people killed in a Tsunami here. A hundred thousand dead from a chemical spillage on the shores of the Black Sea. The Sleeping Flu of Northern China that took the children from tens of thousands of families. Which of these, and other appalling tragedies, was the work organisation? Jan knew he had to act.

He had contemplated gathering the necessary evidence and handing it to the authorities. Coincidentally, the Global Regulation Board was headquartered in Oslo, his hometown, and he had some contacts there that he had initially tried to sound out. But the smallest of steps that he took in this direction confirmed that the Regulation Board was as much an employee of the organisation as he was. Something much more direct, something more creative was required.

17

Exit

Jan and Sandeep walked in silence together through the auditorium and then headed for the Fire Exit. They disappeared along the corridor and took a series of turns that led to a storeroom. In the room were stacks of promotional leaflets, cartons of drink flavouring, sacks of popcorn, some cleaning equipment, a safe on the wall and some uniforms. They pass through this room into another at the back that had a single table and two plastic chairs. Jan sat down, took out a small wrap of tobacco and some rolling papers and effortlessly constructed a cigarette. He put it between his lips but didn't light it. Sandeep looked visibly nervous. Sitting at opposite sides of the table they stared at each other. It was going to be a difficult meeting and they wore the strain on their faces. These were two people from separate sides of a divide, both skilled in reading and in suggesting, and both trying hard to hold a 'normal' conversation.

"I think this would work best for both of us if we did this." Sandeep said this as he stood up and took off his jacket to reveal that he was unarmed. Jan followed Sandeep's lead and did a similar twirl before sitting down again. "Back a bit!" Sandeep instructed. Jan dragged his chair back providing more space between the two of them. This way they could both cross out of the storeroom at any time without having an unwelcome passenger. Jan stood up again and took two steps towards a switch on the fascia of an extractor and air conditioning unit. He turned it on with a pointed finger, lit his cigarette and returned to the table. "Stop fucking around" Sandeep said impatiently, "What did you bring me here for?"

"Why so irate, Sandeep?" Jan probed. "I'll tell you why Hjarand" Sandeep pronounced his name like it was a swear word. "The new recruit that you sent me this morning to pass on the message, some bloke called Robin Mann? Well he tried to kill me. Which I assume you knew about?" No response. "I was preparing a nice breakfast, and the fucker pulls a gun on me. Just like that. He had no clue either that he'd been used to pass on the location of our little private chat. Is this how you treat your recruits these days? And why meet in this fucking freezing, dark nowheresville country? That's why I'm irate!" Jan smiled thinly. Sandeep had a shiny film of sweat on his forehead. He now had his back against the wall, maximising the distance between them. "Well, if we're going to talk about who's trying to kill who, what about Larry?" Jan blew a lungful of smoke from between his teeth. "I can't have that Sandeep. No one deserves that." Jan shared with Sandeep some mental images of Larry when he was recovered. Bloodied face. Broken nose. Shattered fingers. A dark purple knot of skin where his implant had been removed from his wrist. Jan's face wore a rigid expression. Sandeep's eyes flickered for a second as he appreciated the horror of the image brought to him. "And of course Edward?" Jan paused waiting for a response. It didn't come. He held his ground. A few more seconds and Sandeep cracked. "That has got nothing to do with me. I've got no idea where he is." Sandeep confidently asserted. "I don't know. Maybe he went on vacation. Have you checked his cellphone?" This riled Jan.

As they spoke occasional incidental music from the movie would drift along the corridor into the storeroom. It added a strange form of dislocated drama to their discussion. Questions would be accompanied by some rousing orchestral music, while Sandeep's throwaway comic remarks would be followed with a tense bass line. A conversation with its own backing track.

Jan knew how the meeting needed to go. He'd been building up to this for a while now. The organisation, that he had unwittingly created, had become too powerful and too much of a threat to his work. He'd always been aware of the allure of the technology, and he'd even fallen prey to its charm. The ability to be anywhere. To walk the earth as if it belonged to you. The sense of invincibility that it bred. All of this explained why he needed to exercise care, and why he and Victoria had so diligently watched and researched their recruits. One by one. But he had learned that you cannot underestimate peoples' vanities.

The killings had started a few years ago. While in this line of business, it was an inevitable collateral consequence, they had got more frequent, to the point that it was clear that the organisation intended to eliminate everyone that stood with Jan. There had been numerous attempts on his life, but as the inventor of the technology, and someone that knew better than anyone what it could do, he had so far been able to evade capture. But he could feel them closing in, if not on him, on those closest to him; Larry and Edward had been the most recent casualties of this, and he feared for what might happen to Georgia and Victoria.

If any of this can be spoken of in terms of irony, then this was it; there wasn't a single member of the organisation that had turned against Jan that he hadn't personally recruited or endorsed. In the beginning, at least in this time band, they had been a tight group of some forty or so activists. Activists with a difference. The ultimate campaign was to make it impossible for the GenCo's and Al Habs of this world to exist. None of the group fully appreciated this of course, not having crossed forward in time with Jan to witness the ramifications of the work of these companies. Recruits were chosen as people of character. People that were politically motivated. They were people that Jan and Victoria had observed at different stages in their lives before they were even approached. As vetting processes go it didn't get much more reliable than this. But, power does corrupt. And as Jan came to appreciate, humans made in the crucible of neo-liberal, consumerist and anxious times corrupt quicker than most.

"I have a proposition to make to you Sandeep." Sandeep lent forward a little signaling his curiosity. "You've always known that there was more to the technology, right?" Jan's eyes dropped to his hand as he flipped it over exposing his wrist. Cigarette ash fell onto the table like a flower shedding its leaves. "I'm prepared to tell you what more there is. I'm prepared to show you what you can do. And believe me, it will blow your mind." Sandeep's interest peaked. "So for example, watch the switch on the air conditioning unit. Are you watching?" Sandeep nodded. He focused his eyes on the white switch. Nothing. Then, it happened. The switch turned off. Jan remained still in his seat, and the unit had shut down. No one had moved. "And the uniforms?" Sandeep was encouraged to nudge his gaze to the uniforms that sat on the shelf. "Fuck! How did you do that?" The uniforms were no longer on the shelf but were sitting on the table between them. Still folded neatly. They had moved about six feet seemingly at the behest of Jan. "And that's just the beginning Sandeep. Can you imagine what else is possible? Can you? I'm pretty sure you can." Jan took a long drag from the hand-rolled up cigarette. He knew that Sandeep wouldn't be able to resist. He'd studied him for the best part of five years before he'd recruited him.

Sandeep stared at Jan, weighing up the proposal. His eyes searched the ceiling seeming to look for inspiration. He was silent for a moment, and then spoke "Okay, okay. And what do you want in return for this? What do you want from me?" Sandeep asked. "It's simple." Jan explained. "I want you to call a meeting of the key people in the organisation. You know who they are, and I want all of them to be present including our good friend Ryan." Jan enunciated the word friend mockingly. Sandeep probed "Is this a meeting that you will attend Jan?" "You could say that." He replied quickly. "Although, I think it would be best if you didn't mention that." Sandeep nodded with a half-smile. "And what's so essential about Ryan? You've always had your doubts haven't you about Ryan. In fact, from the second you crowned him with the implant. But I never really shared your concerns. Why such enmity for one of our flock?" With his head tilted to the floor and eyes closed as if in prayer Jan spoke quietly, "On the very first day I gave Ryan his implant he used his capabilities to settle a vendetta. He'd lost his brother you see, a few years earlier. An engineer in the army on leave from a tour in the Gulf. He'd headed out to Dublin with some friends for some fun. Kicking back, you see, until the early hours of the morning. But he'd got into a fight with some locals who had been sick of yet another gang of army lads taking over their drinking hole. It turned out it was a particularly tough bar and in the confusion from the fight Ryan's brother had been fatally knifed. Four of five Irish men were involved but no one had been charged. And so Ryan, implant in wrist, and with an immediate form of transit out of the scene, located all of the men that were involved and executed each one of them. Some were found crumpled in the streets, others murdered in their homes, their children sound asleep upstairs. That's when we discovered who Ryan was."

Sandeep searched Jan's eyes to read his feelings but was met with an expressionless wall. "And if I set up this meeting, Ryan in tow, what protection will you give me? How do I know you won't just send one of your idiot recruits to have me killed when I've done this for you?" Jan listened and pointedly extinguished his cigarette by crushing it into the plastic table top. "Do you think my abilities stop short at turning switches off and moving clothes? How long do you think it would take me to sever your windpipe with that screwdriver?" Jan's eyes direct Sandeep to the black handled screwdriver lying on top of a pile of leaflets. "Believe me, if I wanted you dead. You would be." Sandeep understood. Jan offered a few words to soften the threat. "If you do this, you have my

word that you'll be left alone. All you need to do is keep
out of my way. You carry on doing whatever you do - an
organisation of one. And I'll forget you ever existed."

"Well" said Sandeep, "Most of these guys are
Libertarians at heart, not Anarchists. You know that
don't you? I think that was the mistake you always made.
They don't like meetings. They don't like being told what
to do. They don't like being summoned. That's what
fucked them off when you were in charge. We were never
an 'organisation' and thank God for it. But you made the
mistake of thinking we were." Jan's patience was wearing
thin. He took out the wrap of tobacco, started to roll a
cigarette and spoke. "Will you fucking do it or not?"

Jan had first spotted Sandeep when he was a bicycle
courier in his late teenage years in central London. At
the time he had an athletic figure and was an active
member of various anarchist movements. He took his
political commitments seriously. He would hack corporate
computer systems, picket the gates of arms manufacturers,
organise anti-Capitalist protests and so on. He was an
artist too and would creep out in the early hours of the
morning to decorate the dullest of streets of London with
beautiful seditionary art. From a safe distance as always,
Jan checked him out again when he was in his early
twenties. At this point he had re-located to Barcelona
and was writing for *La Quinta Columna,* an anarchist
newspaper, while also continuing his direct action. A few
years older again and Sandeep was ensconced in some
quite technically complex work that involved frustrating
transactions between despotic governments and arms
suppliers. He would pose online as the supplier in the
course of an illicit transaction and introduce unexpected

and difficult demands. This would cause relationships to become damaged, often irrevocably, and the deals would crumble. Result achieved!

Sandeep was very effective at covering his tracks and as far as Jan could tell he never attracted the interest of the authorities. He was one of the most skilled individuals that he'd recruited and Jan had been impressed by his resourcefulness, if a little wary of how much he could be trusted. In the end Jan asked Victoria to recruit him, which of course she did expertly.

Sandeep grinned from ear to ear and held out his hand to Jan. It looked like they were about to make the deal. Jan smiled back but held his hands up, as you might do if the police had asked you to do so. In this instance though it was to signify that making physical contact wouldn't be a good idea. "We have a deal then!" Jan pronounced. It looked like it was done. But then, without the slightest warning, Sandeep literally threw the weight of his entire body at Jan, wrapping himself around him. Arms and legs trapping him like an octopus. They both slammed into the wall. Sandeep was yelling into his ear. The words were difficult to decipher and probably just an echo of what Sandeep was using by way of suggestion. He screamed, "Stay here. Stay here. Stay here!" repeating it over and over. The plaster on the wall crunched. The two bodies began to fall and then nothing. The incidental music from the cinema screen climbed to a crescendo. They had disappeared and left what was an empty storeroom and the dying embers of a cigarette end.

18

The Stone Circle

My career in filmmaking was short-lived. I never really had my heart in it and the more I saw, the less I liked. This was becoming a theme in my career choices.

If you look at being employed as a means of getting money, then in some ways it doesn't matter what you do. Providing the job is tolerable, on the right side of ethical and you get paid enough then what's there to complain about? And in fact many would argue that if the money was right then the rest is way down the pecking order. Alternatively, if you take the view that spending most of your waking hours engaged in the kind of activity that you wouldn't ordinarily touch with a barge pole if you didn't have to, then it puts a different spin on it. Philosophically, it's hard to feel comfortable with exchanging most of your time, energy and talent for cash. At least that's where I'd got to in my thinking.

By the time I took my next career turn I had forged a different relationship to money. Spending nine months as a student again, this last time studying film, had reminded me that you don't need much money to live. You really don't. More than this, I had developed an uncharacteristically stoic outlook. Consider the lilies of the field, while they do not labour or spin. That kind of thing. I was developing faith. Not in a Supreme Being. But in being. Over doing. The realisation took me by surprise, but I came to appreciate that I didn't need to engineer my happiness, or my living circumstances, through working. I had come to the view that I didn't need to reach for anything.

So my next career was one that entailed no work at all. At least not in the terms that work is usually understood. I committed to doing nothing. It's a hard one to explain. And harder still to live this way in societies where people who do not work are regarded as idle or parasitic. This life I lived for five years.

I moved to the country. To the Highlands of Scotland. I spent most of the money I had left on a train ticket to Perth. Four hundred and sixty miles north of London. I left the station and hitchhiked my way to a small collection of houses near the Spittal of Glenshee. It was extraordinary. A place of dark greens, deep reds and golden yellows. Perpetually undulating terrain. Tall ferns. Bracken. Fences. Ice cold rivers bustling under bridges. Moisture on the ground, in the air or on its way. Smoke rising from the chimneys of stone houses in the hills. Compared to London it was empty, and yet it felt like more than enough was going on.

I had made my way to a small pub. It was called The Steading. Excluding the barman and myself there were three other customers. As I walked in I had expected an American Werewolf in London moment. But silence did not fall on the room as I entered and no one seemed to

*notice my arrival. It was mid evening and early springtime.
I ordered a pint of lager and sat at a table near to the
fireplace. I had a small knapsack with me with a few
essential items and that was it. I was exercising my faith.*

*That evening I got chatting to the barman who offered
me a place to stay. I had explained that I didn't have
any money but this didn't seem to matter. It transpired
that the accommodation that he was offering was a small
kirk that had nearly burned down the previous spring.
It needed a lot of reconstruction. The roof was more
or less watertight but the timbers needed strengthening,
numerous tiles replacing and insulation. Built in the early
1800's, it had ten rows of pews, all intact, and an altar that
had been singed by the fire. The fire had ravaged all the
tapestries that had been hanging on the walls and there
were a handful of half burned bibles that had been liberally
scattered around. Towards the back of a church was what
resembled a bedsit. This was the best comparison I could
make. It was a small room that contained a single bed, a
small stove, a sink, a couple of wooden armchairs and an
old fashioned black and white TV. The barman didn't ask
me to help repair the kirk. He didn't need to.*

*I set to work initially on the roof structure. It perhaps
goes without saying that I had literally no experience of
roofing. It didn't share anything with the skills I'd acquired
in my former life as an employee. And the same applied to
the vegetable garden at the rear of the kirk that I brought
back to life. Tomato plants. Onions. Garlic. Potatoes.
Pak Choi. Lettuce. Carrots. I would read books that I
borrowed from people I met in the pub about roofing and
growing vegetables. All I had to do was mention what I
was doing and they would appear. Sometimes they would*

be posted through the letterbox of the kirk. No message or inscription to say whom they belonged to. Just there on the mat. In the early days I would get at least a book a week through the door, and another Do It Yourself book in the pub each week. I could have started a library by the time I finished.

Early one Sunday morning I set out on a walk. I had heard about a stone circle not too far from the kirk and I was intrigued. I put on most of the clothes that I owned and with a battered old map of the area in my hand, given of course to me by one of the locals, I strode out into the wilderness. Initially following the flow of the road, I took a dirt track and then weaved in and out of farmland, woods and dense grasses. I had navigated my way using a combination of landmarks and the sun which hinted at its positioning through the intermittent clouds. It was a privilege to have eaten breakfast from the food that I had grown myself, to repair the roof above me, and then to make my way to the stone circle without any electronic devices or navigation systems other than what sat in my head.

The stone circle comprised four rocks on top of a small mound. Like the posts on a four-poster bed. Without the bed. From what I had read the circle had been there for between four and five thousand years, when most of Britain was covered by woodland. At the time there would have been perhaps a hundred thousand people at most living in Scotland. Within a ten-mile radius of where I was, no more than a hundred people. Records suggest approximately one thousand two hundred sites of stone circles around Britain, all of different sizes, and with the majority being located in Scotland. The purpose of the stone circle monuments has never been fully understood.

The mound on which this one sat was apparently naturally formed – a moraine from the process of glaciation. In this sense it is unlikely that the stones marked a burial ground. Furthermore, there was no evidence of people having lived there. The two most likely explanations were that the stone monuments were either created for ceremonial purposes or that they possessed a kind of talismanic value – warding off or appeasing nature's spirits. I preferred the latter.

The particular site of the four-poster stone circle felt special. Auspicious. Energetically still. Four stones that had seen time in the making. If I stood in the centre of the mound, I could look down and see the shape of a shallow valley. A smooth curvaceous landscape edged by trees. The scenery took the form of interlocking bodies as if at any moment the land could stand up and walk away. The wind would pick up and dance furiously around the fabric at the neck of my shirt like a bird frantically taking flight through the branches of a tree. My hair waving and separating like fingers, then falling flat as the wind disappeared. In the sky, in the distance, I could see muscular clouds lined up on an elevated horizon. They advanced slowly but unrelentingly. They too had presided over the formation of this land, and the ants that had come to inhabit it. As I stood there as part of nature I wondered what would become of this place in another five thousand years. Whether these stones would remain. Whether the trees would disappear. Whether the fused bodies of this land would in fact have got up and walked away.

By the time the summer came I knew most people in the area. I would be asked to help out with various chores that needed an extra pair of hands – helping to pull a tractor out of a ditch alongside of the road, cleaning up the debris after the early summer storm, even occasional babysitting. I would visit the local market on Saturdays to sell surplus food produce. At the market there was seemingly no rhyme nor reason to the pattern of stalls there. Next to mine was a candle stall. Next to that Crystals. Then a health elixir derived from rare Amazonian plants. Then Olives in every variety. Hats. An exercise gimmick. Mad Davey who would predict football scores. Almost always incorrectly. Vinyl records. Cute pig themed carvings. Massage chairs. An anarchist bookstall. Used shells, cartridges and replica guns. Family planning devices and guidance issued by Joy. And Steve who offered tuition to children studying for exams. Steve's marketing tagline, emblazoned across the top of his stall was – "Have Something Up Your Sleeve. Achieve with Steve!" Next to the word Achieve was a small asterisk and at the bottom of the banner in miniscule writing the asterisk was reproduced with the warning "Please be aware that Steve cannot guarantee your child's exam results."

Between the stall owners there would be a sense of esprit de corps. People would lend small change to one another, they would look after each other's stalls while the owners nipped out, they would batten down the plastic sheeting if the wind picked up and threatened to endanger stock, they would bring one another coffees and homemade cakes and biscuits and tissues and gifts of all varieties.

I found myself talking a lot to the woman that ran the anarchist bookshop. We were roughly the same age. Her name was Grace. She was a Scottish woman born in Oban, a coastal town a hundred or so miles west of where we were. She had dark shoulder length hair and despite being Scottish, born and bred, she looked South American. Tan coloured skin. I assumed she had ancestors that hadn't come from Scotland. She had deep dark brown eyes with bright points in them. Curved. She had a small horizontal scar on her left cheek and a certain vigour to her. Our conversations were always highly animated. Something about the tempo that we both thought at created a kind of chemistry. She was an author of a short story as well as bookseller and brimmed with ideas and a rich vocabulary. She put it all out there too. Without a fear in the world and frightening honesty she would declare how she felt, what excited her, her mistakes or weaknesses, what she hoped for and so on. And all without the usual self-protectiveness or low-level deception that the vast majority of the population employs. Her presence at the market became one of the main reasons I returned week after week.

One day we went for coffee. We left our stalls in the capable hands of Steve and wandered along the river towards the coffee shop. I described how I had ended up living nearby and she told her story. She'd been brought up by hard working parents who ran a hotel in Oban. As a young girl, probably as early as ten years old, she'd helped them clean the bedrooms, look after the reception and take orders in the hotel restaurant. Much of her earlier life had been occupied by schoolwork, homework and hotel work. When she hit sixteen years old she took the opportunity to leave home and she travelled around Spain and then Morocco, ironically funding her travels by working in hotels and bed and breakfasts. After a few years, she had met a Spanish man called Juan and had fallen in love. They rented an apartment initially in

Barcelona and then in Marrakech where they lived for a few more years. However, the romance between Grace and Juan simply ran out of steam, and they staggered on in a relationship far longer than they needed. Neither of them wanted to admit that the magic had long drained out of the friendship. They liked each other enormously but eventually parted ways.

At this point Grace felt more alone than she had for many years and so she had returned to Scotland. At the time in her early twenties she came home to find out that her parents had been taken seriously ill. Knowing that she was going through a difficult time with Juan, they'd kept it to themselves. They had both developed Cancer and the prognosis had been gloomy. The medical verdict had been announced to each parent just a few weeks apart. Grace then spent the following year nursing them. While it had been a grueling and sad period for all three, Grace described their time together as 'blissful', and she cherished every moment. I admired the way she had seen the experience in these terms. It was hard not to like someone like this. Both parents passed away within a few weeks of each other. Grace had sold the hotel and moved east to where she was now. In the town she owned a small bookshop that clocked up only a handful of visitors each day. There weren't many anarchists in the Spittal of Glenshee.

I was keen to take Grace to the stone circle. I think I'd described the site as 'prodigious', and as a lover of words, this had made Grace laugh out loud. But I'd said enough to make her curious so we arranged to go there one day later in the summer. The day came. It was a Sunday and it was dusk by the time we arrived at the circle. We'd planned to get there earlier, but Grace had been fascinated by everything at the kirk and so the tour had taken hours. She wanted to see the work I'd done to the roof, the vegetable plantation and the birds that I'd managed to lure into the garden. On that particular day it was like a scene from a Disney film. There were Blue Tits, Bullfinches, White Thrushes, Blackbirds the colour of coal and Blackcap Warblers making the most amazing fluting song. All were flitting in and out of the trees or hanging from the feeder. At one point a young Roe deer strode nonchalantly behind the trees at the foot of the garden. It was idyllic. Grace immediately warmed to the Kirk, and to me it seemed.

When we arrived at the circle the colours in the sky had turned from a dark pastel purple to burnt orange and then to a shimmering grape. It was like someone had blown into the embers of a fire. There was a gentle hum around us. The traffic on the roads nearby had all but disappeared, and the pre-dusk chorus from birds and other wildlife had died down. When Grace first saw the stone circle she had been as moved as I was. Characteristically she had said exactly what was going on for her. She said something like "It's so beautiful I feel like sobbing." It's a strange thing as after all they were nothing more than four stones in the shape of a rectangle, and yet they conveyed something. Perhaps it was a sense of timelessness. Or maybe they hinted at human life in the heart of all this wilderness. The stones meant that you weren't alone.

I remember that Grace had turned toward me with shiny eyes and a thin oblong tear that had lined the scar on her cheek. It had reflected the colours of the sky. We kissed then. It seemed natural and inevitable. We were standing in the centre of the circle and we held each other. My hands were around her waist, and hers hung onto the belt around mine. Under her jumper, her body was warm and her skin was impossibly smooth. Goosebumps rose up at the bottom of her back and tiny down-like hairs stood to attention. As we'd started to undress each other I remember that Grace had given a kind of running commentary of what she was thinking. At times it sounded like a sexy farce. She'd lurch from saying how desperate she was to 'feel my arse' to announcing that 'the clasp of her bra is caught in her vest top'. Talking about her knickers at one point, she had yelled 'Just rip the fuckers off!' There were giggles and frantic gasps for air and the sounds of material being stretched and pulled. Holding ourselves up against trees and then stumbling into the bracken it looked like we were in a wrestling match in the final round of a fight. And by the time we'd finished it was like we'd dived into a dressing up box. Clothes half on and half off. At jaunty angles. And exposed skin where you wouldn't expect to see it. It was exciting and liberating. It was unforgettable. We didn't come down from the hill until it was the early hours of the morning. It was before the sun had fully risen and we were shivering cold, but we didn't want the time to end.

It hadn't been long before Grace had moved in with me in the kirk. She would drive to her bookshop every day in a clapped out Morris Minor, while I would continue to renovate the building. She too had been accepted by the locals without hesitation. There was something instantly charming about her. We would stride up to the pub in the dark, and stagger back at closing time in the pitch black, snorting and guffawing as we would stumble into shallow ditches and rocky walls. Sex continued to be intense, furious and bordering on the hilarious. Hands all over each other. Wildly honest and intimate comments from Grace. Like messy play for adults. In bed, we would embrace each other tightly, sleeping with arms and legs wrapped around one another.

We continued to live in the kirk for three more summers. The repair work had been mostly complete but we feared that if we confessed this to Ken in the pub, then he'd ask us to move out. We loved it too much. So we invented 'critical' repair jobs that needed to be done. I would shake my head and suck my teeth in when talking to Ken about the heating system or the damp coursing. He would give us the benefit of the doubt, but we sensed our time there was coming to an end. Interestingly, the aspiration of purposelessness and detachment that had motivated me to come to the Spittal of Glenshee in the first instance, was beginning to be eroded. In fact, if I was honest, it had long gone. I had fallen for Grace and had started to worry about what might happen if we lost the kirk. And what the future might hold for us. It was difficult seeing my philosophical position of virtuous cluelessness being challenged so effectively. We were both blissfully happy.

During this time, I had also developed the strange sense of being watched. It's hard to explain and this might simply have gone with the territory when you live in an old kirk in the middle of the Highlands. The kirk constantly creaked and the joists in the rafters would bend and move with the wind. Strange noises would be carried on the air from the villages nearby. Car lights would play tricks on you at night-time. But every now and then I would catch the shape of a person in the driveway. Seeming to be looking at me. Usually a man's shape but not always. If I ran out to confront them the shape would disappear in the blink of an eye. Even in broad daylight at the market I would get a sense of someone in the crowd, perhaps fifteen metres away, observing me. To be honest though it was but a small oddity in our otherwise enjoyable lives.

Early in the New Year Grace had agreed to go to a demonstration weekend in London. It was an anti-Capitalist march and something she cared about greatly. It was a beautifully crisp and bright Saturday. I had agreed to look after the market stalls and Grace had got on the road at about four am. I had been worried about her, as I knew she'd be driving for close on eight hours, and in her Morris Minor. I'd begged her to fly but the truth was that we didn't have the money. She was due to get back in the early hours of Monday morning. I spent the weekend manning the stalls and then making the kirk look nice. We had kept the main area of the kirk – the pews, the altar, the font and so on - exactly intact and wherever possible sensitively restored. But we'd also expanded the bedsit area into a further back room, and I wanted to finish the work we'd started there.

There wasn't any reason to imagine that anything had gone wrong with Grace's trip but I felt uneasy all weekend. It came to midnight on Sunday and I was already beside myself with worry. Although it was still a few hours before she was expected I was nevertheless on the verge of panic. One am came and no sign of Grace. Two am. Three. Four. Five am then sunrise. Not a sound was carried on the wind. It felt like a lifetime had passed before the news got to me.

My heart sunk to my stomach when I first saw the police car pull up onto the driveway. I rushed out hoping that if I was quick I could undo the news I was about to hear. From the stained glass windows, you would have seen me on my knees weeping at the feet of the two officers. Grace had been involved in an accident on the motorway less than fifty miles away. Her car, it seems, had caught fire. The officer mentioned something about its age. The vehicle had veered off the road and down the side of a hill into a ravine. It had exploded on contact and the car had been almost unrecognisable. Following the explosion, the fire had raged for almost an hour leaving a charred chassis and little else.

My first reaction, of which I was convinced at the time, was that Grace had exited the car before it hit the bottom of the hill. And that she was wandering around the Highlands with concussion. Ken had given me and a small local search party a lift to the site of the accident where the wreckage had already been removed. We spent the best part of twelve hours searching but drew a blank. I had continued searching returning there every day for that week. I contacted the friends in London that she had stayed with. I called service stations where she might have stopped to fill up on petrol. I retraced her steps time and time again. But nothing. Another theory I had was that someone else had been driving Grace's car. But who else would be driving her car? At that time of night? In this direction? As pure desperation struck I took a walk up to the stone circle, imagining somehow that she would rendezvous with me there and tell me that everything was okay and there had been an enormous mistake. If she was lost in the wilderness this is where she would *gravitate. But the beauty and wonder of the stone circle had disappeared along with Grace.*

Time pushed on, and half accepting the reality of the situation, I signed the necessary forms. In the weeks that followed I attended to the remaining formalities. I still visited the site of the crash hoping that something might change. My visits became less frequent. I stayed on in the kirk long enough to complete the final works. The vegetable garden would surely die in time but I set it up as well as I could. A few months later I sold Grace's shop and gave half the proceeds to an anarchist foundation, the other half to Ken in the pub, and left the Spittal of Glenshee for good. My world had collapsed. Utterly. There was nothing.

19

Ameena

Hjarand, or 'Jan', as Victoria had long since labelled him, closed the door of the lab behind them. Victoria, now in her early twenties and Yo Yo and Pandi, in their mid-thirties, followed closely behind. The lab was situated on the outskirts of a small village called Ameena located near Hazarganji-Chiltan National Park in Grand China. Jan had taken them to the experimentation zones. He hesitated over whether this was entirely necessary. Whether it might be too much for them. They'd seen the evolution of GenCo and Al Hab, sometimes witnessing developments over hundreds of years in just a few crossings. And they'd got the picture. Travelling forwards and backwards they'd seen the colossal changes that the world had undergone. The growth of mega companies, the ultra-wealthy takeover, population expansion, the early and the mature off-earth projects. And Jan had escorted them using pinpoint accuracy and diligence to make sure that they didn't transgress some important conditions of using the technology.

Jan had attempted on a number of occasions to explain the science behind the ability to cross in time, but he hadn't had much success; something he'd put down to the way in which scientific knowledge had developed over the centuries, becoming increasingly abstract and hard to relate to even for people born in his time. Nevertheless, Jan had shared with the gang that for many years GenCo had been exploring the possibilities that arose from the fantastically high speed travel capabilities that they had developed with their sister company Al Hab. First this found expression in the transportation vehicles that travelled from Earth to the settlements on the Moon, then over the course of decades to the rapid voyages to Venus and Mars. This had led them to work on near light speed travel; travelling as close as possible to the cosmic speed limit of light. They had solved the problem of the enormous power needed to travel at such speeds by using harvested hydrogen energy from sources like Jupiter and Saturn; planets that hung silently in space alongside web-like constructions that captured and processed vast hydrogen emissions from the two gas planets. And they had minimized too, to a tolerable level, the strain on the human system associated with expeditions approaching this velocity. This had given the company its first breakthrough.

The second breakthrough had come largely from Jan's work in the field of quantum wormholes. In contrast to the scientific theories that dominated much of the late twentieth and early twenty first centuries, rather than wormholes being the stuff of Science Fiction, it had long been recognised that not only did they exist, but there were a seemingly infinite number of them. Each wormhole was comprised of two mouths; an entry and exit point joined by a kind of neck through which matter would travel under particular conditions. The entry and exit stages of wormholes had pre-existing spacetime coordinates and therefore were a lottery for whoever had the means to make use of them. However, the coordinates of each wormhole could be engineered so that entry and exit points could be specified by the user, theoretically making planned time travel possible. They were fairly unstable though and could only be used if the passage of matter through them was more or less instantaneous – a problem which had its answer in the form of the near speed of light technology that Jan had worked with during his time at GenCo. The more significant issue though was that wormholes were extraordinarily small, and the challenge that Jan had faced had been to enlarge them so that they could accommodate large objects, working up from protons to atoms, from minute Water Snails to Fairy Flies, and eventually to people. Success was found by bombarding these tiny time tunnels with profoundly intense bursts of energy until their expansion could fit the size of the object being transported.

This is what Jan had been experimenting with for years, using the considerable resources of his employer. His last task before he left had been focussed on how to download this immense capability into what became the wrist implants, that would, amongst other things, piggy-back off the energy source located in humans. Jan had been a pioneer in his field and while once he would have been proud to score these immense discoveries for GenCo, no doubt securing his place in the upper reaches of the company, this had long since passed as an aspiration, and instead he had meticulously covered his tracks and concealed the truth of what would have been their greatest and most potent discovery.

While most of what Jan had shared with Victoria, Yo Yo and Pandi, had been met with a polite but faraway look, the small number of inelastic rules relating to crossing in time had been given due attention, not least because of the practical implications of ignoring them. The most important was what Jan had called the *Circle of Influence* principle. This stated that if you attempted to cross back to an earlier point and place in time, where you or others close to you had existed, you would die. Or more accurately you would be ejected entirely from the material realm. Where you would wash up was unknown. Jan had explained that this was related to a glitch in the technology itself that couldn't cope with the computational permutations that would arise from contradictory or circular event sequences. It was a routine that the technology had effectively written itself to guarantee its own survival. As the architect of the system, this discovery had taken Jan by surprise and he had theorised that this had occurred in the process of the technology fusing with its human host causing it to borrow from some of the stronger human biological imperatives, specifically the instinct to survive. Put simply, contradictory events were interpreted as a threat which was responded to by triggering an immediate escape from the situation.

This feature of the technological system had meant, for example, that Jan was not able to cross back in time to save Victoria's parents on the clipper. Doing so would contravene the Circle of Influence principle. Once they had shared a relationship, both of their circles of influence had become intertwined, denying Jan access to earlier events involving her parents. The same principle applied to the fate of Yo Yo and Pandi's children. Understandably, Victoria, Yo Yo and Pandi had struggled with this for some years, but ultimately they had no option but to accept the limitations of the technology.

There were two exceptions to the Circle of Influence principle. The first was that if you crossed backwards in time in an entirely observational capacity, that is, without at any point affecting the turn of events in your circle of influence, then the technology wouldn't eject you from the prevailing reality. The risks were significant though, and hard to predict, but providing that you managed to stay in the shadows then you were safe. The second exception was that within a bandwidth of just a few seconds you could cross forward or backwards whilst staying within your own timeline and your own circle of influence. The computational permutations were much reduced over such a short period of time for which the technology gave you a temporary reprieve. So, for example, if you dropped a glass on the floor, you could immediately travel back to the moment before it happened to prevent yourself from doing it. You and time would move with you. But the window available for you to do this was literally one or two seconds, and once it was gone you were subject to the Circle of Influence principle. The technical term for this was what Jan called Micro Time Shifts (MTS). It took quite some effort, training and bravery to use this capability, as the risks associated with getting it wrong were considerable.

In contrast, and as far as the user was concerned, the technology attracted no limitations with regard to forward crossings in time. No amount of alterations to history could impact upon the user. If Jan, for example, had travelled back in time and removed every last vestige of the GenCo corporation – the same company that had unknowingly funded his research activities – to the point where GenCo no longer came into existence in the future, Jan and the technology would remain unaffected. The system creates a bubble of protection around the user from the very first point at which they make their first time crossing. Jan had called this principle the *Circle of Protection.*

In her mid teens, after hounding Jan for a long time, Jan had conceded the battle and had given Victoria her own implant. Yo Yo and Pandi had resisted the offer of an implant for some time but eventually capitulated after Jan made a dramatic case highlighting the risks of being stranded in a place or time that neither he nor Victoria could access.

Jan continued to lead the group through the building that they had just entered. Compared to the time in which they had grown up, the technology around them was dazzling. They walked along a sleek grey windowless corridor with subtle lights that lined the ceiling, floor and walls. It gave a totally convincing effect of being in natural daylight, and with the same light quality for this time of the morning. There were no other people in the building, which gave an eerie feel to the place. They bunched up a little knowing that if anything happened and they needed to escape then they would need to be within arm's reach. At the end of the corridor was what looked like a sheer glass door that Jan, at the head of the group, walked through without any sign of impact. The others followed and similarly passed through the glass. Victoria let out a small yelp and a giggle as if she had enjoyed the experience. She assumed that Jan had somehow neutralised the door. She had no idea how. Jan strode boldly forward and in an understated way he reached round to the back of his trousers and retrieved a gun. He didn't know what he would find at the far end of the corridor, but as unexpected and illegal visitors to the site, he knew they needed to take precautions.

The thin corridor opened out into a larger room, which then expanded into a much bigger space, about the size of a football pitch. The ceiling was around twenty metres above them. As they entered it caused all of them, including Jan, to gasp out loud. It was a sight to behold. To Victoria's mind it had the appearance of an enormous engine room, but she found it impossible to determine what the apparatus in front of her represented, or did. There were over thirty large grey rectangles that sat at waist height, that were scattered around the area. There were a series of metallic pipes that linked up the rectangles and the occasional metal bollard, randomly positioned in the arena. There were almost no distinguishing features to the objects in the room. Each rectangle looked like the next. Each bollard like the next. Each pipe like the next. What was clear though was a purring noise that consumed the space. An unbroken, low level, and constant thrum. A sound of energy passing through the building.

In a manner entirely consistent with the way that Victoria was developing, she shattered the background noise by letting out a shrill whoop. The sound echoed around the small stadium as Jan jumped decisively towards her and cupped the palm of his hand around her mouth. He paused for a second weighing up the answers to two related questions – Had anyone heard them? And should he cross back to the moment before she cried out to stop her? He reprimanded her with a thought and assuming there was no present danger turned his back and then walked on. Pandi scowled at Victoria.

Jan was taking them to observe for themselves what the company had done to thousands of experimentees. GenCo built laboratories in remote regions of Grand China on the edges of a village – typically one with ten or twenty thousand inhabitants. In the media this would be reported as a good news story. A huge influx of jobs. Investment in the region. Improvements in healthcare and education. Modern infrastructure. The whole deal. This would last for a while. They would establish a good reputation. Secure the support of the movers and shakers – people in public office, the key business owners, the wealthier residents. And for three or four years they would run their operation without a hitch. The media interest would fade to the background leaving an overwhelmingly positive impression. Something the company internally called the 'GenCo Warm Glow'. Then GenCo would press on with their main programme that would entail experimentation on hundreds and sometimes thousands of people – some of which were locals but often people that had been shipped in from more distant regions.

At this point in time, the period that Jan had selected, GenCo had been developing their research in a range of fields, but specialising in human energy management. This involved a diverse set of exploratory trials looking at technologies that would significantly reduce the requirement in humans for sleep, food and water. Subjects would be deprived of all three, for weeks at a time, while nanotechnologies were injected into the subject to slow down the body's call on regular sources of energy. Effectively blocking the usual signals to the brain such as hunger, thirst, lethargy, muscular fatigue etc. At the same time, energy substitutes were introduced into the body's system and subjects were required to undertake extreme and demanding physical challenges. This would deliver data on the limitations of the substitutes. The attrition rate would be very high and the labs would lose scores of people every month.

There were other streams of experimentation. The most grotesque was undoubtedly the Lazarine trials. GenCo had toyed for some years with the idea of post death resuscitation. In fact, they had already established that this could be accomplished relatively easily within thirty or so minutes after death, but this had exclusively been applied to subjects that had died of natural, or at least naturally occurring causes, principally arising in old age. The Lazarine method had departed from this in two major respects. Firstly, it encompassed people of all ages, young and old. And secondly, it included people that had been pronounced dead for up to a month. In order to undertake this work therefore, GenCo would terminate a proportion of employees and store their bodies for extended periods, in anticipation of their revival. Importantly they were held in conditions that did not in any way slow the process of physical deterioration. This was critical. No cold rooms or sealed environments. GenCo needed to allow the prevailing atmospherics to have their effect in order to understand the range of circumstances in which the resuscitation treatments worked. Practically this meant that the stench of human decay would fill the laboratories every day, reminding everyone that worked there of the gruesome horrors that occurred within the walls. And as if this wasn't morbid enough, the efficacy of the technology was further tested by analysing the impact of different causes of death on the treatments – coronary heart failure, cancer, lethal virus, fatal beatings, modern diseases like Sybola, drowning, gunshots and on the list went. All were administered by fellow employees under the firm direction of the GenCo management.

When success was found in the Lazarine trials, it took on a frightening form. The name given to those that survived was Wài Decedents, or Wài D's for short. Wài in Chinese meant beyond or foreign, and the phrase stood for beyond dead. They would haunt the corridors of the facility, still human, with all the characteristics of living humans. But remote. Displaced. Hollow. And in pain. The GenCo science teams would engage them in psychological analyses and therapies. Trying to reconnect them to the world they had left. Trying to discover what caused their existential secession. In most cases Wài D's would end up taking their own lives, in one way or another. For some it would take a few days. For others their torment would last for months. They were empty, tortured vessels. Created by GenCo. Not brought back to life but plunged further into death. But this wasn't the end. For some, GenCo took the extreme measure of attempting second, post-suicide revivals. This tested the scientists. Pushed them to their edge of what were already flexible ethical limits. The subjects would beg and plead to be released from their living hell. They would be placed in soundproof containment cells so the screams and the wailing wouldn't be heard. This was the work of GenCo. And one of the very many reasons why Jan wanted them stopped.

But this isn't what they were here to see. They tiptoed through the mysterious engine room. Victoria calmer now. Jan had slipped his gun back under his belt, comforted by the fact that Victoria's outburst hadn't drawn any attention. The operation had ceased here about one month prior to their crossing and Jan had imagined that there would be a skeleton crew of employees, but it seemed that no one had remained. This was the third facility like this that he had seen. All ending in the same way. At the exit to the arena was a vestibule area presenting a set of lifts. Jan waved the group through into the first that they saw. He swiped his finger over a panel at the back of the lift. The doorway they had passed through flashed once and the entrance became opaque. There was a gentle shudder and the sensation that the lift was travelling upwards. Fourteen floors and three seconds later the lift had come to rest and the opaque door flashed again revealing a darkened room. Lights buzzed into life as they stepped out of the lift. It looked like an abandoned control room. There were a handful of empty chairs and desks all arranged in a semicircular fashion pointing towards a blackened viewing window. A large pair of wrap-around sunglasses, protecting the eyes of the building from the view beyond the window. Towards the far side of the room were more than ten slender lockers that looked like vertical black keys on a piano. Jan wafted his hand over the central desk. A series of screens sparked into life and glowed in a cool blue colour. As if casting a spell, he flexed his fingers and the viewing window subtly shifted its colouration from dark to grey. He did it again and this time the greyness of the window drained away to be replaced by bright morning sunlight. The group shielded their eyes as a reflex.

Initially they found nothing unusual about the scene that confronted them. It was a view of Ameena - the village where GenCo had chosen to build its facility. It was laid out in front of them. Gentle hills to the rear. Housing in the middle of the picture. Tracks. A centre of commerce. Religious buildings. Tall metal poles carrying wires. Vehicles. All the usual features of life. Even with Victoria's set of anachronistic reference points, it all seemed very normal to her. Jan remained silent. He was waiting. Victoria, Pandi and Yo Yo looked at each other blankly. Jan almost imperceptibly tilted his head towards the window as if suggesting that they take another look. They stepped forward and squinted against the sunlight. Still nothing unexpected. And then, as their eyes adjusted, and the glare subsided, they started to see the problem. There was no one there. A town built for perhaps twenty thousand people and not a single sign of life. The vehicles were still. Motionless on the roads. There was no bustling in the commercial centre. No evidence of shoppers. No haze of pollution. No smoke. No dogs lolloping at the sides of the road. It was a ghost town.

But there was more. Pandi noticed it first. After stepping closer again to the window and studying the town, she quickly recoiled. Her face pallid and eyes glassy. Yo Yo was next and he pulled her into his chest walking her away from the window and back towards a befuddled Victoria. She didn't understand their reaction. Victoria shuffled forward half keen and half anxious. With her nose pressed against the glass she squinted, summoning as

much concentration as she could muster. Then she started
to see something. It started as specks in the picture. Blobs.
Which then took on form. They looked like human shapes,
scattered around town, but she couldn't be sure. She
raised her arms to Jan as if it were a question and under
Jan's instruction two of the lockers opened behind her.
Inside each were translucent suits hanging like human-
sized plastic bags. Victoria couldn't describe the material
they were made of. They appeared thin and flexible. At
the top of the suit, above the neck, was a similarly formless
and malleable looking face mask. Jan checked with Yo Yo
and Pandi to see if they would like to come, but they both
sat down indicating their decision.

They crossed holding hands, fully kitted up and able
to breathe through the skin of their suits. Their outfits
were designed to filter out all impurities in the air, and
this was needed. They were in the heart of the commercial
district, at ground level, perhaps a mile from the tower.
There were low and mid-rise office blocks and scores
of shops lining the entrances. As they started their
reconnaissance it immediately became clear what the
shapes had been. A shudder had run down Victoria's
back. She knelt on one knee catching her breath and Jan
placed a warm comforting hand on her shoulder. She
motioned to Jan that it was ok and stood up. She had
never seen such annihilation. It was all around her. She
was inside it. Everywhere they looked there were dead
bodies. These were the outlines that Pandi had seen,
but now filled in colour. In three dimensions. In detail.
Literally scores of dead people within the scope of their
vision, and the same number again each time they turned.
Mothers holding children in their arms. People frozen

with horrified looks in their faces. Bodies were slumped. Against walls. Buildings. Vehicles. Stairways. Some face down as if asleep on their noses. Others less peaceful. Contorted. Bent double. Clutching themselves, and wearing expressions of pain. Victoria fixed her attention on a group no more than ten metres away. She could barely make out where bodies started and finished. Adults and children together, clinging onto each other, trying to block out the event that had caused their end. Victoria was reminded of the stories of Pompeii with people trapped in the lava as they went about their business. Frozen in time.

"Every last one of them." Jan said in a somber tone. "GenCo killed every last one of them." He paused, taking a mental run up to the next sentence. "They have to ensure that no one has the chance to escape or tell the outside world what has been happening. So they have to be quick. They use something called a blanket spray. From the control tower we just left. On the roof, above where our heads were, they fire the spray jets. Incredibly powerful and with a reach of three or four miles square. It takes less than a few minutes for the initial effects, and within fifteen minutes the entire population is slaught..." Jan corrected himself mid-sentence. "Actually that's not true. There are usually a few people that have an unpredictable reaction to the chemicals. They might have a tolerance of sorts or have somehow avoided the full blast of the blanket." Victoria interjected, "What happens to the survivors?" Jan lowered his head and spoke softly "They are executed. A handful of GenCo security patrol the streets armed with guns and breathing devices and destroy everything that moves. Men, women, children, babies. No one is allowed to survive. And they leave the bodies here for the cleanup crew. They'll be here in a day or so." Victoria took in another view of the scene. Like drawing in a lungful of air. She felt she owed it to the people there to remember what she'd seen. Their hips touch. And then a punch to the stomach. Nausea. Whiteout. And they are back in the tower with Pandi and Yo Yo. Stood in the same positions as they were a moment before this time wearing disapproving expressions.

After the trauma of the clipper, Pandi and Yo Yo had taken Victoria as their own child, albeit one on the brink of becoming a woman. They had committed to making her life complete once again after losing her parents. In some ways too Victoria was a surrogate for the children that Pandi and Yo Yo had lost. And so while Pandi and Yo Yo tried to protect Victoria, they saw Jan introducing her instead, and at a young age, to the cruelty of the world. Each time that Pandi pulled her close she would feel Victoria drawing away a little. Attracted to the excitement and the drama of the world that Jan could provide for her. For a young woman growing up it was terrifying and thrilling in equal measure. Pandi had worried, and still did, that it had twisted Victoria. That it had bent her out of shape. Giving her the ability to cross at such a tender age, Victoria being barely sixteen years old, was a lot for a young mind to take. At least this is how Pandi judged it. At times too Victoria had become a little confused about her relationship with Jan, although Pandi didn't hold Jan to blame for this. When Victoria first met him she was impressionable and Jan had saved her life. He was a hero. And one that then went on to display spectacular powers the kind of which no one in her time could fail to be dazzled by. When she had first asked Jan if he was God this was because to her, he was God. He may well have laughed, but to her he was young, tall, handsome, intelligent, selfless, magical, caring and more - a potent combination of qualities for such a young mind.

For Victoria, the age gap of twelve or so years between them had started to narrow quite quickly. For every year that they aged it felt like three to her. Jan was well aware of her muddled feelings for him. They sat in the front of her mind where they were easily picked up and read by Jan. And while he did not and would not for a second, take advantage of her, he could no longer regard her as a little girl. The twelve-year-old daughter of a captain, that once wore court shoes and ribbons in her hair, had become a force to be reckoned with. She had become a woman that, without really meaning to, would stir up and toy with the desires of a single man in his prime – always on the right side of the line, but only just. A quality that would come to characterise Victoria. All of which created some tension within their unconventional family unit.

Pandi and Yo Yo had put their own interests aside for the sake of Victoria. They had made the decision not to have any children until Victoria no longer needed them, which in the event lasted for a decade or more. This had been a tough path. The loss of their own children had nearly destroyed them and the dream was to have children once again. As they aged they started to feel this drifting away, but they persisted with the hope that one day the time would be right. As former teachers they had educated Victoria. They had become her carers, her friends, and her confidantes all wrapped up into one.

After all, with their unique lifestyle, she wasn't set up well to form enduring relationships outside of the unit. However, granting Victoria with an implant was akin to coming home one day with a tattoo, a motorbike and the wrong kind of boyfriend. Pandi blamed Jan and they fought furiously. Both loved Victoria dearly and in entirely different ways wanted the best for her.

"I have one more thing to show you." Jan announced while scanning their thoughts to check whether they accepted his suggestion. They agreed and crossed forward. It was about one year later and although they remained in the tower it was different. The air was dank and stuffy as if no one had been here for a very long time. Jan summoned the lights to turn on. They did but even with the lights on it seemed dark. It was even more bare than before. More unused. This wasn't all that was different.

The entirety of the facility, excluding the tower had been removed. At the foot of the lift shaft, rather than an entrance to the vestibule and then the large engine arena, there was a door to the outside. The tower stood like a solitary pole plunged into the ground. The scene from the viewing window had changed too. Where Ameena once stood there was a valley filled with trees. The type of trees that looked like they would take twenty or thirty years to grow, but here they were, just a year later. The village, in its entirety, had disappeared. No physical evidence of it ever having existed. Twenty thousand lives wiped out, and replaced with trees. The media would be silenced in a variety of ways. Digital historical reports that were held would be removed by GenCo. This was easy for them. Individuals that were able to offer a different, counter argument to the line that Ameena never existed, would mysteriously vanish. Business that had traded in the region learned that if they challenged the story then they would financially suffer. GenCo claps its hands and the world does what it commands.

20

Stammheim Prison, Stuttgart

Jan wanted to know what worked. What made a difference. In fact, this is what had become his preoccupation. But unravelling causality on the scale that he was interested in was complicated. Maybe even impossible. He'd learned that it wasn't enough to match up an intervention at one point in time with an outcome some years later and assume that one had caused the other – no matter how clear the relationship seemed to be. All of the other variables that might have intervened. All of the unintended effects. All of the difficulties of choosing the focus of your attention. All of the quantum particle-wave, Schrödinger's cat - looking, not looking stuff. It was enough to send him insane.

So Jan decided that he wanted to get a bit more grounded in his thinking, and speak with some of the important architects of change. The very people that had in some respects attempted what he is attempting. To understand their method. To get a different kind of insight into how to halt the seemingly unstoppable march of wealth and colonisation and all the various forms that it takes. His meeting with Ulrike Meinhof had caused a seed of possibility to grow within him.

It is 1974, some two years before the death of Ulrike Meinhof; the former journalist, eponymous collaborator, and enigmatic voice of the Baader-Meinhof gang. She is held in a newly renovated high security wing of Stammheim prison along with other members of the gang that include Andreas Baader, Gudrun Ensslin, Irmgard Möller and Jan-Carl Raspe – all awaiting trial; a process that has controversially stretched out over some years even before the trial has commenced. Collectively they have been held responsible for setting fire to department stores, a trail of bank robberies, the manufacture of bombs, gun running, and amongst other activities, over thirty politically motivated murders and attempted murders of Police officers, Judges, Bankers, Army officers, officials and so on. A few weeks earlier Andreas Baader received a visit from Jean-Paul Sartre who has joined the list of intellectuals that publicly support the cause. All five are showing the effects of repeated hunger strikes protesting against the conditions that they have been kept in for years.

Jan had come to the decision that he wanted to speak to Ulrike Meinhof as, in his view, she had been the intellectual engine beneath the cause. Rather than appearing unannounced and without any apparent means of entry into her prison cell, he had chosen to pose as a journalist seeking to obtain the truth about the cause of the Red Army Faction and Ulrike's role in it. He knew that he would be unlikely to be given permission by the prison authorities to do this, even if he were a bona fide journalist, but he needed enough of a back story so that when he eventually showed up in her prison room she would accept this as normal, perhaps even as expected. After all, what would she know about what the authorities had or hadn't sanctioned? And so some months earlier Jan had befriended Ulrike's lawyer Klaus Croissant on the outside, frequently raising his journalistic interests with regard to Ulrike with the hope that he would mention this to her, which, after a short period of time, he did. He gave himself a distinctive false name – of Lenny Shines - so that Ulrike couldn't fail to recognise it when she eventually met him.

Jan crosses into her room just prior to her return from her daily trip to the prison yard and waits quietly in the corner, out of view of anyone opening the door. In a cell close by is Gudrun Ensslin, who Jan hears mutter a few words as the two part company and as the prison officers jangle their keys to assist the return of the prisoners to their box rooms. Jan first notices Ulrike's short, scarecrow-like dark hair as she enters the room; far removed from the much publicized images of her as a young and successful journalist with silken, luxurious waves of hair. He'd expected her to appear downtrodden and frail but the person that walks into the room seems more damaged than he'd expected. The hunger strikes and psychological pressure have taken their toll. Her clothes are not prison clothes but her own; a pair of faded black trousers and a similarly coloured heavy cloth blouse. Ulrike is immediately aware of Jan's presence but acts as if he is not there. She shuffles over to her bed and spins around slowly coming to rest with her back against the pale, unadorned wall, her body in a semi-horizontal position. She continues to avoid eye contact as her left hand snakes towards a pre-rolled cigarette on a knee-high table. She lights the cigarette and coughs, her thin frame shuddering as she tries to compose herself. Jan is aware of the guard walking nearby and so chooses to remain silent.

A moment passes before Ulrike speaks with a strong but slightly irritated-sounding voice, looking down as if her visitor is a speck on the floor. "What do you want to know?" She says. Short and to the point. Clearly having tired of the circus of visitors. Jan steps forward lowering himself so that he can sit on a wooden chair that is just a few feet from Ulrike's face, hoping to meet her eyes. Mirroring her pithiness, he replies "I want to understand whether you think it has worked?" Ulrike, still with her eyes on the ground, responds in a German accented English. She appears to show no interest in who she is conversing with. "I'm here aren't I? In a high security cell. With people queuing up either to speak with me or to torture me in one way or another. Do you think they'd do this if it wasn't making a difference?" Jan feels like he needs to explain his interest, in part to underscore his cover as a journalist. "My readers would want to know whether it has been..." Ulrike interrupts Jan, this time, for the first time, raising her dark eyes in the direction of his. They offer no warmth and do not care if it is given in return, "Mr. Shines, I don't give a shit what you think your readers want. You and I know they really want some gossip and a way to feel like they're part of the action here. But of course there is no action in words and we're all tired of words. You would do better by recognising this yourself." Jan feels inclined to remind Ulrike that for most of her life her weapons had been words, and her work had been her journalism, but he knows it won't help.

Ulrike continues without encouragement. "Anyway, it's the wrong question to ask. You should be more interested in what would be possible if there were not one but a hundred Red Army Factions. An organisation of activists unafraid to use the tools of violence against the power system. And I draw no distinctions between the imperialist state and the owners of industry, or between the things they produce or the people producing them. All must become targets. We must turn our hearts black to lead us into the light. This is what we should be doing."

For Jan this is exactly what he wants to understand. He reflects, with a flutter of excitement in his chest, on the implications of an organisation that could multiply the effects of an entity like the Red Army Faction. Not one that operated according to the same principles, one that exercised more care over human life. But an outfit that could enjoy the benefits of operating at scale. He had always known that in dealing with institutions and enterprises like GenCo something ambitious would be needed. Anything less would be batted away with a casual swipe of the hand. Did he need an army of like-minded people? This was his question.

Jan is still following his own train of thought when Ulrike intervenes again. "When we rob banks with our *Firebirds* shoved in peoples' faces, or when we light up an Army barracks with pipe bombs, this is the language that makes us understood. The Capitalist ruling system is deaf to any other communication. When the enemy carries guns and wields instruments of repression, what would you suggest that we reply with?"

Jan breaks into her monologue with his own question "And what of the morality of killing people to satisfy your interests?" Ulrike delivers her response without a moment's hesitation. "This is a false morality that the enemy relies upon. This is the morality that our captors invoke to vilify our actions. Meanwhile they drop napalm on the poor in Vietnam and drive Palestinians into the sea. Ours is a higher morality. It is higher because we see the relentless campaign of brutality that the power elites wage against the common man, and we are prepared to do what is needed to restore a morality that has been used against us. If you want to throw around accusations of immorality, then you really are talking to the wrong person." With this she directs her gaze to the prison door, presumably suggesting that Jan should speak about morality with those wearing uniforms.

Wanting to making best use of what is a limited amount of time, Jan jumps in. "What if your actions empower the security services to greater levels of authoritarianism? What if the Baader-Meinhof experiment serves only to justify a hardening of the power of the state? That would make the situation worse right?" Jan expects Ulrike to return her thoughts with increased force, but instead her voice lowers and her pace slows. "The 1967 demonstrations in Berlin that saw Benno Ohnesorg shot in the back of the head by the authorities was a moment of clarity; the police were pulled out of the shadows and a glimpse of their intent was declared to the world. Action forces the authorities to break cover and with that we have the basis for collective action. Tens of thousands of people marched in recognition of this. Imagine if we could get this many people on the streets in opposition to the military-industrial complex but carrying rifles instead of student banners? How would your readers feel about that?"

Ulrike is testing him. Her eyes flitting across his face. He hears some noises coming from along the corridor leading to her cell. He senses that his time may be nearing an end. One last question he thinks to himself. "What should you have done differently Ulrike? Any advice for a budding activist?" he whispers so the presence approaching beyond the door can't hear him. "Just one thing" she replies. "Just one thing. Choose your company well."

As a key is turned in the cell door Jan disappears.

21

Lantau - Hamburg

We are stood facing each other in the garden to the rear of the temple. Victoria has a vacant look in her eyes. She is frightened for Pandi and Yo Yo, but this isn't her main emotion. Beneath the mask she has made of her face she is simmering with rage. I can see it. Her jaw is tightened. Her lips pinched. I have never witnessed her like this before now. She mutters just a few words. "How dare they? They walked right into their home and kidnapped them. And in front of the fucking children." Although she hadn't seen who it was she has a good idea who is involved. "Romanov and Mary." She declares. "It has to be them. This is exactly their M.O. Always throwing in a bit of drama. The smoke from the other temples on the hillside. Such a giveaway." Her monologue continues, "And Ryan too. Fucking Ryan! He'll have a hand in this. His brutality was off the scale. It was something we thought we could tame and channel. We needed something a bit extra in the old days. And you accept that people like us come with sharp edges. It goes with the turf. But like all of them he couldn't resist it. The technology. It makes you feel invincible. Like you're no longer mortal and held to the laws of regular people. And the imagination takes over and while we were creating a better place for others. While we were trying to prevent pain and suffering, Ryan, and each one of them in turn started thinking about themselves. The possibilities. And what they could get out of it. How they could have everything they felt they'd been denied. Wealth. Adoration. Respect. A slice of the world all to themselves." Her mind returns to Pandi and Yo Yo. "They're going to pay for this."

I can see that while she is standing she is rocking backwards and forwards. Victoria is seething, and at the same time trying to work out what to do next. She continues talking to herself as much as to me. "And you know the funny thing. The really funny thing?" She stretches her enunciation of the word 'really' to give it emphasis. "I recruited them. All three of them. I spent years of their life making sure that they were our kind of people. That they were trustworthy. That they were good people. And they do this!" She kicks over a low metal table, and as it's about to strike my ankle it flips back to its original position – defying all that we learn in science about objects in motion. She has used one of Jan's Micro Time Shifts. "Sorry! I didn't mean to hurt you" she says. "I'm desperate Robin. I don't know where to start." From looking like a wild animal a moment ago, she now looks like a little girl.

I steer her towards the bench. I feel like my main role in this whole episode has been to prevent Victoria from going into a flat spin. She yields as I pressure her to sit. The hottest part of the day has passed but it is very humid.

I feel damp under my shirt. My hands are sweaty and my eyes feel tired. Victoria looks worse than I feel. I sit down next to Victoria and gently raise her chin so that she can look into my eyes. I don't know what I'm going to say but start talking anyway. "Listen Victoria. We have to be strong. If anyone is going to find them, it is us. The children are safe aren't they?" Victoria has slipped into a kind of trance. "Aren't they?" I raise my voice. Her attention snaps back to me and she confirms her relief about the children by loudly expelling her breath and nodding her head. "Do you know where they might be? Any ideas at all." Victoria is drifting away again, this time shaking her head from side to side. "When did you last see them?" My question sounds like I'm helping her to find some lost jewellry, and it doesn't help. "Do you know the location of anyone in the organisation? Anyone at all?" Her head sinks even lower. "Think Victoria!" I realise that in trying to comfort Victoria I'm losing my cool.

I slide back to the other corner of the bench. It's a small seat so we are still touching knees. If I had a beard I would stroke it, and in doing so I imagine that an idea would come to me, but I don't, and it doesn't. We sit in silence. The sound of bells from temples that described the scene an hour ago have ceased. We are left with the chatter of insects, the distant muffled sound of ferries bashing against the wall of the harbour, and our thoughts. Victoria's ebb and flow into my own, rising and falling like the boats. We sense the darkness of each other's mood and a dearth of hope. With the ability to cross we know that Romanov, Mary and Ryan could be literally anywhere on the earth. And if they had any sense they will have taken Pandi and Yo Yo to a place that we would have no knowledge of whatsoever. They just needed to be somewhere that we couldn't imagine and they would be safe. It was impossible. It would be like trying to find a needle in a haystack but with a haystack the size of a football pitch.

And then it comes to me. "Christ!" I pull frantically at the pockets of my jeans. The front pockets relinquish nothing but pocket fluff. I twist to my right and lean forward. The first back pocket is empty. I switch to the other and with the precision of a surgeon, and fingertips in the shape of a beak, I retrieve a folded piece of paper. It has become molded to the shape of my buttocks, has started to disintegrate at the edges and has soaked up some of the dye of my trousers. Victoria frowns at me. It doesn't look very impressive on the face of it. "It's the list!" I proclaim. Victoria's expression remains unchanged. And then her eyebrows twitch. And lift. Her eyes widen. She's got it. She speaks. "You mean the list that Georgia gave you? I nod vigorously. "But didn't you track them all down?" she continues. "No, that's the point. I did track down Carlos. And I messed up with Sandeep. But there was another. A third person. Someone I didn't get around to." I delicately unwrap the package and trace my eye down the page of Georgia's writing. I am distracted for a moment wondering what has happened to Georgia. "Here. Here. Listen! Their name is Stefan Baden in Hamburg. The location is an office block. Georgia described him as being tall and bony faced, with dark eyes and an awkward gait. And the notes say, smart, tricky, can read, and can cross. But you know this right?" Victoria nods her head vigorously suggesting I should keep talking. "And there are some location details." I say. "That's it"

Victoria asserts triumphantly. "Hang on a second though," she corrects herself "This was his location when Georgia wrote the list, how do we know he'll still be there?" It is a good point. I hear myself saying. "It looks like the location might be a place of work, and if it is, then there is no reason to assume he won't be there most weekdays. This might be our chance."

After Grace I returned to an office life. I understood how it worked there, the rhythm that it followed. I could appear to be normal in this world, even though it meant nothing to me. It was a massive multi-player role-playing game as far as I was concerned. The only benefit was that it was a game that I could play. From the outside you might mistake me for any other employee – professional and focused on the task. Keen. Wanting to 'make a difference'. But that wasn't me. I thought of Grace every day there. I missed her so much that barely a moment would pass without thinking of her or, out of habit, imagining that she was close by. She was the life I had chosen to live, and the most wonderful person I'd ever met. But the end to it was incomplete. It's one thing to know that someone has gone for certain, to have the evidence of your own eyes that they have departed forever, and to understand how they had died, and what had led to their passing. But with Grace it was a question mark rather than a full stop.

I started off working in Security for retail banks. Grace wouldn't have been pleased. I would spend day after day asking people questions on a telephone to verify their identity. "What is your current address? Your previous address? Your date of birth? The second letter of your password? The eighth letter of your password? No, you don't need to tell me the whole password. What was your

mother's maiden name? Of course she's still alive. I'm
sorry. I mean what is your mother's maiden name? That's
right her second name. Can you tell me two transactions
you have made in the last week? How about in the last
two weeks? No, they would need to have been paid for
by a card. It won't work if you bought them with cash"

And then I would get bored so I would vary the
questions, just for my own idle amusement. "Could you
repeat the sixteen-digit number on your card working right
to left? Yes, that's right in reverse order, it reduces errors.
I am getting some interference. Are you near any electrical
equipment while making this call? Could you please
go into the bathroom there is usually less interference
there? Do you recall having ever forgotten anything?
Perhaps a friend's name, your telephone number, your
wife's birthday? Yes, it is necessary; I need to establish
your reliability. It's standard procedure. What was the
name of your first cat? Well, I have you down as a cat
owner. It was one of your security questions. And to
proceed I would need to know their name. Would you like
to guess? If you're telling me that you have never owned
a cat then I'm afraid, that would be a serious matter. We
will have to escalate this. Yes, that would take some time.
Would you like to see if you can remember what the cat
that you can't remember was called? No, that wasn't it.
You have three more attempts. No, I don't have that either.
Geoffrey, did you say Geoffrey? That matches my records.
Yes, I'm sure, that's what it says on the system."

Once I had verified the identity of my callers I would
place a release on the transaction they were trying to
process. In the event that there was a genuine fraud I would
be required to cancel all of their payment cards, which

*would always cause immediate distress. "I understand,
of course." I would say. "It is difficult to buy anything
without a card. Can you avoid shopping? If you do so
you'll need to pay in cash. Do you have any cash? Perhaps
in a jar? Do you have money that you keep in a jar? Or
a drawer? Or in some trouser pockets? In a sock? Do
you give your children pocket money? Might they have
some? There really is nothing I can do I'm afraid. We are
very sorry. Your new card will be with you in five working
days, can you wait until then?" It is fair to say that I was
disengaged from my work, but I would only do this with
the aggressive or rude callers. More or less.*

*In spite of my unconventional behaviour, which largely
went unnoticed, I was promoted to supervisor and then
to a different, and more senior role, again in customer
relations. Ah, the irony, I thought. You have to wonder
sometimes how organisations operate. At one point in the
company a major change initiative had been introduced.
They'd decided that they'd lost sight of their customers.
Divisions within the company had become isolated from
one another causing an uncoordinated service to the
customer, and regulatory demands had made interactions
with the organisation too bureaucratic. It had all become
about forms and inflexible processes. So it was my job
to re-humanise the relationship with the customer. After
years of de-humanising customer interactions through the
removal of bank tellers, the introduction of automated
cash machines, online banking, outsourcing of telephone
service to somewhere else in the world, they now decided
they wanted closer, more intimate relations. I was one of
the people leading this. Where I was leading it to I had
no idea.*

I spent a lot of my time talking to customers about what they wanted. I would corner them in different branches or piggyback on existing meetings with other employees. I thought I would be a most unwelcome inconvenience to their otherwise busy lives but it transpired that people loved to complain. It was a cathartic experience. I wasn't there to solve the problem rather at that stage to learn about it, so I would stoke the fire as much as I could. For every complaint they had, I'd squeeze another four out of them. It wasn't difficult. I would look disappointed if they said that they were happy and sure enough they'd come up with something. Opening times. Branch location. Durability of payment cards. Colour of cards. Size of cards. Tone of letters. Frequency of letters. Absence of letters. Friendliness of service staff. Overfriendliness of staff. You name it, I would get a complaint on it.

The more I did this, the more it dawned on me that people didn't really want closer, more intimate customer relations. They didn't view their dealings with their bank as a relationship. And who could blame them? Why would a business arrangement entirely centred on money be likened to a relationship? Why would a transaction be thought of as a relationship? Is this what it's come to? Literally speaking there was a relationship, and by that I mean a connection, between the customer and their bank, but how many of our relationships exist only because payment is involved? Relationships involve emotions, feelings, obligations, commitment, effort, engagement, trust, openness, toughness, tenderness, hope, meaning, and more. Is that what the bank wanted me to introduce. Should the bank be open about how much money it's making from the customer? Should the bank trust that the customer is who they say they are? Should the bank teller storm out on the customer for no recognisable reason? Should there be heated disagreements followed by passionate making up? Should there be inappropriate texting?

To add to this, what I discovered from retail bank customers was that they really quite liked an arms-length arrangement. They just wanted cards that worked, security that didn't fail, statements that were correct, lots and lots of faceless automated cash machines, and to be left alone. On the rare occasion that they had to interact with the bank, they just wanted the thing fixed that they had called up for, without fuss or complication. I'm pretty sure too that they didn't want someone enquiring after their health, or an idiot asking them what their non-existent cat was called. The only type of relationship I could discern that customers wanted with a bank, beyond this, was the ability to complain about anything that got their goat. If banks were like a punch bag full of money, then that would be the best vision of the future I could paint. And they can draw a face on it if it makes them feel better.

I would tell the seniors all of this, but they would think I was joking. I wasn't joking. I would tell them I wasn't joking, but they still wouldn't believe me. "I'm not joking" I would say, and they would laugh. "I'm being serious" I would say and they would laugh harder. In fact, my boss's boss took a shine to me. I think I reminded him of a younger version of himself so without asking for it, he took me under his wing. I was to be nurtured. To be molded. I explained that I was fine without his support but I'd already been signed into the club it seemed.

I was bumped up the hierarchy, transferred to the investment bank side of the company and put in charge of change. Such a wonderfully odd term change. I'm pretty sure that some things change in ways we might like, but also in ways that we might not like. I assumed, on being given the role, that I was meant to be batting for the good change side. It sounds like a pedantic point but it's crucial to get this right. For example, when I was younger I changed the brand of trainers that I wore. I did it because everyone else had migrated to the new brand. It transpired that the new brand was really uncomfortable, and the trainers wore out really quickly. The change went well, but in the wrong direction as far as I was concerned. I had the same worry about the company and I asked my boss about this. I said, "Since I am responsible for change, is it my job to decide what we change into?" He paused and then chuckled, no doubt thinking again that I was joking. I wasn't joking. I was responsible for the continuation of the change that had already been started. In many ways this felt like the opposite of change.

The company was a global outfit. Of course. Who wouldn't be global in these times, with this technological capability? So rather than flying around the UK like a bee picking up complaints from customers, as I had before, I would literally fly around the globe finding out what the company's employees thought. I knew what to do here. There were lots of meetings to be had. I was very good at meetings. Every so often during a conversation I would find myself drifting away and thinking about mending the roof of the kirk in Scotland, or how the vegetable garden was getting on. If I pictured the scene and breathed in slowly I would recall the smell of the wet mud on the ground. The sharp, biting wind that cut across my legs. The birds making their early morning call. The wood instrument sound of a cuckoo that would announce the start of the day. Just for a few moments I would experience a sense of bliss. Despite being surrounded by chairs, whiteboards, markers pens, tables, wall mounted screens, bottles of water and all the man-made accoutrements of the modern office space, I was out in the open air, the light flickering and glowing as the clouds pass by overhead. And the stone circle would come to mind. And Grace would be there. I would suck in every detail of her face. The tiny silvery scar on her cheek. The bright points of her brown eyes. The minute soft hairs around her mouth. Her olive skin, flushed in places from a long hike. Her walnut brown hair, messy and silken, tumbling down onto her shoulders.

We are holding onto each other in the empty stairwell of the building. A place reserved for technology-free exit during a fire or similar emergency. A pattern of concrete stairs and utilitarian metal bannisters repeats itself for the fourteen floors beneath us and the ten above. It is like we've been dropped into an Escher sketch. As the nausea subsides we release the grip on each other. Victoria playfully pushes her hips into mine as we de-couple. Her disposition changes almost immediately and she grips my upper arm firmly. She has something important to share, "I didn't know Stefan too well and to be honest, although what I did see, I didn't really like. However, he was very effective. He tended to get more involved with the disruptive side of our work; smashing logging equipment in the Amazon basin, posing as a buyer to foil human trafficking operations, exposing secret meetings of the corporate elite, that kind of thing. He was good at it but he loved the thrill of it more than what we were trying to accomplish." As Victoria is talking I absent-mindedly take my gun out from the back of my jeans, eject the magazine and press my thumb into the end. There is a cold tension against my thumb. It is full with fifteen rounds in the magazine. I shove the magazine back in its place. I am reminded of the struggle with Carlos and his crew. I notice myself tracing the grazes and cuts on my neck with one of my fingers. I flick the position of the safety lever so it is ready for use. My attention drifts back to Victoria.

"This is what we need to do." Victoria wanted to get this right. "Both of us need to stay in contact with him at all times. The best way to do this is by hooking your hands under the waist of his trousers. Grab his belt or even his hair, just make sure you have a tight grip. With both of us trying to cross to the same place he won't be able to divert us. But even if he does manage to, he won't be going anywhere without us. There is a safe place in Kibi in Ghana. It's a disused school on the outskirts. If you keep that and Southern Cross in mind you won't miss it." She pauses briefly pondering something. "Here, it will help if I show you." And with that Victoria thrusts her hand towards the front of my trousers, grabs my belt and yanks me towards her. The stairway is replaced by the inside of a wooden hut. There is no one there apart from the two of us. Through the window I can see dry dirt on the ground, a couple of seemingly uninhabited buildings and in the distance a ridge of lush green trees. Inside there are a handful of rows of desks and seats in a dark wood. It takes me a few seconds but I realise it is incredibly hot in here. It must be forty degrees centigrade, and I am already sweating and scouring the room for an indication of water or something cooling. Nothing appears apart from the words Southern Cross that are scrawled clumsily in chalk on the blackboard. "This is where we come, and where we keep returning if we get crossed anywhere else. And leave the questions to me. This is our only lead" Victoria has pronounced. And then we are back in the stairwell.

Moving through the doorway the atmosphere changes from one of relative peace to the kinetic bustle of an office floor. No one notices our arrival. We are instantly absorbed into the scene. We had walked into the middle of an open plan office area comprising at least a hundred and fifty workstations. Most are filled with people glaring into screens or talking loudly on the phone, or both. And many have adapted to the rather chaotic environment by wearing headphones. Those that aren't fixed to their chairs are purposefully striding, or in some cases almost jogging, about the room. The sense that I get from this place is that there is never enough time to get the work done. Everyone is a few notches away from blind panic. Both Victoria and myself share the same thought that it is going to be difficult identifying Stefan in this crowd of clones. "At least he is tall," I suggest to Victoria. She returns a half smile, appreciating my positivity.

We split up. I patrol the right hand side of desks and Victoria the left. We walk slowly and assuredly, like we've spent years working here. One glimpse from Stefan, at least of Victoria, and he'll be gone. We do one circuit, crossing in the middle, and arrive back where we started. But nothing. No Stefan. No sign of him. There is a kind of corporate marketplace of identical meeting rooms at the far end. Each has a thick horizontal yellow band on the glass concealing the upper half of the people in there. If he is in on the floor, he'll be in one of these. Without uttering a word, I suggest to Victoria that she gives me an image of Stefan, whatever she can remember, and I'll look into the rooms on my own. This way if I get spotted by Stefan then he won't flee on sight. Victoria agrees, downloads a number of visual clues for me and makes her way back to the stairwell where I will cross to once I have Stefan. This is the plan.

There are perhaps eight rooms in a row. I can see as I approach them that there are only two that actually have people in them. This should make things easier I think to myself. As I get closer it dawns on me that if I walk by on my tiptoes trying to peep over the top then this will only look suspicious. So I decide that I'll make up a story, knock on each door and somehow put myself in a position where I can shake Stefan's hand. If I can do this, then I can get him out to Victoria and onto to the Southern Cross in Kibi.

I rap my knuckles on the first glass door and wait. I see under the yellow modesty board that a few legs and knees turn in my direction. There is laughter from the group. The interruption has provided some light relief. The door opens and a lady in her fifties dressed in a grey trouser suit smiles at me. She doesn't say anything, waiting for me to explain myself. "Ah, I'm very sorry to interrupt your meeting, but I have a message for Herr Stefan Baden." As I talk I smile with my eyes and scan the room looking for a tall, gaunt and bony faced man with dark eyes. There are a couple of people that are tall but that is where the comparison ends. I remember too that in the description from Georgia that he has an awkward gait, although with everyone sitting down this won't help me. A room of puzzled faces look back at me. I've already decided that this is the wrong room but I'm committed now. "And your name?" I am asked by the lady at the door. Swinging into corporate meeting mode I reply. "Of course. My name is Robin Mann, I'm the new head of change. Not that we need any more change around here." There are wry smiles of recognition. A smile returns to the face of the door woman. "Well, I think he must be in a different meeting room, he hasn't graced us with his presence today," We are all veering dangerously close to being mildly amusing at this rate. I grin knowingly while having no idea of why she would say that. "Well, I will thank you and take my leave." I find myself doing a strange bow. I don't know why I'm doing this but it may be because I'm picking something up in her thoughts. It seems to go like that sometimes. As I reach to the door handle to pull it closed she holds onto the door. I tell myself to remain calm. She leans forward "Do you have a business card; I'd like to offer some of my own thoughts about our change programme?" I know this routine. "If you let me have your card I'll throw a line across. I'd love to take you for coffee." She presses her card in my hand and I'm gone.

I nonchalantly walk to the next occupied meeting room and repeat the process. Legs swivel towards me. There is the sound of laughter and I am met at the door this time by a tall man. My heart flutters for a moment thinking it might be Stefan but it's not. I can see straight away that he's not in here and to avoid wasting any time I mime hitting myself on my forehead with the palm of my hand. I look goofish and exclaim, "Wrong room!" I step backwards pointing to my temple with my finger in a circling motion. Acting stupid makes everyone feel good about themselves.

The door is closed in my face and I am left staring at a reflection of myself. I look different from how I remember. I can't connect the image in front of me to the office worker I once was, or the filmmaker, or the drop out. Gazing back at me is a rougher looking version of myself. The bruising from the incident with Carlos has subsided, by my skin looks thicker, my eyes narrower. I simultaneously appear both tired and alert. It's a strange impression. As I'm staring at myself like a dog that has seen their likeness for the very first time, the corner of my eye catches a movement; a shadow swaying in an irregular manner. It looks like an old-fashioned animatronic toy, jerking as it moves. I'm confused for a second. I can't place where the shadow is emanating from. I turn one hundred and eighty degrees and cast my eyes over the office. There are at least fifteen people walking about the room. A pair of women joined at the shoulders striding away towards the fire exit. A young man dressed in a brown uniform carrying a package. He is whistling as he passes two, then three men walking in single file, they are wearing sharp suits and polished dark shoes.

I've lost my bearings completely and as I'm about to return to the reflection to retrace my steps, I see him. Unmistakable. Tall, gaunt, bony faced, dark eyes, awkward gait. That's him! I launch myself forward on a collision course for him. Keeping my steps measured and controlled. I need to look like every other person. I need to be invisible. We are ten or so desks away from one another. He looks at me but doesn't see anything unusual. I flash my eyes up and down as casually as possible. I make a right-angled turn to my left so that we are opposite each other and now fewer than five metres away. I'm closing in on him. Eyes down. I focus my thoughts on something banal just in case he tunes into me. Four metres. I push thoughts of Victoria and then my gun out of my mind. Three metres. A young woman carrying a stack of papers cuts across me. She looks sternly at me like I've done something wrong. Two metres. I can nearly touch him. I'm reminded about Victoria's advice about going for his belt. I wiggle my fingers in readiness. One metre. By accident I look directly into his eyes. I can't help it! Shit! He realises that something is up. I feel him hacking into my thoughts. My right hand grabs at his hair like the talons of a bird. I wedge my left hand in the front of his trousers. Holding on for dear life. From his mouth comes a deep rumbling sound. More of a roar in fact. He stumbles backwards onto an empty desk, his scrawny neck exposed as I fall on top of him.

Before our bodies hit the surface of the desk, I cross us both into the stairwell. Victoria is waiting. As soon as we appear she propels her left hand forward and hooks a claw-like hand onto his ear. It is such a violent movement that his bellow turns into a scream. In the struggle I expect Victoria to reach for his belt, but instead she lashes out with her boot towards his shin, then to his groin and then to his stomach. It's such an incredibly fast and brutal sequence of movements, I can only assume that she has used a few Micro Time Shifts. I certainly can't work out what has happened. There is a fourth blow this time with her elbow to his cheek. It's so powerful that his head ricochets against the stone wall, backwards and then downwards towards the floor. There is a snap of gristle from somewhere in the area of his neck, and although my hand remains wedged in his belt, the sudden flick of his torso causes me to lose my grip of his head. I am left with a large clump of his hair between my fingers. Stefan is conscious but groaning now. As I crane my neck towards Victoria expecting a signal to cross to Kibi, I am horrified to see her swinging her pistol towards his face. She smashes it into the bridge of his nose leaving a bloody gash. Thump! He is lying flat on his back now and Victoria straddling him jabs the barrel of the gun into the swollen cheek that she struck a few seconds earlier. "Don't fucking move!" Victoria barks at him. "If you attempt to cross anywhere. Any. Fucking. Where. I will blow your brains out. Do you understand me? Have you got it?" Stefan whispers yes repeatedly. "Right, let's go!" Victoria says in my direction.

It's only been a few minutes but it's even hotter now in the hut. We are squashed on top of each other like a pile of dirty laundry. Stefan is panting. His face is bleeding and his head is at an awkward angle against the wall. Victoria and I shuffle around so that we are now lying on each of his arms. Victoria is still holding the gun to his head, and I have my hands down the front of his trousers. The knuckles of my hand are pressed into his pubic hair. In any other situation this would be sending a very different message. No one speaks while we all try to catch our breath. I feel a bead of sweat trickling down the side of my face. It runs quickly until it reaches my jawline then it leaps to the floor. There is no sound as it lands. Stefan looks like he's in a trance. He may be thinking about his next move but with the hammering that Victoria just gave him, he's more likely trying to manage the pain that he must be feeling.

Stefan is the first to speak, "I think you've broken my collar bone." He addresses this in a matter of fact manner to Victoria. He tries to change his position to relieve the pain but with two bodies pinning his arms to the ground it's fruitless. Victoria slowly drags the barrel of the handgun away from his face and across to his collarbone. He watches, incapable of doing anything to stop her. It comes to rest. My heart beat quickens. Feeling really uncomfortable about what I think Victoria is about to do, I open my mouth to negotiate with her, just as she drives the end of the gun into flesh. His eyes flash and he lets out an unholy squeal. Shocked by the noise I jump back momentarily losing contact with Stefan. Victoria's face remains emotionless. I roll back onto Stefan's arm. He is weeping now and begging for mercy from Victoria. "I don't know where they are Victoria! I had no idea that they were doing this." Victoria has quizzed him about Pandi and Yo Yo in her thoughts. "Then why are you trying so hard to block me out?" Victoria pronounces each word emphatically.

As I observe the standoff between them I find myself thinking of somewhere else. My mind is going to a crowded space. There are policemen and women milling around. It's the entrance to a police station, but I don't recognise the uniforms. The police are dressed in black and are carrying guns. It has a strongly paramilitary feel to the place. I squint in my mind's eye and read the words *Policía Federal Preventiva* on the breast pockets and upper sleeves of the people around me. I'm flicking through possible matching countries in my mind; Spain, Argentina, Mexico...when I realise what is happening. Stefan is attempting to cross and using suggestion so I'll support him. I literally shake my head trying to eject the thoughts from my mind, but it has no effect. The fuzzy resolution of the image fills out and bang! The three of us are on the floor of the police station. It's a brilliant move, I think to myself, as Stefan has brought us to the place most likely to get us separated from him. Sure enough, as he starts yelling in Spanish "Ayúdame! Ayúdame!" two, then three, police officers have their hands on Victoria and myself trying to pull us off Stefan. A fourth police officer is pointing his rifle at Victoria bawling commands, "Caer el arma. Ahora! Dejar caer la maldita arma!" In the chaos, I can feel Stefan trying to shake my hand loose. Victoria is still sitting on top of him. The officer with the rifle is losing her cool and she starts yelling again even louder, no doubt instructing Victoria to drop her gun. Victoria turns to me looking me directly in my eyes. "Do not let go of Stefan. Whatever happens hold onto him like a fucking limpet and think only of Kibi. Kibi!"

I see an officer swinging a baton furiously towards Victoria's head. It is so fast it looks like it is going to take her head clean off, but as it is about to connect, it suddenly changes course cracking into Stefan's legs. Two of the officers are now on their backs on their floor. There are spots of blood on the tiles next to them. Then there is a blur in front of me. I know Victoria is involved as I can see the outline of her body and the swish of her hair. Two gunshots ring out in quick succession. The female police office that had her gun levelled at Victoria is lifted fully off the ground as a bullet strikes her. She is wearing body armour although it's not easy to see where she has been hit. Now with one hand free, Stefan is reaching into the back of his trousers. It didn't dawn on me that he might be armed. I lunge at him grappling with his hand, trying to bend it backwards. His long skeletal fingers sliding out of my grip. It's just him and me now as Victoria is throwing herself around the room neutralising a growing crowd of police. When I finally have his hand under my control I feel a familiar sickness. He is crossing us out of here.

We are slumped against one another on a cliff top overlooking a vast expanse of sea. We are surrounded by tufts of thick grass. And the wind is high. I have no idea where this is. My best guess would be somewhere in Europe. It all seems vaguely familiar. It might even by the South West coast of England, but there is not enough information to go on. I am still clinging on to Stefan. My hand squeezing his hair and my fist around his belt pushing into his stomach. He's clearly injured and his breathing is laboured. The past few minutes of Victoria's viciousness had mystified and sickened me. I knew she could be decisive. I'd seen that much, but this didn't seem necessary. Although perhaps she knows what he was capable of and is entirely justified. He'd certainly been cunning and here we were now separated from Victoria. And if it hadn't been for her ruthlessness I would most likely be on the wrong side of his gun. While thinking about this I suddenly remembered that this is exactly what he'd been reaching for just as we crossed. Without hesitation I leap on top of him, my knees pinning down his arms. He squeals. I have twisted his collarbone. Foolishly I lean back to release the pressure from his collar and torso and no sooner have I done it he violently strikes his knee into the centre of my back. The shock is so great that I black out for only half a second, but long enough for him to pull his arms up in front of him and smash both of his elbows into my chest. I know I can't break contact with him so as I fall backwards I grab at his clothing pulling him towards me. We started rolling down the cliff. We are both so focused on hanging on to each other, in my case, and prizing each other apart, in Stefan's, that we make no effort to stop the momentum that is building as we tumble and bounce along the grass.

Stefan lashes out with his fists striking me on the ear. The pain is intense. It is like someone has thrust a red-hot iron into the side of my head. I feel an agonizing burning sensation and the sound of the wind and our bodies crunching through the undergrowth become muffled and distant. I tighten my grip on his clothing as he rolls over the top of me. We were gathering pace and propelling ourselves faster the more that we struggle. As his head cartwheels over mine I take my opportunity, and with all my strength I unhook my right arm and deliver one almighty thump to his body. I have no idea where my punch will land but I know that simply hanging on to him will leave me too vulnerable. My fist connects with his groin and there is a dull, almost wet sound that follows. Just as I sense a tightening in Stefan's body, I feel a sharp cutting jab into my kidney that is too hard to have been caused by Stefan. I rebound off a rock that dislodges the moment we hit it. We are careering down the cliff at an uncontrollable rate. The tufts of grass are becoming smoother and more slippery and we are reaching a point of no return. I estimate that we are perhaps five or ten metres from the edge. I don't know whether it is a sheer drop into the sea or a series of rocky steps that will take us down, but either way I know that our chances aren't good.

Uncharacteristically, particularly in the circumstances, clarity comes to my thinking. We have to cross. I have to make the crossing back to Ghana. And I cannot afford to disconnect from Stefan. Everything I know about crossing, and every ounce of focus that I have left in me, I pour into the school hut in Kibi. I make my entire existence about Kibi. Stefan may well have had exactly the same idea and a totally different destination in mind, but as we hurtle towards the edge of the cliff, and I see the vertical drop beneath us, we disappear and re-appear at the front of the classroom in the hut. Before my mind has caught up with my body and accepted that I am not about to have my brains dashed at the foot of the cliff, Victoria, who had long since returned from the Mexican police station, pounces on Stefan, her gun jammed into his chin and her other hand around his throat.

Stefan looks petrified as Victoria speaks. "Okay Stefan. You've used up all of your lives now. And you've worn out my patience. So this is what is going to happen." With this Victoria repositions the barrel of her gun against Stefan's balls. She's obviously picked up on the thoughts in his head and the excruciating pain he must have been feeling. "I'm going to count to three. And if you don't tell me where Pandi and Yo Yo are by the time I reach three, I am going to turn your manhood into a bloody gnarled mess. And after that, when you have no strength to cross out of here, I'm going to tie you up outside for the rats to eat you."

"One!" Victoria starts the count. Stefan's mouth opens but nothing comes out. "Two!" she spits out. Stefan stutters I d-d-d-don't. I haven't got..." Victoria smiles. "I'm about to say three Stefan. Are you ready? Here it comes. Thr..." The pitch of Stefan's voice winds upwards. "They're, they're at the old music store in Delhi. On 316. The instrument store where we had our meetings." Victoria speaks more slowly. "Isn't that a bit obvious

Stefan? Who is holding them?" She asks. He fumbles his words but manages to get out the key details "Romanov and Mary. They took them there. I promise. I promise" Stefan sounds more desperate as Victoria sounds calmer. She now knows he isn't lying. "Okay Stefan, but you told me you knew nothing about this. How can that be?" It wasn't a question and Stefan knew it. She pauses. An eerie silence befalls the room. It feels like something is coming to an end.

"You know what's got to happen now don't you?" Victoria is speaking to Stefan. I look at Victoria. Then Stefan. And I look back to Victoria. I can't believe what I am hearing. "He's told you Victoria" I say, "Just let him go now. We have what we need. Victoria! Victoria!" She looks me directly in the eyes, her gun firmly pressed against Stefan's crotch. "They are torturing them now. As we speak Robin. The whole time that Stefan has been trying to drag us through Mexico to get us killed. They have been torturing my parents. And I bet when you crossed out of Mexico he didn't stop then did he? Did he? He wants us dead. They want us dead. And after Edward, Larry, Georgia, Jan, Yo Yo and Pandi. It's you and me. We are next. It is hesitation that will get us killed." I hear Victoria twist the gun in her hand and three explosions fire out. I jump. Two bullets plunge into Stefan's stomach, and a third up through his chin into his head. He jerks, twists and comes to rest. His body is still. The life has drained from his eyes. "We need to get to Delhi!" These are the only words that Victoria utters.

22

Clavius

Victoria had killed for the first time at the age of seventeen. It was not long after she had witnessed the desolation of Ameena. They had crossed forward in time and in location to the off-earth settlements. To Clavius. Which was in the central southern region of the moon. It was the place where wealthy people from the earth would go to relax. In Clavius there were skillfully fabricated lush green rolling hills, beautiful wild rivers, forests, sandy beaches, warm seas and cool lakes. In fact, everything there was the opposite of what would naturally be found on the moon. The roofs of the pods were so high that it was easy to imagine that you were in an idyllic unspoiled resort back on earth.

It wasn't to everyones tastes though. Many preferred the virtual retreats that were available at considerable cost to those that could afford them. These would simulate any location that was desired with breathtaking accuracy, and to all the senses too – sight, touch, smell, taste, everything. A scrumptious meal could be summoned out of thin air.

A lifelike massage. A romantic encounter. A gunfight with an imagined foe. And of course it offered the added capability that the user could manipulate fundamental laws of physics at will. In doing so you could leap great distances, fly, breathe underwater, be irresistibly attractive, have the physical appearance of your choice and so on. And so the comparatively tame Eden of Clavius tended to be quite sparsely populated, something that stood in stark comparison to the frighteningly overcrowded cities on earth, and the slums that housed over billions of inhabitants.

Jan had taken the group there in the hope that he would be able to make contact with one of the most influential corporate players alive at that point. Her name was Tè Sūn. She had business interests in GenCo, Al Hab, Arkform and three of the largest outfits in Great China. Her personal history was an interesting one. She had been born, and had grown up, in one of the poorer regions of central Great China. She had spent some ten years of her life in an orphanage where she was one of nearly five hundred children that for a variety of reasons had ended up there. In her case her father had been expelled from the country for taking in political refugees from the North. And not long after his expulsion her mother had picked up a virus from a polluted water supply, and it had progressively attacked her organs until she fell into a coma. There were no family members that Tè could turn to, nor friends that had the resources to support her, and so at the age of five she was enrolled into the *New Hope* orphanage.

Jan had observed her from afar at different stages in her life and this had caused him to believe that she could be an ally. The intelligence that he had gathered had indicated that she had actively sought to shape political opinion on matters of corporate monopoly behaviours, ethics and social responsibility. She occupied an unusual position seemingly being both an advocate for the forces of neoliberalism while also being a surprisingly bold and radical reformer. It was a wonder how she had straddled these two tracks without finding herself on the wrong end of corporate hospitality. But more than this, he believed that she had a grand plan in mind, and one that belied her apparent corporate persona. His work to date had suggested that she had links to more extreme political groups, the type that Jan had a lot in common with – Environmentalists, Neo Anarchists, and what had come to be known as the Discontinuists. The Discontinuists were a particularly interesting movement whose singular ambition was to break the power of the ruling classes. That was where it started and ended. And they did this in an assortment of ways but always by looking first at what oiled the Capitalist system. They would hack corporate systems in order to lock them out of action for as long as they could. It was surprising how quickly a large company would grind to a halt if its computer systems failed to work. The Discontinuists would keep this up for days and sometimes weeks. They would acquire and feed critical business information to competitor organisations, and where possible stoke animosity between the major players. Over time this had become increasingly difficult though as the volume of competition had narrowed in many industries to barely two and sometimes none. Their most ambitious strategy was to recruit and train agents to work at senior levels on the inside of the corporate world, often living in that world for decades until they were influential enough to sabotage the organisation from the inside. The Discontinuists were well supported too, and Jan suspected that Tè Sūn had been a long time backer.

As a result of his ability to move in time Jan himself had been able to accumulate a fair amount of wealth for his cause. He did this by speculating on some of the financial markets with the considerable advantage that time travel lent him. And so Jan, Victoria, Yo Yo and Pandi checked into the disgustingly expensive *All Seasons* resort on Clavius. They were a strange looking 'family unit' and certainly not your average group of guests. They were taken by a passenger vehicle through a series of heavily armed security outposts before they entered the visually exquisite world that had been created. An oasis on a grey lump of rock floating in space. Jan had selected the temperate zone where he believed Tè Sūn would be located. They drove into what resembled a Mediterranean village, similar to Southern Italy or Greece. There were Olive groves, Cypress trees, dusty tracks, white painted buildings, brightly coloured flowers lining the streets. There was literally nothing to hint that this was a reconstructed world, apart however from the lack of people. Short of hiring actors to complete the illusion it wasn't possible to fully mimic the Mediterranean lifestyle. There were employees of course of the Clavius resort serving in the bars and tavernas, and projected impressionistic three-dimensional images of people, called *buddies*, but there weren't any 'locals' to finish off the picture. For most though this was sufficient.

They had been shown to their villa, their swimming pool, and the carefully designed views, and also made aware of the places of social engagement, where other guests would be found. This is what Jan had been listening out for. All he had to do was engineer a chance encounter with Tè and strike up a conversation. He knew that with his ability to read her thoughts he would be able to adjust his script accordingly to win her trust. For someone as important as Tè he knew that he would have to take it slowly and choose his moment carefully to make his proposition.

The first four or five days had all the characteristics of a regular holiday. As a group they ate together, lay next to the pool, took walks into the village and imagined they were in the Mediterranean. They didn't talk about crossing or the environmental disasters that had wreaked havoc on the earth. They enjoyed each other's company and forgot about the war that they were waging, under Jan's leadership, against the corporate giants and the corrupt political system. But on the fifth night, Victoria and Jan made contact with Tè Sūn. It was expertly set up by Jan who had been tracking her movements by crossing around the resort mapping her habits. She was sat in the outside of a restaurant under a pergola draped with flowers and vines. The edge of her table was less than a couple of metres from the pavement, and as they walked past Jan caught an authentically decrepit and small lamppost as it was toppling over into Tè's table. It was a rather surreal incident, although less surreal when you know that Jan had spent the last few days weakening the base so that with the additional help of a Micro Time Shift he could both be the cause and the solution of the problem. As it crashed towards Tè's head Jan made the point of injuring himself as he wrestled it to the ground and at a safe

distance from Tè. It looked entirely genuine and a pretty
heroic move by Jan that earned him a thank you place at
her table.

The three of them chatted alone comfortably for
much of the evening, although it was apparent they were
not entirely alone as Tè's plain-clothed bodyguards had
revealed themselves earlier. Fortunately, they were slower
to the scene than Jan. As they parted Tè invited Jan and
Victoria to a garden party the following evening. Tè
described it as a small gathering of friends, although he
knew from her thoughts that there would be some senior
figures there from the various global businesses with whom
she worked. It was an opportunity he didn't want to miss.

Jan hadn't conceived of a plan for altering the course of
history. His conversation with Ulrika Meinhof had been
a source of inspiration for what had become a strategy of
sorts. His best shot so to speak. But after five years spent
gathering intelligence on the scale and strength of the
problem and the studying the work of other people that
had set out to change the world - Martin Luther King,
the brains behind the Stasi, the Generals of the Russian
army – he was left with significant doubts about the way
forward. For some time, he thought that he should work
by funding appropriate political groups at different points
in time, but this had accomplished little as a result. There
were two reasons in particular for this. The first was
that GenCo and its successor organisations had infiltrated
many of the political groupings that sought to stand in
their way, and they worked effectively below the radar to
incapacitate the opposition. Ironically therefore much of
the financial backing that Jan had provided had in fact
gone directly into GenCo's pockets. The second reason was

that very few groups displayed the level of commitment or professionalism that was needed to disrupt such an established and arcane system. The type of fringe political factions that shared Jan's cause rarely possessed the talent that was needed, and if the truth be told, they didn't really appreciate the severity of the situation they were fighting against or the consequences for future generations. If they had seen what Jan had seen, then perhaps things would have been different, but they couldn't. All of this had led Jan to the conclusion that he needed help and this is where he imagined that Tè Sūn might come in.

The following evening Jan and Victoria arrived at Tè's rather sumptuous residence. The garden was enormous and meticulously cared for, and Tè greeted them both like old friends. This was a good sign. As they walked with Tè, Jan became aware of the heightened level of security on the premises and he wondered what had triggered this. There were plain-clothed bodyguards and security staff and surveillance cameras. There were some strategically positioned individuals who watched the party from turrets on the residence, from elevated patches of land and at various access points. Tè made the point of introducing Jan and Victoria to her friends, mainly business people, and one person that caused Jan to choke violently as if some food had become lodged in his throat. This had explained the security. It was none other than Elias Morel, the current Chief of the GenCo organisation, and arguably the most powerful person alive. But what had caused Jan to wheeze and splutter was not only his elevated position in the company, but that he was the grandfather of Benoît Elias Morel, who had (or more accurately would come to) run the operations on the moon when Jan was a scientist

at the GenCo Storm Rooms. Jan had always disliked
Benoît, having met him on numerous occasions when he
had been welcomed into the GenCo elite. As Jan cleared
his throat and marvelled at the connection between these
two people, the Chief in front of him, and his grandson -
Jan's future boss that had not yet been born - he was struck
with sudden panic. He physically stepped back from Elias
Morel with the sharp concern in his head that he might be
crossing into his own circle of influence, a position that
might trigger his immediate elimination. It was a slightly
tenuous link, given that he was two generations removed,
but he really didn't know how tolerant the technology was.
So he turned his back and walked away abruptly.

This had attracted some attention from the other guests
as it seemed like a disagreement had occurred, and as Jan
continued to walk away swiftly with his back to Elias,
this also stirred the interest of the armed bodyguards who
quickly started to move toward Jan. Two, then three,
bodyguards surrounded Jan who attempted to persist
in creating distance between himself and Elias. It was a
confusing situation and although Jan had some attractive
options available to him, such as crossing out of there
back to the villa or deploying some Micro Time Shifts to
neutralise the security, he didn't want to ruin his prospects
with Tè. And so, without thinking it through, he froze
on the spot and turned his head back towards Elias. He
was going to apologise to Elias while praying that in
further engaging with Elias that this wouldn't qualify as
re-entering his circle of influence. He raised both his hands
palms upwards in a gesture to Elias that was to signal an
apology, but as he did this, the bodyguards misinterpreted
the motion and leapt on him propelling him face first to

the ground. While the first two knelt on his back, the third searched Jan and immediately fished out the handgun stuffed in the back of his trousers. This was disastrous and left Jan with no options other than to blow his cover and exit the situation.

He crossed no more than two or three metres away to escape the grip of the bodyguards, but of course as they were in physical contact with him the effect instead was that a clump of four people disappeared and then reappeared in a different place on the lawn still struggling and fighting. The bodyguards seemed un-phased by this change in location and they continued to press him into the ground, only this time they now had three guns trained to the back of his head. Throughout this Victoria had remained immobile and unnoticed. She had been forgotten about in the chaos and this was her greatest advantage. And so with unimaginable speed she attacked the bodyguards who weren't able to make any sense of what was happening to them. Arms flailing, legs lashing out, Victoria went berserk on the three men unleashing a battery of punches, kicks and swipes with the base of her own handgun. As a bystander it was literally impossible to understand how in less than a couple of seconds three trained, burly men had been disarmed, beaten and ditched onto the ground at a safe distance from Jan.

As Jan saw it, there was no point trying to repair the damage that had been done or attempting to approach Tè to explain. It was a busted flush. But as he turned to Victoria to indicate that they should cross back to the villa, Victoria squared up to none other than Elias Morel. And standing at arm's length from him she fired three shots directly into his forehead. The white tablecloth behind him and a seventeen-year-old girl was sprayed with dark, sticky blood and GenCo's most senior person crumpled to the grassy floor like a plug had been taken out of him. Jan was torn momentarily over his next move, but before he could decide whether to turn back the clock on what had just happened the window of opportunity closed, so he crossed to Victoria, grabbed her tightly and exited the carnage that they had created. Mission fail, you might say.

The death of Elias Morel was reported in the GenCo-controlled media, as the consequence of a cardiovascular illness that he had apparently been born with. Tè Sūn had spoken publicly about his bravery in battling the disease and the good philanthropic work he had done to support other sufferers. It was a whitewash but loyalty to the truth had long since been abandoned and constructing a story around what looked like a crazed execution was too tough to spin. The GenCo machine stuttered for a few months with the loss of its leader, but was back on course soon afterwards.

Jan learned two important lessons from this experience. The first was that if he wanted to have a real impact on the course of history, he needed to start at a much earlier point in time, before GenCo, Al Hab etc. had cemented their power. In the current period of time they were more or less unassailable. The removal of their Chief had as much of an effect as taking a pebble out of the sea. The oceans of corporate hegemony were untouched. The second lesson that he learned was that he had exposed too much of this to Victoria and at too young an age. Pandi had been right in her suspicions all along and that evening when he returned to the villa with a blood-caked and distraught

Victoria, he knew that he had gone too far. Victoria of course wasn't to blame. She had done exactly what Jan had unwittingly been training her for over the last five years. He'd made a killer out of Victoria and she'd played her role flawlessly. This was when he first understood this.

23

Delhi Music Store, Road 316

We are standing on the street while Tuk Tuks, people and animals of all sizes whirl around us. It is some twenty degrees hotter than Hamburg although a few notches down from the blistering heat in Ghana. This had been the site of various meetings in the early days, when Victoria and Jan had recruited a significant proportion of the operation. To Victoria's knowledge it hadn't been used for the best part of five years, but clearly the organisation had continued with its use. "What a lack of imagination" Victoria mutters. The atmosphere between the two of us had changed after Victoria had shot Stefan. She had been right. Stefan would have killed us both given half the chance, and in fact he nearly did. But there was something stomach churning about the manner in which Victoria took away his life. And the problem of course with people that can read minds is that there is nothing in my thoughts that Victoria cannot detect. My feelings of distaste are as transparent to us both as her feelings of righteousness.

Victoria speaks first, focusing on the task in hand. "We don't know what we're going into here, but my suspicion is its just Romanov and Mary inside. Ryan will have moved onto somewhere else. What I suggest is that we split up. You grab them as soon as you see them, and you move them to the Southern Cross motel in Arizona. Do you remember it? Back in the days when you liked me?" Victoria smiles a half smile. She is trying to summon her characteristic sassiness but her expression reveals the hurt she feels by my new perspective on her. I wait for her to finish the plan but nothing comes. "And what will you do?" I enquire. "I will be stopping Mary and Romanov from killing the three of you." Once again I feel conflicted about Victoria. She will be protecting us at considerable risk to her own life, and in fact this is what she has done throughout. "Besides" She says "We can't have you all shot up for your girlfriend can we?" I don't understand what she is saying, but I'm starting to believe that this is how it will always be with Victoria.

She squeezes my hand and looks into my eyes to confirm that I am ready to cross. Stomach punch. Nausea. Whiteout. It's a gloomy hot basement and we are the only people here. There is a murmur of activity above us in the main part of the music shop and the occasional flutter of a trumpet sound. Without having to speak Victoria suggests that I investigate the adjacent room to my right, and she informs me that she will go in the opposite direction. The basement stretches the full length of the shop. From the deep rumbles reverberating through the floor I assume that I am moving from the brass section to the bass guitar section. As my eyes start to get used to the low light I see the cavernous passageways that lie ahead, and the twisted wooden arches bracing the walls and ceiling. There are fetid smells that wander across my nose as I edge along the walls. I can no longer see Victoria but we continue to silently brief each other from afar. Her voice is in my head describing the broken furniture that is lying around her, and the insects that she fears might scuttle out without warning.

I'm starting to believe that we are in the wrong place when from the corner of my eye I detect a small movement. I have to stand still and tilt my head from side to side to see if I can locate it, but it has become lost in the gloom. I keep walking forwards warily and hoping that something will reveal itself. I take small steps and hold the back of hand against my face for protection. A cobweb tangles itself around my hair and I duck as a reflex. A beam brushes against my ear and I crouch a little more. I am half expecting a nail or shard of wood to snag my clothing when my knees come into contact with an angular and hard surface. I stop in my tracks. There is something about the shape that I recognise but it eludes me. In the dark the most mundane of objects takes on an unfamiliar form and I cannot place this one. And so I stretch out my arms to feel whatever it is with my fingers. My heart sinks, and I brace myself. It is a knee, a woman's knee. I am petrified. My hope is that it is Pandi although the quiet is disconcerting. I try to determine whether there is warmth emanating from the knee but in the humid, close environment it's just too difficult to call. Barely holding back my anxiety I whisper "Pandi? Pandi? It's Robin. Is that you?" There is no response and so I grip the knee more tightly hoping that it will trigger a reaction. Initially it is inaudible, but as I lean forward I hear an infinitesimally small noise. A squeak. It is a tiny sound but my relief is palpable. I throw my arms around the body in front of me and lift it up in a bear hug. I need to get Pandi out of the darkness. I reverse out of the space backwards carrying the person with me and summoning Victoria with my thoughts although she doesn't respond. As I drag the body out of the pitch black I take my first glance at the person in my arms to confirm for sure that it is Pandi. But as the light improves I see the harm that has been done. Her arms are limp, her neck is at an unnatural angle, and the delicate features on her face are lumpy and bruised. It's a wretched sight.

I lay her down, silently calling for Victoria who again is nowhere to be seen. It is only now that Pandi recognises me. Some life returns to her eyes and she attempts to cup my face in her hands. Her arms are damaged in some way and as the pain rises within her, she retreats and folds them back on her chest. She is holding herself like a baby. It is clear that she has been hurt too much for her to contemplate crossing out of here. I know that she isn't okay but I ask her anyway. She smiles a surprisingly broad and bright smile in the circumstances. But as her face starts to shine I hear the thoughts in her head. She tells me that Yo Yo is not far from where she was dumped, back in the gloom. Her thoughts though are fuzzy and she seems to be struggling to remember whether he has been moved. Feeling somewhat fearful at re-entering the space, and also leaving Pandi on her own, I move as quickly as I can again with my arms around my head to avoid crashing into anything. I estimate that I am back at the spot that I found Pandi and I return to making small steps. I must have walked no more than two metres before I tread on what feels like an arm. I jump in the air rather overdramatically and let out a gasp. This must be Yo Yo. I'm afraid to see what state he is in and pray that he is alive.

I scoop him up, and as I am carrying him a sense of dread comes over me. I have made a realisation that I don't want to face. There is no sweat leaking from his pores. No resistance as I twist his torso. No sound from his lips as I haul his body. He feels lifeless. I am a few steps away from Pandi and I don't want to go any further. I can't bear it. I tell myself that I may have got it wrong, and that he can be revived, but as I stretch him out next to Pandi a deathly quiet descends. Pandi rolls on her side and stares into his face. It is immobile. Fixed. Static. She moves closer, the tip of her nose briefly in contact with his cold cheek. It causes her to flinch. She understands what has happened. I kneel down next to Pandi without speaking. She has started sobbing softly, her shoulders quivering, and her chest tucked into his. I shudder thinking about the treatment they must have received. Yo Yo's final hours in this fusty dungeon.

I can't work out what seems to have killed Yo Yo. He has dried blood on one of his ears and lacerations to his neck. His other cheek is sunken. I pluck at Pandi's hair clearing it from her forehead and stroking her in a consoling fashion. She is lost in grief. I am reminded that I haven't heard from Victoria, although I am grateful she is not here to see the desperate sorrow in front of me. This was her greatest fear and what we had come here to prevent. We were just too late.

"Victoria!" I say out loud in a breathy voice. "Victoria?" I repeat my call, this time as a question. I scan the thoughts in the room but silence is returned. I try to find my way back to the plan. What was the plan anyway? What is happening here? Larry. Edward. Carlos. Stefan. And now Yo Yo. This cannot be right. My mind is wandering. But Victoria was clear. Find Pandi and Yo Yo and get them out of here. That was the plan. I look across to Pandi and place my hands on both of Victoria's parents and cross to the motel in Arizona.

In the hours that follow I move between Arizona and Delhi as many times as I have the energy to do so. But Victoria has entirely vanished. And there is no sign of Mary, Romanov or anyone else from the Organisation. Eventually, Pandi intervenes and asks if I can take her and Yo Yo back to Lantau. She has children that need her and she needs them to come to terms with Yo Yo's death. I patch up her cuts and bruises as well as I can and we exchange no words as I do so. We cross to the temple and after a short while Pandi releases me with an instruction to bring Victoria back safely. We part ways and I return to the motel.

24

Epiphany in the Diner

I sleep fitfully in the night, worrying about Victoria and Pandi, and wake fully clothed still clutching a Beretta in my hand. I must have been dreaming about it, as the second that I open my eyes a realisation dawns on me that I am entirely separated from what is left of the operation.

The number of people that I know has been consistently whittled down. And I am at a loss to know how to find Victoria, or for that matter how to discover where Jan and Sandeep disappeared to after entering the cinema shoulder to shoulder. I search the available options in my head. The Southern Cross safe place under Sydney harbour has been burned down. Carlos' residence offers no leads. The Delhi music store is empty. I work through every location I have been to, but draw a blank. I need to come up with an idea. Something. Anything, that will help me pinpoint either Victoria or Jan.

The morning passes and still no one arrives. I leave a note on the bed for Victoria in case she finds her way to the motel and stroll out of the door to find a local diner.

I am starving and haven't eaten a proper meal for days. I am shown to a booth and before my back is pressed into the back of the seat a cup of coffee has been poured for me. The menu is expansive to say the least. There are English, American, Scottish, Mexican, Oriental and Vegetarian Full Breakfasts on the list. Pancakes, eggs, ham, bacon, pulled pork, cheese, patties, smoked salmon, herrings, toast, porridge, fruit, juice, maple syrup, hash browns, eggs Benedict, eggs Florentine, crumpets, muffins, baked beans, refried beans, spinach, grits, tomatoes, mushrooms, black pudding and even haggis. I choose haggis in memory of Grace. She hated it in fact, but in a strange way by choosing such a quintessentially Scottish dish, it brings me closer to her.

As I eat I recall the diner that Victoria and I drove to, the first time we crossed into the motel. She explained to me then how the operation worked and what they had been trying to accomplish. Hearing it was thrilling, and it was then that I was persuaded that they had a cause worth fighting for. And then of course there was Jean-Paul and his men who had abducted and beaten Larry. The speed with which Victoria had dispatched them had been unfathomable to me at the time, but of course since then I understood that I had been witnessing her skills in Micro Time Shifting. I find myself lingering on this point. It feels significant but I can't figure out why. And so I wait. And wait. And then, with a rush of adrenalin, a thought rises within me. It is obvious. Blindingly obvious. How can I have missed this? It would make so much sense of everything I have come to know about Jan and Victoria. The futuristic technology. The unshakeable belief that the world is headed for disaster. Their meticulous recruitment strategy, as if Jan and Victoria had known their recruits for years. For their whole lives. All of them. What if Jan and Victoria aren't only capable of Micro Time Shifts, but also macro time shifts. Of being able to cross to any time they choose?

I feel my hand shaking as this idea unfolds in front of me. Everything falls into place. This is absolutely stunning, I think. And if all of this is possible, and if I want information on the whereabouts of Victoria or Jan, all I have to do is be in the right place, and importantly, at the right time. If I can observe the initial arrival of Mary and Romanov at the music store in Delhi, or even the meeting between Jan and Sandeep in Reykjavik then I will know what was planned to follow. Or better still, if the music store has continued to be used by the organisation to conduct their current campaign of terror then I just need to be a fly on the wall when the plans were conceived. I have my answer! I leave fifty dollars on the melamine counter and bolt out of the diner and across the car park to the motel.

Back in the room I prepare myself, for the first time, to cross in time and location. I haven't done this before, but I assume that the principle is similar to locational crossing. Victoria always said that the technology was smarter than the user, and it would fill in the gaps for you. Before I do anything I make a point of registering in my own mind the current time and date, just so I know when to return to. And then I retrace my steps to when Victoria first taught me to cross. Picture the destination, that was the advice that she gave me. Having been to the music store before, the details come easily to me. The street. The building. The furious activity around. The animals and Tuk Tuks whirling in the road. And now the time. I think about this carefully. I envisage two days ago. I have no idea if this is right, but it would be about the time when Sandeep would have passed the information to Mary and Romanov about Pandi and Yo Yo's whereabouts.

I picture an early morning version of the scene. I focus my attention on the physical and temporal coordinates. I let the scene fill my head. I let it become everything. I am entirely absorbed in the destination. The edges of my vision become speckled, like I am having a migraine. It hasn't happened quite like this before. I feel the throb of the pulse in my wrist, which jumps and then pounds. There is a sound in my head like a whirring jet engine. The noise gets louder and starts to become overwhelming. I feel like I'm having a heart attack. A powerful surge happens within me. There is no punch to the stomach, but I feel excruciatingly hot and I can't breathe. I'm struggling to breathe. I feel claustrophobic and trapped. I pull at the collar of my shirt from my neck. I must have done something wrong. There is saliva rising in the back of my throat. I'm going to vomit. But I don't know where to throw up or even where my physical self is. My thoughts are climbing on top of themselves. I'm going to pass out. I feel like there is no oxygen left to breathe. And then, it all ceases. Instantly. There is whiteness. A nothingness. Then the colours rush back. The air returns. My body prickles like I have pins and needles. Now I am bracing myself against a corrugated iron shelter outside of the music store. I am here. I pray that it is two days earlier. I will need to find out. I slide down the shelter to the floor, safe but exhausted.

The heat in Delhi is starting to rise and with it a yellow light caused by the pollution. The shelter that I am leaning against is a makeshift bus stop and behind it is the music store. The street is a hotchpotch of shops, industrial estates, empty patches of dry scrub and pathways that crisscross one another. My arrival from thin air is entirely unnoticed; the street that I crossed into is filled with busyness and distractions for all the senses. There is a continuous buzz of motorbikes, cars and people and across the street from me are some mobile food kitchens with a short queue in front of each. Behind the low display glass windows are pastries of one sort or another and what appear to be dhal and breads. Behind the food stalls are more shops that have a jumble of signs and advertising hoardings above them. They are painted in purples and reds and yellows, and there is beautifully ornate writing on them, I assume in Hindi. Because I don't understand what the signs say I can instead enjoy the scene as if it were a piece of art. While I am here and in Delhi, I feel like I am also standing outside of it, perhaps this dislocated feeling is a consequence of crossing in time, or maybe just a result of being so dog-tired.

I am the only European face around but so far I've attracted no attention at all. I much prefer it this way. I find myself focusing back on the task in hand, that of locating Mary, Romanov or anyone from the organisation. I notice that across the road, there is café on the third floor of a building. It is tucked away underneath a large sign that has the word 'vegetarian' incongruously inserted between five or six Hindi words. I am surprised to see it there as on my first scan of the shop fronts all I could see was banners. It would be a perfect viewing point. I notice my legs carrying me across the street. The road is gritty underfoot and as I pass the food stalls I become wrapped up in exotic smells. There is a narrow passageway that leads up to some concrete stairs. I am guessing that this will take me up to the café. As I ascend the stairs a young Indian woman, dressed in a beautifully flowing shocking pink Sari, walks carefully down the stairs. We squeeze past each other exchanging slightly awkward facial expressions. It feels rather too intimate an encounter in a such poorly lit stairwell. We break free from each other and I continue to the top of the stairs. The café is relatively quiet although the seats at the window overlooking the street are mainly occupied by young men and women with laptops. The contrast couldn't be more stark.

Without speaking to the woman at the counter I gesture with my hand towards the group of tables. Her face lifts with a bright smile, her teeth shining white, and she nods her head at a forty-five degree angle which I take to mean that it is ok. There is a vacant table in the corner next to the window. It is hard to see but private. She is keen for me to sit here and in broken English I hear her say, "There is a better view here." Fair enough, I think. Using my clearest English accent, I ask for a coffee, some pastries and an English newspaper. I am keen to find some verification of when exactly I have arrived and this seems a sensible way to do it. The food and drink arrives and for some reason, an Indian newspaper. I thank her as if it was exactly what I asked for. My eyes wander across the paper looking for clues. Just some numbers to illustrate whether I have travelled in time or whether I have just crossed in the usual fashion. Then I see what I'm looking for. Buried at the top of the front page in some incomprehensible words is the date. It's the twenty third! Exactly two days prior to when I departed the motel.

I'm surprised and pleased although can't fully accept what has seemed to have happened.

My cup of coffee is replenished more times than I can remember, each time with the same smile and composure from the server. At about lunchtime she brings me some more food without having asked her. I guess she thinks that if I'm going to be occupying a table then I should consume more than coffee. Or maybe I look like I need feeding up. I am at about the five-hour mark now and there is no part of the view from the window that I haven't examined in great detail. I've even started to detect some routines in the behaviours of the people out there. The young boy, no more than twelve years old, who runs between the food stalls along the street seemingly carrying change for the owners. The old men sat on the pavement outside of what looks like a Laundromat playing cards and smoking cigarettes. The arguments that spark up almost on the hour, every hour, between a father and daughter working in the tiny key cutting shop. As for the music store, I haven't seen a single non-Indian person pass through the doors. And given that at least a handful of the members of the organisation are European, it doesn't bode well.

I had been trying to kill time waiting for a flight I had later that evening. I'd spent a week working in Marrakech, of all places. The company had a small presence there and a workforce of less than thirty people. The trip was symbolic more than anything, to show that we cared about the more remote international branches. Of course they weren't remote if that's where you lived, but the company was essentially a British one and it struggled to ever really grasp the global concept. It's fair to say that I had become adrift in my life. I had become what might be called a functioning depressive.

I worked for a company that bought, borrowed, lent, sold, and invested money. Money. Money. And more money. Apart from that being the dullest thing imaginable, it was also a soulless activity to be involved in. The company would have the odd corporate social responsibility project. The occasional fanfare when they chucked a few notes in the direction of a charity. And the online newsletter would feature a small business in a rural African community that had thrived due to the company's investment. There would be the picture of a face, all smiley, with a quote from someone that said the company had saved their business. But I'm pretty sure that very few people got up in the morning here with the ambition of making the world a better place. And after having spoken to nearly a thousand employees I had heard nothing to contradict this view. Perhaps everyone was depressed.

The company did have values though. Really good ones. Integrity. Stewardship. Professionalism. Empathy. Respect. All of the good things you'd hope for. Solid values. Comforting values. Laminated values. And none of it meant a thing. The real values, the lived values, were entirely different. Competitiveness. Wealth accumulation. Avarice. Winning. This was the engine of the industry. But these values wouldn't look particularly impressive carved into the marble block that stood outside the company headquarters. Alongside the expensive commissioned cool street graffiti. And the anti-homelessness spikes on the ground. It would be hard to inspire on a platform of avarice or the accumulation of wealth. But it seemed to me that that is what it was ultimately about.

I'd been in a trance since Grace's departure and sleepwalked into the job. The previous month I had handed in my resignation. A very matter of fact letter to my boss. I said something about wanting to work independently and then something about having appreciated the support that he had given to me. I had made up both of these sentiments. My boss, I think, had understood my resignation as a negotiating position. That kind of thing happened a lot around here. So he arranged for me to be employed as an external consultant at higher rates and asked that I undertake just a few more projects in Marrakech and then Sydney. He no doubt thought that I would find it hard to refuse the next batch of assignments he had in mind. In fact, in recent months he had expanded my responsibilities to take on a kind of scouting role for potential new acquisitions. This stuff bored me but I could do it in my sleep and I suspected that the kind of detached stolid demeanor that I brought to the job assured my boss that he would always get the truth, plain and simple. Oh yes, espionage. That was another company value I forgot to mention.

I had wandered around the central market in Marrakech enjoying the heat, the smells and the colours. It was strangely cleansing to be in this place. The square was dotted with men and women chatting in separate groups, children playing, snake charmers, smoke rising from cooking equipment, stalls selling dates, figs, raisins, nuts, olives, lemons, oranges, herbs, rice, couscous and more. There were passageways that led to huge emporiums containing treasures. The sun was caught in the reflections of ornate pans made of copper, brass and silver. There were a thousand clay coloured, tall cooking pots shaped like cones. Enormous carpets that must have taken months to make were rolled up and stood leaning against buildings like giants. The scene was electrifying and as I walked through it I soaked up the atmosphere. I had no idea of what I might do after I had completed the Sydney job. I had harboured the idea that I should return to the Spittal of Glenshee. I had loved it there. But I didn't know if I could bear it without Grace. If I was honest, a part of me believed that if I waited there long enough she would turn up at the door of the kirk one day. On that famous bereavement change curve, I was probably making another run at denial.

It wasn't long that evening before I had got lost. I had indulged in a few drinks of Mahia, a rare and potent liqueur made from distilled figs. The streets out of the square all looked the same, at least at this time of the evening. I had been staying in a Riad with a terracotta exterior seemingly identical to every other Riad in the area. On the way back I walked into a small kiosk to ask directions and found myself instead buying some cigarettes, the name of which I didn't recognise. It was incredibly embarrassing, as I couldn't remember the name of the street where I was staying, and all that I could recall was the word Maheer, which I knew was also similar to the name of the local liquor I had drunk. I had left to the sound of giggles.

I had learned once in SCUBA diving that if you get separated from your buddy you should swim in a circle before making for the surface. Thinking of the Riad as my buddy I had done a circuit of my present position only to find myself in an even less familiar part of the city. My flight was due to depart at just after midnight and I needed to get back to the Riad, grab my luggage, my passport and *tickets, jump in a taxi and board the plane to Sydney. I guessed that had about thirty minutes to get to the airport which was only really feasible if I had found my hotel in the next five minutes. I had bent my knees, sunk to the floor, sat crossed-legged on the dusty ground, and I had cried. Not small tears, or sniffles of sadness. But big honest ones. The Mahia certainly had a part to play, and the desperation too at knowing that I stood little chance of making my flight. But if I was honest, it was Grace that was at the centre of my thoughts. Living without her was what it meant to be truly lost. This was the moment that I had faced this. I was a well-dressed western man, by that point with clay and dust caked into my trousers, sat sobbing in the less salubrious side of town. It must have been a surreal sight to behold. And as my body jerked and shook, the most unusual thing happened. Something that baffled me at the time and continued to do so afterwards. The owner of the Riad, a lady called Nehma, walked up to me like an angel, holding my travel documents in her hand. It was like a dream. Behind her was parked a yellow taxi that I discovered held my luggage in the boot. I knew I wasn't near the Riad. It must have been at least a mile away, and yet Nehma had somehow anticipated my need and seemingly tracked me down. It didn't add up. But there she was. She had consoled me with a warm embrace and then hurried me into the taxi. I boarded the plane and immersed myself in as many films as it took to send me to sleep.*

It is dusk now and I am still being tolerated by the woman in the café who I now know is called Ania. As I'm looking at the entrance to the store I see that the owner, or perhaps one of his staff, is bending down to bolt one of the main doors, and then the other. It must be closing time. He finishes the job and with a rucksack on his back he walks purposefully away from the building. I wonder if I'm just in the wrong place. Perhaps the store was only ever used the once to hold Pandi and Yo Yo. I squint with my eyes as I pick up some movement to the side of the store. It looks like there is a side entrance that I couldn't see before now. The light from the door is now set against the darkening sky and so not only can I see movement, but as the door opens there is a flash of orange light on the faces of the visitors. There seem to be a group of maybe four people, and I can see that at least two if not more are European looking. This has to be it.

I hand a wad of US dollars to Ania and she smiles once again. "Good luck" she says. It seems like an odd choice of words to bid someone farewell with but I don't have the time to pursue it. As I descend down the tight stairwell I see that I am alone and I take my opportunity to cross. A moment later I am standing in the passageway that leads up to the side entrance of the music store. The area where I am is too busy and dark to be noticed. The last person in the group is stepping towards the open door. The artificial light reveals that he is a tall man wearing light blue jeans, white trainers and a sports hoodie. I can't see his face well but he has thickset features and unkempt brown hair.

As I stand fixed to the ground, I detect some thoughts that are moving around someone's head close by. I hear the scrape of shoes on the ground and I remain still. Two people walk past me, and my shoulder is gently brushed. I freeze hoping that no one turns to apologise or work out who they have just nudged. Both individuals continue without breaking stride and I now see the backs of a man and woman walking side by side towards the closing door. Thankfully they haven't acknowledged my presence or picked up on any of my thoughts, but I hear them both thinking about none other than Jan. I sense a complex set of emotions within them both that stray from confidence to fear. It feels like a tense meeting is about to take place. The woman's thoughts are focused on an awareness of the gun she has in her jacket that then shifts to a pain she feels in her ribs. The man is rehearsing what he is due to say when he gets inside. I hear my pulse beating faster in my neck. He is walking through his plan that involves Jan. This is exactly what I want to hear. I can't believe that he is about to give me everything I need. And then his thoughts become disjointed and I cease to hear them. He has moved out of range and because I can't afford to be heard following him, my feet remain stuck to the ground until both members of the organisation have been let into the building.

There is a row of six windows at head height that extend along the side of the store. The first four windows have no sign of life, but the final two are lit up and this is where I guess the meeting is taking place. I creep along the line of bushes marking out the alleyway. The night is humid and heavy and as I disturb the bushes insects and mosquitos take to the air. The heat causes me to check my pace and I use this to compose myself. When I get to the fifth window I stand on my tiptoes and peer through the glass. I see six people sat down at a dark wooden table and a seventh person that is pacing the room. It is the man that brushed past me a few moments earlier. Behind him there is a carpet on the wall and two mounted sitars. There is also a lot of wicker in the room. Chairs. Low

tables. Baskets. Picture frames. A lot of wicker. I inspect
the gathering making a point of fixing their physical
appearances in my mind. If this is the organisation, then
I want to remember every single person.

There are two men seated with their backs to me so
I shuffle along the brickwork of the store toward the
final window to get a better view. As I poke my head up
I instantly recognise them. And in that moment I feel a
sickness deep in my stomach. It is Sandeep and Stefan.
The very same Stefan that Victoria had shot in the belly
and the face a few days earlier. Or later, depending on
how you looked at it. It surprises me but I start to feel
sadness and a longing. I want for Stefan to be alive. The
image of the fear on his face in Kibi has burned itself into
my memory. This sits alongside the disgust I had felt as
Victoria taunted and then shot him. This is what I think,
at least until I hear him speak.

Stefan addresses the group in perfect English and I listen
intently with my ears while summoning all my powers of
reading. "We are so close from working out what they are
really capable of." Stefan rotates his wrist so that everyone
can see. "And it's clear that even those closest to Jan and
Victoria - Edward, Larry, Georgia, whoever – haven't got
the faintest idea. Not a clue. And I should know. I put
these fuckers through the mill. They hung on for dear
life. So sad!" He says this mockingly. Sandeep and the
others remain quiet as Stefan continues talking. "So this
is my plan." He turns to Sandeep as if double-checking
something with him. "Jan has requested a rendezvous
with Sandeep. He always had a soft spot for him." He
winks at a stony-faced Sandeep. "Apparently Jan has
used a new recruit to carry the message that he will be in

Reykjavik." That's me he is talking about. I realise that *I am* that new recruit. Stefan continues. "This has got to be our best chance. I don't know about you but it's been impossible to get a lead on Jan's location. The guy is a master of disguise. He's the fucking invisible man." Stefan laughs out loud but no one joins in. He recognises that he's misjudged the mood. "Seriously, it's been years and this may be our only opportunity".

And then the thickset man stands up to speak. He looks Russian to me so I assume that it is Romanov. He too looks across at Sandeep before he speaks. This is becoming a strange routine. "And more than this, Jan's new recruit also unwittingly disclosed to Sandeep the location of Pandi and Yo Yo. Apparently they live in a temple on Lantau." My shoulders drop and I grasp my forehead with my hand. This is awful. What I am hearing is that I am responsible for Yo Yo's death. I am the reason that they knew where to go. After a pause for dramatic effect, Romanov delivers his proposal. "And what better way to lure in Victoria than to steal the people that mean the most to her? If we do this right, in just a few days from now we can have wiped out the entire opposition and found out all we need to about the technology. With enough pressure on them, we might even get what we need from Pandi and Yo Yo." He turns to the woman at his right with a question. "Mary, this job has your name written all over it" Mary nods in a definite manner.

For someone that has the gift of the gab, Sandeep is unusually quiet. Maybe he thinks his work has been done in delivering the two most useful pieces of information the organisation has had for years. The man that brushed past me outside in the street then pushes his chair back to announce that he is about to speak. "And after we have removed the opposition, what then?" The group looks confused by the question. He picks up on their reaction and develops his point. "I think we've all done our bit in helping the world." Some of the gathering nod in a hesitant but curious way. "In the early days at least." He adds. "We sacrificed some good people, some good friends along the way. And since then we have been united in a purpose, but one that has been defined by opposition alone. Opposition to Jan, Victoria and the rest. Without any of them on the scene we have a chance to create something afresh." It sounds like a bid for leadership.

"I think it's time for a change of direction. This is an opportunity for us to finally release ourselves from the baggage that came with Jan." I still don't know the name of the speaker but listen closely. He continues to prosecute his case. "Fighting against bad corporates was his agenda, not ours." His face grimaces as he pronounces the word 'bad'. "The arrogance that he routinely displayed in imposing his personal world-view on everything always sickened me. And I know I'm not alone in thinking this. If we fought for anything it was for collective change, not to serve the agenda of one man. And if we pull together as a group we don't need to have such modest ambitions. Let's stop being so coy about creating wealth. Christ! We've put in the work haven't we? Let's get some collateral behind us and get organised." The support of the group is hanging in the balance. "And I'm not afraid to squeeze the truth out of Jan. There is more to this technology, we just don't know what. If this is what we all want, then it would be a privilege to put myself forward for this." The balance tips in his favour. There is a ripple of agreement and heads are nodding. But the greatest feeling in the room, the most overwhelming current, is a sense of relief that someone is prepared to take on Jan. The speaker is cutting a deal with the organisation and it seems to have bought in.

Sandeep stands up and speaks for the first time. "Okay. I'll bring Jan to the old recording studios in New Mexico." Everyone looks blank. He looks annoyed that they don't recognise the venue. He reminds them. "Our first ever big meeting. The Southern Cross in Dexter? New Mexico? Remember?" The group recovers its collective memory loss and concurs loudly. Sandeep addresses the person that had been holding the floor, "Ryan, if you can prep the equipment and bring anyone you need to, I'll be there in twenty-four hours. If Victoria falls for the parent trap, then bring her along too. She might be a weapon we can use against Jan" I watch through the window as in turn everyone in the room disappears. One by one. Stefan is the last to cross. The sympathy I had for him has evaporated.

25

The Recording Studios

Back in the motel, the second note that I had written for Victoria is in exactly the same spot on the bed that I left it. I am not pleased to see it there, as it means that Victoria is still missing, but it does at least comfort me that I have crossed into the right time.

The process of temporal travel is punishing and so I allow my eyes to shut for a couple of hours. My dreams are filled with grotesque images of people being tortured. I wake up with sweat on my brow and the shitty feeling of being more tired than I was when I fell to sleep. I gobble up some nuts, chocolate and Coca Cola that is waiting in the mini bar. My stomach groans as I splash fizzy drink down my throat. I think to myself that I need to gain some kind of advantage if I am to be of any help to either Jan or Victoria. I am conflicted over what I had heard in Delhi and experienced for myself in Kibi - the suggestion that I was used by Jan to carry a message to Sandeep troubles me. The brutality of Victoria has caused me to question, once again, my assumptions about her. These thoughts run like an engine in the back of my mind.

In the afternoon I cross in and out of New Mexico to familiarise myself with the place where Jan will be taken. With the first couple of crossings I make sure that I'm some distance from the recording studios. No one expects me to be here, but I can't afford to be spotted at any point, so I am tentative in my approach. Or maybe I'm just terrified about what lies ahead. I'm definitely terrified. As the day goes on I pluck up the courage to cross inside the studios. They are empty, and have clearly been disused for a few years. There is no one I can see here for the time being. With the exception of the entrance reception, the facility is entirely underground. I assume this is for the purposes of soundproofing, although I sense a twinge within me in thinking about why this place has been selected. It is built like a catacomb with numerous dingy practice rooms that branch off a main passageway. Each room has a heavy metallic door barring the entrance and a small glass window at eye height. Towards the end of the darkened passageway is a fully kitted-out recording studio. There are desks with sliders, old-fashioned tape machines, clumps of cabling disappearing into metal boxes, worn out sofas and shelves of books. Everything has a thick layer of dust on it. It seems strange that the equipment in here hasn't been removed or cannibalised. Perhaps the organisation had aspirations to cut an album at some time. I try and calm my nerves with this quip to but it doesn't work.

The main mixing room looks out through a soundproofed glass window into a performing space, and both the mixing room and the performance area are overlooked through another window by a kind of narrow, elevated viewing gallery. I assume it was designed so that visitors to the studio would be able to marvel at the band and the sound engineers as they worked. There are a few interesting things about the viewing gallery. Firstly, you can only get to it through a set of stairs that are tucked away from the entrance to the main studio. Secondly, it is only big enough to accommodate two or three people. And finally, it is hidden from sight by a one-way mirror system. You would only know that it even existed if you had taken the other set of stairs to get there. I imagine that this was so neither the engineers nor musicians were disturbed or distracted by the arrival of an audience. And this gives me an idea. I remove the fluorescent tube of lighting leading to the stairwell rendering it almost invisible, and to make doubly sure I shift, by a couple of metres, and with some considerable effort, a drinks vending machine that stands in the passageway. While this doesn't fully block the route to the viewing gallery, it makes it appear to be a dead-end. If Ryan brings Jan into either of the two recording spaces, I will be hidden from sight in the viewing gallery hopefully at a distance that doesn't allow my thoughts to be skimmed.

I return to the motel to gather my thoughts before I intend to cross back to New Mexico. I flick the TV on to try and zone out, and quickly regret it. The first six channels are international news programmes interspersed by fast moving, garish commercials. As the news returns the screen lights up with images of mass urban expansion in China, collapsing arctic shelves and the next corporate scandal, and this makes me think of Victoria. And Jan. And I muse on their cause. If Jan has seen where our current trajectory is taking us and this terrifies him enough to travel God knows how many years to the present to try and fix it, then I shudder to think what's coming next. And if the organisation is successful in either extracting the time shifting secrets from him, or killing them both, what will become of their cause? If the personal reasons for wanting to attempt saving Jan and Victoria weren't enough, then this surely should strengthen my resolve.

Before I cross out of the motel for what may be the final time I leave a third note for Victoria, this time giving the location of the organisations' rendezvous in New Mexico. My hand is trembling as I spell out the words, knowing that Victoria may in fact already be held captive by Romanov and Mary. I take a deep breath and summon an image of the viewing gallery. Stomach punch. Nausea. Whiteness.

A lot has changed in the last few hours. It now looks more like a hospital than a recording studio. Jan is there. And he is lying on a gurney with a series of tubes and wires taped to his wrists, chest and temples. There is a portable monitor presumably tracking his heart, pulse and other vital signs. Attached to the tube that is protruding from his right wrist is a large syringe, and feeding into the other wrist is an intravenous drip. His eyes are forced shut with some cumbersomely applied duct tape. I can see that there has been a struggle in getting him here as Jan has dark grey and yellow bruises along the line of his jaw. There are fresh cuts and puncture holes on the inner part of his arms that suggest a number of failed attempts to get the lines in. His round glasses are bent out of shape and I can see that the fingers on his left hand are twisted into a claw. Up until this point I have been able to keep my emotions in check, but as my eyes scan the room, and

I see a pair of jump leads under the trolley lying next to a twelve-volt car battery, a hiss escapes from my mouth and I wrap both of my hands around my face to stop the noise. The soundproofing protects me on this occasion. I feel tears collecting at the corners of my eyes. It is an agonising and pitiful scene to watch.

Jan is barely-conscious and periodically appears to stir from his slumber. Each time that he does Ryan, who is stood next to him also sporting injuries to his face, steps forward, applies some pressure to the syringe and Jan seems to quiet down. Sedating Jan must be their strategy to prevent him from finding the strength to cross. In addition to Ryan, there is Sandeep and two other people in the room that I recognise from the music store. They are positioned close to the glass window separating the mixing room from the performance space. There are a further two women and men who are each holding onto Jan's arms and legs. They look tired like they have crossed about as many times as they are able. There is no sign of Mary and Romanov.

There is a lot of milling around in the room. It seems undirected, or at least like they are waiting for something to happen. I can't fathom it. I see Ryan bend over and whisper into Jan's ear. I try desperately to read his thoughts but can't quite get them. Ryan then reaches down and pulls a lever on the side of the gurney up towards him. Jan is raised to a half-sitting position. He looks like a ventriloquist's dummy, with the regular features of a man, but lifeless and disjointed in his occasional movements. The two colleagues adjust their orientation to accommodate this move, while remaining in physical contact with him. Ryan produces a scalpel from the arm of the sofa. I wince as I see the flash of the blade. I grab myself again to stop making a loud noise.   He runs the blade along the length of his shirt pulling and cutting at his clothing. Jan's long and sinewy chest is exposed. With a final and expert flick of the scalpel, Ryan separates the top of his shirt collar from his neck. He looks even more vulnerable than before.   He places the scalpel to the side of his face and tugs at the duct tape and although the tape loosens, in his eagerness, the blade catches his ear and in an automatic response Jan jerks up, forward and squirms. Ryan quickly reaches for the syringe and pinches it to deliver another dose of sedative. Jan 's body relaxes as the bright blood drips heavily down his ear onto the bench. He rips the remainder of the tape from his eyelids.

I'm furiously trying to calculate the odds on disarming eight people and crossing out of here with Jan without being gunned down. Perhaps with four, or even five people it might be possible. Perhaps if I used Micro Time Shifting, which I would be attempting for the very first time, I can't be confident that I wouldn't end up dead, and very quickly. My reticence is tested as I witness what happens next.

Ryan lifts the car battery up and swings it into place on the gurney between Jan's legs. Jan's head is lolloping from side to side. He is trying to regain consciousness but the drugs are keeping him under. Ryan produces from the table behind him a slim wire that he stretches around Jan's neck, twisting the ends together. This is fiddlier than he expects and it takes him a few minutes. The four people maintain a tight grip on Jan's limbs as they can see that the other end of the leads aren't, as yet, attached to the battery. Everyone else in the room looks on mesmerised, with expressions of faint disgust decorating their faces.

Ryan takes the black and red crocodile clips on one end of the jump leads and snaps them around the metal necklace around Jan's neck. This is becoming too much for me to watch. I take the gun out from my trousers and grip it with both hands. I don't care how this ends up; I cannot do nothing while Ryan electrocutes Jan. I am repulsed and terrified by what's happening in front of my eyes, and I have to act.

I stand up to my full height and feel the adrenalin thumping around my body. I focus. And just as I'm about to cross, there is a commotion in the room. I pause. A second later and I would have been down in the main room. Ryan is turning the trolley away from me and towards the glass window. He is clearing Sandeep and the other members of the organisation out of the way. He is waving his hands and issuing orders. "Get out the way. Shift yourselves. There's work to be done here. Come on." He then reaches for an old-fashioned chrome microphone sitting on the mixing desk. It looks like something from the 1950's. "Testing two, two, two," he says. "Stormy weather…" He's singing now "Since my man and I ain't together, Keeps rainin' all of the time…" He sounds unhinged. "Alright!" Sandeep says. "We can do without the dramatics." Ryan ignores him "Oh, yeah, Life is bare, gloom and mis'ry everywhere…Stormy weather…Stormy weather." He turns back to Sandeep "That's rich coming from you. You are the reason why he's here. You're the reason why this lanky fucker is here." He punctuates his sentence with a sharp slap to Jan's face. Jan's head bobbles to the left and right but he doesn't wake up.

"Come on Jan, its wakey wakey time!" He yells, "Wake. The fuck. Up!" Ryan lunges at the car battery with both leads in his hand. The four people holding Jan spring back and relinquish their grip on him. As the clips connect, the current shoots along Jan's body. He squeals in a high pitch at the top of his voice. Ryan keeps the pressure on the connectors for a few seconds more. Jan, still not fully conscious, scratches at the clips on his neck but immediately throws his arms wide open with the pain. Ryan removes the jaws of the jump leads from the battery and Jan is violently thrown against the back of the gurney now panting. The four holders return to their original positions. I swallow hard to prevent myself from vomiting on the glass. My legs feel weak.

Then beyond the glass window that separates this room from the performance area, some artificial strip lights flicker into life and another voice comes across the sound system. It is Mary's voice. She is singing as well, an echoed response to Ryan. "Stormy weather...stormy weather... since my man and I ain't together, keeps rainin' all of the time" I feel like I've entered a never-ending horror film. I squint to see what is happening in the other room, but struggle to work it out, so I quietly shuffle along the narrow viewing gallery, four or so metres, so that I am overlooking the performance space, still on the right side of the one-way mirror. And then I see what this is all about.

In an almost identical pose, Victoria is strapped into a wheelchair, now staring at Jan from the other side of the glass. She is seated in a more upright manner than he is and her hands are free. She seems considerably more alert, but her characteristic vigour and attitude has entirely vanished. She looks broken. She hasn't been physically beaten in the same way that Jan clearly has, and so I am wondering what she has been told about Pandi and Yo Yo. I can see

Romanov lurking in the background of the performance space and I double-take when I see what he is carrying in his hand. It is a machete. About a metre long with scuff marks on the blade and small amount of rust near the handle. He is prowling the length of the room with an impatient look on his face. The tension in both rooms is palpable.

Ryan and Mary talk to each other through the microphones in each room. They seem to be enjoying themselves. I do not physically hear anything through the soundproofed window but I continue to pick it up through reading as if I were there. Ryan is directing his words to Victoria. "It's lovely to see you Victoria. I was very sorry to hear about your parents. I know how very close you were." Ryan laughs and jabs Jan with his elbow as if he were part of the joke. Jan's eyes are now half open and he is beginning to appreciate where he is. Victoria's face is motionless. Ryan is relishing the power that he has. "And I suppose that it would be an even sadder day if you were to see your saviour, namely Hjarand, burnt to a crisp in front of your very eyes. That wouldn't be something to write home about. Although who exactly you'd write home to is somewhat academic now, given the circumstances. Don't you think?" Victoria lifts the heavy lids on her eyes and inspects his face with a look of contempt. Her eyes drift towards Jan. She had been avoiding looking directly at him before this point. It is a painful sight to accept. There is a silvery red burn mark around his neck and a thick clot of blood on his ear where Ryan cut him. His eyes are fluttering as he desperately attempts to climb back up into consciousness.

There is a growing sense of unease in the room, but not enough to dissuade Ryan and Mary from the path

they are on. "Okay Victoria!" Ryan announces loudly.
"This is what's going to happen. I'm going to carry on
electrocuting Jan until both his eyes fry and slip out of
his face like broken eggs. Or, and this is where you come
in, you tell me what else this technology, these implants,
are capable of." He pauses to draw breath. "Now, I
don't expect you to part with this secret easily, and you're
probably thinking that you might even just cross out of
here to a coral sandy beach and put your feet up. Well.
If you attempt to disappear for just one second. One tiny
second. Then I am going to take this scalpel" He picks
the knife up and dangles it in front of the window, "And
I'm going to drive it into Jan's scrawny stomach until
his intestines look like spaghetti." Victoria is frightened
and her chin wobbles. But she says nothing. "Ah, it
seems you need some help in understanding what your
silence does to Jan." And with that he attaches the leads
to the battery for the second time. Jan's squeal is utterly
horrendous. At least three of the group turn their heads
away from Jan's face, which is now contorted, stretched
and ruddy.

Having already seen what has been happening from the
previously darkened room, Victoria can't take any more
with heavy fists bangs on the glass. "I'll tell you. I'll tell
you!" she yells. Ryan points to his ears indicating that he
can't hear. Of course he can, in fact if he could be bothered
he would have picked up the thoughts in her head, but
he wants Victoria to do the work. "I will tell you," she
repeats sobbing into the microphone that Mary hands to
her. "But, I need to show you. It's the only way. It's not
a trick. Honestly." She is pleading with him. Without
hesitation and in a rather dramatic manner Ryan invites

her in to the mixing room. "Romanov! Please show the lady in" he says. Mary flips a handgun out from behind her back and levels it at Victoria's head, while Romanov uses the machete to saw away at the tape and rope that is pinning her to the wheelchair. As I watch this, I sense my thoughts becoming jumbled. It's like when a lot of people talk at the same time and it derails your ability to think, to hold on to your view. I don't know what's happening until I hear a thought edging its way into my mind. A thought that I haven't fathered myself. It seems to be coming from Victoria. She must have detected my presence in the gallery, although how, I have no idea, as no one else has. The suggestion is as bright and clear as a diamond. Without any introductory pleasantries Victoria speaks to me, "Kill Romanov, Mary and Sandeep. I will do the rest." The request causes my heart to race. I feel panic rising within me. I count the number of people in the room. There are ten people excluding Victoria and Jan. Ryan has a scalpel, Romanov a machete, Mary is holding a handgun, and I assume that other people are armed too. Victoria sends another message. "Don't worry. You'll be fine. Just cross in when I raise my hand." I am staggered by her calmness.

I wipe the sweat from the handle of my gun on my jeans and quickly pinpoint the positions of Romanov, Mary and Sandeep. Mary and Romanov are stood next to each other behind Victoria in the entrance to the mixing room. In some ways it will be easy to get to them. Tackling them is a different matter, but at least they are close to one another. Sandeep is leaning against the wall at the rear of the room, and difficult to gain access to, not least because he is effectively shielded by Ryan and the long gurney on which Jan is strapped to. This leaves the other people in the room that Victoria must have a plan for. Ryan troubles me most of all in this. He is unpredictable and hell bent on removing Jan and Victoria from the face of the earth. My eyes are drawn to Victoria, awaiting her sign. She has a final message for me, "When there is no one holding on to Jan, cross him out of here. To anywhere that's not here. Do you understand?" I do understand, but what does this mean for Victoria? Why isn't she suggesting that we all cross out of here together? I don't want to leave her here.

Victoria has all eyes on her as she starts talking, and as she propels her arm upwards, "The secret that THIS holds..." I realise that this is it. I focus with everything I have. I cross instantly. I fire two bullets, one into the centre of Mary's back, the other into Romanov's head. In both cases they lurch forward towards Ryan and I deliver another bullet into them both to make sure they stay down. I have no idea of what Victoria is doing but she appears to be moving at a remarkable pace around the room. Ryan is knocked backwards over the gurney by the combined weight of Romanov and Mary. The gurney pitches on its side and then clatters to the ground with wires, tubes and the portable monitor being dragged to the floor with it. The glass in the monitor smashes and this sprays out towards the two people that were holding on to Jan's right arm and leg. Jan's face and then body hits the floor causing a single slap sound followed by a deep, throaty grunt. He is now trapped under the trolley and is wriggling to break free. There are gunshots from the other side of the room. Victoria seems to have got hold of a weapon, and three people bounce off the wall and drop to the ground.

My attention goes to Sandeep and as I launch forward to get a clean shot at him, I skid on a stray fragment of glass. This throws me off balance and I veer off towards the glass panel between this and the next room. I hit the window awkwardly and I am ricocheted back towards the gurney and Ryan who is raising himself off the ground. Ryan falls back again this time with me on top of him. He seizes his opportunity and grabs at my head, twisting and pulling at my neck and hair, trying to lock my head in the crook of his forearm. He sees the gun in my hand, relinquishes the hold on me and lashes out with an open hand trying to catch the gun. I extend my arm as far as possible to put it of reach but he is incredibly strong and now is above me and a moment away from prizing the gun from my fingers. In the struggle, I see the scalpel that he was holding, that must have been knocked from his hand in the fall. It is lying to my side within arm's reach. Ryan is pulling at my gun that comes free in one clean tug. I snatch at the scalpel and as Ryan swings the gun in my direction poised to pull the trigger I belt him in the chest as hard as I can with my knee. This winds Ryan and distracts him for a second. I aim the knife at his throat and thrust it towards him. I am sure that is going to land but as it connects with his skin he throws himself to the side. The scalpel nicks his throat but misses the target.

I am unbalanced again and as I attempt a second lunge for Ryan, I feel an excruciating pain in my groin. Ryan has smashed the heel of his boot into me. I pull my legs up towards my chest in a reflex reaction, and Ryan swipes at the knife with his boot, but because this doesn't loosen my grip he stamps and then kicks at my hand until I feel the knife fly away and hit the wall. I am completely defenseless and in extreme pain. Ryan leaps onto my knees first with my gun in his hand. I twist my shoulder towards him so that as he lands he has to steady himself with his hand. He misjudges his positioning and his elbow buckles and his body crumples onto mine. We are face to face with one another. I smell his dank breath and his greasy forehead is pressed up against my cheek. In a quick movement that I do not expect Ryan folds his body around mine and twists so that he is behind me. He clamps me in a headlock, straps his legs around my waist and with his free hand pulls the gun to my forehead. The unyielding tip of the barrel is locked in position against my head. This is it, I think. This is how I die.

There are two other people left standing in the room. Victoria, who is stood to my right about five metres away, and Sandeep who is the same distance away but on the opposite side of the room. He is holding a gun that is pointed directly at Victoria. This is the second time that I have failed to kill Sandeep and the second time I have regretted it. Once again, I am unwittingly the engineer of our downfall. There are bodies piled up on the floor. Some have evidently been shot, for others it is not clear to me what has happened, but there is no sign of life. The look on Victoria's face is one of resignation. I have a gun to my head. She has another trained on her. Whatever move she makes one or both of us will get shot. If she goes for Sandeep, Ryan will kill me, and if she goes for Ryan, then Sandeep will finish us both off. Not even Micro Time Shifting will help us now. Victoria makes her final intrusion into my thoughts. She doesn't finish the sentence. The first two words are "Cross Jan" and then the blast of a gun fills my ears. I tense my body.

Ryan's head snaps back towards the door, and a fine shower of blood splashes into my eyes. With Victoria's thoughts in my head I throw myself forward to grab Jan. Sandeep is aiming his gun again at Victoria. I want to, but I don't hesitate. I feel a punch to the stomach, nausea then whiteness.

26

The Schoolhouse

It takes Jan a good few hours to overcome the effects of the anaesthetic, and the treatment that Ryan has subjected him to. We are holed up in the schoolhouse in Kibi. It is the last place that I want to return to but in the chaos it was the only place I could think of. Jan is seriously hurt and passes in and out of consciousness a couple of times before he becomes more stable. When he is strong enough we cross back to the recording studios but there is no one left alive. No sign of Victoria or Sandeep. I had tried to make sense of why Sandeep had saved Jan and myself, and more importantly why he had killed Ryan. It occurred to me that he might even have been responsible for removing other members of the organisation. Even for Victoria that would have been a lot of people to deal with single-handedly. Perhaps he just couldn't bear seeing Jan being murdered in front of his eyes. Or maybe he wanted no part of the organisation's new future.

We are both harrowed by the experience but before agreeing to part ways Jan makes a final request of me. An unwelcome request that comes with some urgency. Jan needs to locate Victoria. I understand this. And he needs to devote his energies to tracking her down. He has no idea what Sandeep plans for her but his instinct is that it involves revealing the remaining secrets of the technology. This in itself opens up some horrifying possibilities, with Sandeep capable of crossing in time as well as space. Jan also obliquely refers to some other properties of the system that he doesn't want Sandeep to have access to. Above all though, Jan knows that Victoria's time is short and he needs to act quickly, and while he is attending to this, there is no one able to complete some equally time-critical tasks in the fight against GenCo.

This is where the request had come in. Jan gives me the coordinates of three people; John Grimes, Pandora Fontainebleau and His Highness Sheikh Abdulla Al Khalif. He doesn't need to explain what I am meant to do. Jan can see that I 'm not happy about this to which he responds portentously "If not for me, then for Victoria."

Reluctantly. Very reluctantly. I agree. "You'll need a suit." These are his final parting words. And with that the schoolhouse is empty again.

27

The Motel

The motel room is exactly as I had left it. It had felt like months since I had carried out Jan's request, but of course in this time it was hours. The motel remains a strange home from home decorated with cheap paintings on the walls, a red and blue patterned carpet, a candlewick bed spread and heavy beige curtains. Apart from the technology currently sitting in the implant in my wrist and, by now, absorbed in some way into my system, this is all I have left. I consider visiting Pandi, although without good news to give her about Victoria I feel that it wouldn't be of any use. She's had quite enough trauma by now.

I limp into the bathroom and turn on the dial in the shower. Returning to the bedroom, I remove and lay down on the bed the suit that I had picked up in the store outside John Grime's offices. The cuts on my neck that I got from Carlos have been replaced with a fresh batch of grazes and scuffs from the fight with Ryan. It was only through suggestion that I had managed to draw attention away from these marks in my most recent set of 'meetings'.

I stand in the flow of the water and watch the colour as it becomes reddened. The top of my thighs and my balls are bruised and painful from Ryan's boot. It hurts to wash. I feel sick and sickened.

Coming out of the shower I start to feel more human. I towel myself dry and find a fresh set of clothes in the wardrobe. Fully dressed I sit on the bed and against my better judgment switch on the TV. Again I am greeted by a similar set of depressing images to the last time I looked. I never learn. As I sit down I notice the note that I wrote for Victoria. It sends a twinge down my spine. I reach out to it so I can throw it into the wastepaper bin but when I pick it up I see that it is different. In place of my writing, where I had explained where I could be found at the recording studios, there are someone else's words.

I bring the paper closer to my face to ensure that my sight isn't failing me. This is not what I wrote. With a puzzled look across my brow I read the note out loud "Robin. It's about Grace. We didn't tell you. And we're sorry. We did have our reasons. You'll understand them one day I hope and perhaps even find a way to forgive me. Perhaps you two recruits should rendezvous? Try the Stone Circle, Spittal of Glenshee, 27 May 2041. She'll be waiting for you. Love, Victoria"

28

The Day of the Anti-Capitalism March

Within a few hours of first twisting the ignition key in her Morris Minor the sun had fully risen, and the day had awoken. Grace had felt a sense of privilege at being the only car on the road at that time. The only person enjoying the wonder that nature had to offer. Soft light. Long shadows. Vast, slow moving clouds. Curvaceous green hills. Even though the air was crisp and biting, she had rolled down the window to feel in contact with her surroundings. The tip of her nose had become cold and her cheeks ruddy. Her skin tingled causing her to twitch her nose and stretch her face with repeated smiles to get the blood circulating. The tyres massaged the road as she made her way along country tracks to larger roads, to dual carriageways and eventually onto motorways, all pointing her towards London.

She'd flicked the radio on to accompany the rattling of the engine and the sound of cars that whizzed at high speed passt her. Her car had always made her laugh. Its incongruity in the modern age was its charm. It slowed everything down. Put whoever was in the car back in touch with the world that they were passing through. It eschewed the virtual experience of driving in a climate adjusted vehicle, with a smooth suspension, and turned it into something that was real, something that transported you into the moment rather than disconnecting you from it. She had briefly caught a glimpse of herself in the rear view mirror: her tousled dark shoulder length hair, her deep brown eyes reflecting the countryside as it flashed by, and the small horizontal scar on her left cheek. The same scar that Robin had gently traced with his finger the previous night, as they lay wrapped around each other in bed. She had struggled to tear herself away from Robin. Silly really, she had thought to herself, but she'd never been happier and everything about their life - the kirk, their vegetable garden, the market, the stone circle, their comical excursions to the local pub, the playfulness between them, the passionate evenings – all of it. Hard to leave, even if only for a weekend.

She'd arrived in London at around lunchtime and had barely had time to park her car before she had joined the march along the Strand with a group of old friends, most of whom she hadn't seen for years. The procession had trundled along the length of the Strand, looped around Trafalgar Square, stopping briefly to drop some red dye into the fountains beneath Nelson's Column, continued up along Charing Cross Road, Shaftsbury Avenue, to Pall Mall, the red road of the Mall leading to Buckingham Palace and then a sharp left towards the Houses of Parliament. There must have been ten thousand or more demonstrators. There were people singing, people chanting, people yelling, aggressive-looking people, bored-looking people, excited faces, people holding hands, huge homemade banners being waved high in the air, professional looking banners produced by the fringe political parties. Every now and then there would be a flurry of furious activity. There would be a sound of glass shattering, as a group would hurl a clod of concrete at the window of a bank. Police would leap out of vans and rush a particular portion of demonstrators. There would be bugles sounding, drums being banged, expensive cars would get rough treatment as the crowd swept through the streets.

At one point in the afternoon, when a group of police pushed into the line to arrest some seemingly harmless protesters, Grace was separated from her friends and she found herself walking with a woman who introduced herself as Victoria. They had got talking and hit it off from the outset. They talked politics, environmentalism and campaigning, and Grace told Victoria about her anarchist bookshop and her life in Scotland. Victoria explained that she was a hopeless idealist and the daughter of a merchant sailor. Eventually as the demonstration petered out, they both retired to a pub not far from the Houses of Parliament where they collectively put the world to rights. The drink flowed easily and although Grace had messaged her friends none of them arrived. For Grace it seemed like they'd known each other for years which, at least from Victoria's side, they had.

Victoria and Jan had been watching Grace for over three years, and long before Robin had arrived on the scene. Grace had been the most significant discovery that Jan and Victoria had made since they had begun their work. She represented a profoundly fortuitous collision of events. In the first place she fitted the regular recruitment profile in almost every respect. She was politically motivated, she lived off-grid in a remote area, and her close family ties had been severed due to the untimely loss of her parents. She had a clean police record and still possessed the youthful ambition and determination needed to join the outfit. But the principal reason why Grace had come to their attention was something quite different. She bore a striking resemblance to one of the remaining challengers to GenCo's future monopoly position – Scottish-born Maria Gutiérrez, Chair of the La Trobe Corporation. There was an uncanny physical similarity between them both. And it wasn't only about the way she looked. Grace's demeanor, the timbre of her voice, her posture, her facial expressions, her open personality, and even her scent, was like a facsimile of Maria. It was quite extraordinary. A coincidence. But to Victoria and Jan that were familiar with Maria and the role she played, it was an opportunity that couldn't be missed.

In the time zone that Maria existed, GenCo was poised to become the single largest and most influential company on the planet. To the average onlooker this wouldn't be obvious. There were seemingly scores of major players, suggesting a diverse spread of ownership and what might be regarded as healthy competition. But this was just camouflage, that came in the form of complex company structures, falsified legal papers, skillful media-handling, and a tight group of people at the centre of GenCo that guarded their affairs very effectively. With the exception of the La Trobe Corporation there was effectively no competition, and there was little that stood in the way of GenCo's scorched-earth philosophy to create wealth for itself regardless of the considerable human and natural cost. The La Trobe Corporation was no angel. In fact, it had profited greatly from the emerging over-population crisis, and it had participated in the lucrative scramble to set up the off-earth projects. It had mined and plundered resources relentlessly to drive its considerable technical capability. And while a takeover of La Trobe would remove the final plank in the opposition to GenCo, their technology is what GenCo really wanted to get its hands on.

Having spent years studying the course of history first hand, Jan had come to understand some very important lessons about what shaped it. After all, his entire journey had been an attempt to put it on a different path. And this is what he had learned; Every now and then history would arrive at a crossroads where the route that it took would depend on the outcome of a single event. Only a few of these would come along in each century. Moving forward in time this pivotal event would be near impossible to see, but retrospectively, after the event, everything would fall into place. Jan had the rare benefit of hindsight, or what he had come to call *theoretical hindsight* as it only really offered an insight into one of many theoretical possibilities. In all of this Jan had come to recognise that the decision to be taken by Maria was one of those pivotal moments and Grace had unwittingly become the instrument of change.

At the end of the evening Victoria and Grace had bustled out of the pub arm in arm, giggling and jabbering to one another. Like best friends. There was a liveliness to the night air and as they walked around they recognised some other protesters that they had marched alongside earlier that day. They nodded and smiled in a show of solidarity but before they could stop and chat, Victoria had ushered Grace away. Grace wondered fleetingly if she was a little possessive but the thought popped out of her head as quickly as it had arrived. Because Grace had lost contact with her friends she had nowhere to stay that evening and Victoria was quick to suggest that she stay at her apartment. Grace hesitated trying to collect her thoughts, which had become rather scattered since bumping into Victoria. But something made her feel that she could trust Victoria, so she agreed and they bounced along the pavement next to the river Thames admiring the houseboats and the party boats that chugged by. Victoria's apartment was in a Brutalist block of flats, faceless and imposing. She lived on the top floor overlooking the river. When Victoria swiped her card to the main doors they realised that the lift was out of order and so they climbed the urine stained stairwell at an impressive pace. Ten floors in just of couple of minutes. Their ascent was inspired by the desire to escape the potent smell. But for the remaining nine floors their exertion had turned them into old people, bent over and wheezing. The sight of each other just made them laugh all the more.

That evening they sat on the sofa chatting and sipping cocktails that Victoria had whipped up. It was in the early hours of the morning that Victoria had felt that the time was right. Grace would be relaxed enough to listen to her proposition but not too drunk to fall asleep. Suggestible enough too if she ran into trouble. She'd rehearsed her speech in advance and knew exactly what she needed to do. She had a lot to explain. The ability to cross. The dreadful future that they needed to change. The importance of Maria. And the role that Grace would need to play in the La Trobe Corporation. A lot for anyone to hear let alone at two 'O Clock in the morning. Grace listened intently feeling increasingly uncomfortable.

At the conclusion to Victoria's monologue Grace had paused, thinking about her options. Rather than addressing directly her serious concern about Victoria's claims that she could travel in time or transport herself across the planet in the "blink of an eye", Grace spoke instead about the plan involving Maria. She figured that this would be the least confrontational way to handle the situation, after all she was looking to sleep in Victoria's flat and she needed to take any heat out of the conversation. So delicately she had explained that she didn't think she was capable of playing the role of a company Chair and while she would of course want to help, she had her life just the way that she wanted it, and had no intention of leaving her new boyfriend. Grace had invoked Robin as a kind of talisman, an indication that she wasn't as alone and defenseless as she might appear.

But Victoria had been well prepared for her response. She had committed far too much to accept no for an answer. So without warning, or care, she did something that would cause everything to change. She held her by the wrists and crossed them both to the apartment that Grace had shared with her former boyfriend Juan many years before in Marrakech. Victoria wanted to prove that she was telling the truth, that she could in fact travel in space instantaneously. But not only that, Victoria could see that Robin might be a blocker in her mind, and she wanted to remind Grace about the transience of relationships. How wrong we could be about the people. How she had been wrong about Juan. But she knew this wouldn't be enough on its own, so with some persistent mental suggestions she temporarily dissuaded Grace of her feelings for Robin. Unhooked her from her attachment to him, just long enough to let Victoria in. And it proved easier than she expected. The exhausting drive down to London, the alcohol and the disorienting effect of her first crossing had all put Grace at a disadvantage.

With Grace in a more susceptible state Victoria made a decision from which there would be no return. Again, without warning or consent she took her by the hands, and moved her, on this occasion, forward in time. She needed to replace her fading thoughts about Robin with something that would galvanise her. She was transported to witness what was the most extreme experimentation facility that Victoria could find. Far worse than the horrors at Ameena. The site in question was a disused mining settlement at the foot of the Sangar-Haya mountain in North East Russia. It was a freezing, desolate and empty territory apart from the futuristic complex that clung to the landscape. It exclusively housed human experimentation labs with staff that barely observed the scant level of discipline and professionalism found elsewhere in the GenCo family. It was shocking to see, even for Victoria who had seen abuses of this sort on numerous occasions. Victoria needed to jolt Grace and help her see what her actions could prevent, and how impersonating Maria could save thousands of lives, just like those in front of her. Victoria had witnessed the human energy management experiments, the Lazarine Trials and a new low in human research which was a highly communicable sterilisation virus; another of GenCo's contributions to the population control agenda.

But in her haste Victoria knew that she had crossed a line, not because she had exposed Grace to some truly

hideous experiments, and not because she was wrong
about Grace being able to prevent some of these atrocities,
but because in transporting her forward in time she had
made it impossible for Grace to return to her own time
zone, and her own circle of influence. Victoria had told
herself that her single-mindedness and commitment to
the cause had got her carried away in the moment, that it
was the right thing to do, but she knew that what she had
effectively done was trap Grace in time, unable to return
to the Scotland, to the kirk, and to Robin.

From that point forward Grace never spoke again to
Victoria. Not a single word. Lost in time, and with no other
reason for being there, she took on the task of operating
as Maria Gutiérrez, doing so with a steely resolve that
surprised even her. For nine long months she impersonated
Maria, successfully resisting the takeover efforts of GenCo,
and in the face of repeated attempts that ranged from
barely concealed threats to attempts on her life. She held
off the opposition long enough to appoint a successor that
she knew would carry on her work. Jan had followed the
branches of the tree and had been able to see how history
had been altered by Grace's work, how GenCo's expansion
had slowed and how its reduced technological capability
had significantly diminished their pursuit of human
experimentation. Facilities like those found in Ameena
and at the base of the Sangar-Haya mountain range had
still been created, but others that Jan had borne witness to,
had simply disappeared. And other events and even places
that he had seen and touched had vanished without fanfare
or comment. They just didn't happen.

Victoria had been right about their method, of that
there was no doubt. But the big picture, the unbounded

exploitation of natural and human resources to provide for an ever-hungry and ever growing population, remained the same. People and Companies it seemed were becoming adapted perfectly to one another, united in their appetite for more, and complicit in their disregard for the cost. The branches of the trees that flourished may have changed, but from a distance it was business as usual. This had started to become clear to Jan and at the end of her nine months as Maria, Jan gifted to Grace an implant in her wrist along with the honest but unwelcome advice that she would never be able to travel back to join Robin. Any attempt that she made would mean that she, and possibly Robin, would be removed from history.

Grace spent years trying to make some form of contact with Robin. From afar she was a spectator in his life always unable to get through to him, and with Jan's warning ringing in her ears, always too afraid to get too close. She looked on as he frantically searched the wreckage of her Morris Minor – the driverless crash engineered by Victoria to put Robin off the scent. In the week after her disappearance she lay quietly crying to herself on the hillside as he re-visited the Stone Circle, waiting for something that was never going to happen. When he took his first job in banking after selling her bookshop and leaving the kirk, she would laugh until her stomach hurt at the absurd security questions he dreamt up for troubled customers. And she would feel a different pain in her stomach as he became entranced, however briefly, by Victoria and her own particular brand of flirtation. Over time she realised that she could push the boundaries of engagement a little more than she had imagined. And so when he became hopelessly lost in Marrakech and sunk to his knees in desperation, she checked-in to his Riad and with some subtle but strong suggestions dispatched the owner, Nehma, to his aid. Grace had left clues for him too that she was still around. Nehma wasn't the real name of the hotelier in Marrakech and neither was Ania, the waitress in the vegetarian café in Delhi. These names were the result of suggestions, both carrying the meaning of grace. She didn't expect him to get all or perhaps any of these but prayed that these echoes of her existence would at least remind him that he wasn't alone.

But her nightmares came at once when she had looked on from the airless crawl space above the recording studio. Fixed to the spot and unable to intervene in the unfolding bloodbath, she had known that she was helpless to stop Ryan or Sandeep from killing Robin. All her effort to protect him from afar, all this time, would come to nothing. She watched on as Robin struggled and kicked trying to loosen Ryan's grip on him, but she could see, as if in slow motion, the barrel of his gun lining up with his head, and Ryan extending his finger to pull the trigger. And then everything that Grace thought she knew about Victoria vanished in an instant. Every assumption she had about her collapsed.

Grace had tuned in to a conversation between the minds of Victoria and Sandeep. It lasted a moment, at least in regular time. But through Micro Time Shifting, Victoria had opened up a space of about thirty seconds. Unknown to anyone else in the room, she had effectively held time still while she put an offer to Sandeep. The deal that Victoria was offering stunned Grace. She was surrendering herself in exchange for the lives of Robin and Jan. It was a simple bargain, and an irresistible solution for Sandeep.

She would tell him everything that he wanted to know – the technology, its capabilities, all that she had done with Jan, everything. And afterwards he could dispense with her as he wished. And knowing Sandeep that would mean only one thing. But there was one proviso that accompanied the deal. The only condition. Sandeep did not understand the motivation behind it but accepted it nevertheless. Their agreement was that after Sandeep had shot Ryan, and Robin had safely transported himself and Jan out of the studio, Victoria and Sandeep would make a brief visit to the Southern Cross motel in Arizona, before moving on. Victoria had a message she needed to pass on. Just five minutes was her request. That was it.

Sandeep pulled the trigger of his gun and Ryan was lifted vertically from his squatting position and his body thrown against the wall. Robin reached for Jan and they both exited the scene. Victoria cast her gun to the ground and with his pistol trained directly at her head, Sandeep crossed her to the motel.

Victoria laid the note back on the bed, returned the pen to its position on the bedside table, and with her head hung low she was led away by Sandeep.

29

2041

I am standing at the edge of the Stone Circle. Holding a scrap of paper with Victoria's instructions scrawled on it. By clutching the note, I somehow imagine I am summoning Grace. This is what I am trying to do. I know it doesn't work like that but it doesn't stop me. The waiting is unbearable. It hurts just to be here. The last time I waited until the light had been snuffed out and my body shivered violently in the cold. And I was left alone.

As the minutes scrape by I wonder if it is just another one of Victoria's deceptions. I re-read the note for the hundredth time. I check the date. Again. It is correct. I recite the same unanswered questions that I have posed myself over and over. How could Grace have been a recruit? Where has Grace been all this time? How does Victoria know she will be here? As I wait, the doubts take hold. The excitement and optimism that I felt in the motel is beginning to slide away. I scan the horizon for movement for anything that tells me I am not alone. But nothing is returned. The Stone Circle is exactly as I remember it. Time is preserved here. The trees sway from side to side in the wind and the grasses shimmer. Sheep huddle together in far off fields. I cannot see the kirk but imagine it is as I left it. As we left it. A shudder creeps down my back and unconsciously I feel for the note that I have returned to my pocket. I scrunch the thinned paper and expel a glug of air. I find myself leaning against the rough bark of a tree. I do it for company rather than support. The stones stare at me questioning my presence.

And then, from the nothingness, as if carried in on the wind. Grace appears. There. Standing in front of me. Long after she had been assumed dead. Years since I have last seen that tiny scar on her cheek or the points of light in her deep brown eyes. Without a word, we reach out our arms and step forward. Our cold faces touch. The trees are silent as we draw each other closer in to our bodies. The clouds have halted their advance across the sky. I feel Grace's heart pounding through her jumper. It fills me with such joy that I don't have the words to express it. Still in silence we kiss, and I taste the saltiness of her tears and the warmth of her lips. I don't know if I am dreaming. I think I may be, but it is too real. Too exact. The feeling too strong to be conjured by such a frail being as I.

We sit down in the centre of the circle still holding on to each other, afraid that if we let go we will be lost again. I stare into her eyes. She is perfect. That is all that I can think of. She is perfect. We remain silent for a few minutes, not wanting to break the spell. And then for the first time in years I hear Grace speak. In the way that only she can. She tells me everything. All that has happened to her. All that she has seen. All that she has felt. I listen to her words, bathing in the sound of her voice.

The undulating sing song of her speech. The thousand tiny movements of her face that reveal so much about her. We start again. From a different place this time. And as different people from who we once were. As the skies darken we cross to the Kirk. Still uninhabited and more in need of repair than ever before. We return to our conversations. We are making sense of our separate and collective experiences. So much to reflect on. And so many possibilities. So many possibilities.

A thought is taking shape. We have been part of a struggle, but the script hasn't been our own. The strings operated at a distance by others. I turn to Grace, "I think we can do this differently."

A Pool of Diamond Bright Stones

We had crossed to a different place. Far beyond where we had travelled before. The mud and clay that had anchored our feet to the ground, relinquished its grip.

We had been hunting for peace. Tossing rocks aside and ripping the land apart as we did. We were tin gods, and the earth shuddered beneath our feet as we traded blows, and bore our wounds proudly. We hardened our resolve, ever more certain of our calling. Ever more sure of the debts that the world was owed. Mesmerised and emboldened by our dreams. Even as time itself began to run out, our battle weariness held us fast. Our heartache locking us in position.

And the murders. For that is what they were. These were expressions of our anger. Not of our love. They were our first and last mistake. These were the vines that coiled around our legs. Snaking under our armpits. Piercing the flesh of our ears and slithering across our eyes. Clutching us to the sodden belly of the earth and choking us with the smell of decaying leaves.

We were travelling thousands of miles, and leaping centuries, and all the while we remained exactly where we had started. The soil and slime of the undergrowth filling our lungs. Earthly ambitions filling our heads.

But this is not where we are now.

Our anger is useless here. The streams and ponds that are draped across the valley like a necklace of lustrous gems, think nothing of it. The vapour clouds from the waterfalls reflect a haze of colours back into our eyes, and our anger scatters. Drifting up into the deep blue of the sky. Beyond the atmosphere where the blue rolls into black.

Once we swung hammers to shape the molten face of the world. Jamming in rods to make eye sockets. Hollowing out a mouth and chiseling teeth that would sparkle and snap. But now we look upon it. Bearing witness. A conduit and carrier of its momentous presence. We are not bending it to our will or building an army to destroy. We are elves and humming birds drinking in the spectacle. Darting between performances with barely contained excitement. We collapse on our knees, doubled over, caterwauling with an insane laughter. Our cheeks glazed with tears, hands held high pleading for a moment, just a moment's reprieve to catch our breath.

Here, we are friends reconciled. Returned to one another. Delighting and tender in our renewed discovery.

We have no need for love here, nor any such judgements that would create an object to nourish our vanities. The mountains no more touch the clouds than our fingertips interlock as we paddle through shallow streams. The clouds and mountains are already together. Our hands already embraced. The cooling currents, and bleached pebbles, cradling our feet so that we don't stumble. Our feet warming the pebbles so that they do not shiver.

All these things. These manifestations. Shaped and expressed so differently. Coarse to the touch. Silken as we hold them to our faces. Muscular and soft. Panting and breathless. Foreign and familiar. Heavy with odour. Bereft of scent. So demonstrably. So unmistakably. So plainly. So determinedly, different. Separate. Apart.

But here. On this plain. In this place. No longer divided.

Underneath the water a tiger swims. Its fur, golden and white, and sleek against its face. A red Lily, like none we have seen before, is drifting to the bottom of the river. It twirls, and on one side playfully raising its petals to the tiger. A Can Can dancer teasing its audience. In slow motion and with eyes narrowed, the tiger swipes at the flower. Bubbles like pearls escape from the tiger's claws. Encircled by water the Lily is protected. With a tilt and a wave, it side steps the heavied enquiring paw.

On the horizon sits a burnished peach sun. A girl, face in hands, resting on her elbows, looking back across the ocean at this place. Her eyebrows lifted, half in veneration, half in devotion. A tick in the corner of one side of her mouth. A tiny smile of unqualified joy.

A bird, in flight, long before we see it, is carried above the sea by the wind. As it levels off, a few feet from the zig zag peaks of the ocean, it's shadow plays tricks on the surface. First a Pelican, then a snake. A conductor, fingers pressed into the water, directing a lachrymose requiem.

We are felted leaves, a luxurious steely green, sunbathing and wriggling as the wind massages our tips. The clouds yawn, ever so slowly stretching their arms and calming the sun's rays, dialing them down until we are in a cool blue shade. But we do not mind. We are in no hurry. Have no place to be. We have already arrived.

We take our seats at the edge of the pool. The branches of trees leaning in. The wind halting its play with the low grasses that lead to the meadows. Fish, intoxicated with anticipation, leap clean out of the water, gaining such height that for a second it looks as if they will keep going, making for the ice white stars peppering the crimson sky. There is a hush, a pause between heart beats, and then it starts. Diamond bright stones, resting deep underwater, begin the concert. A polychromatic light show.

Iridescent colours start to bubble up toward the surface. Yellows, the shade of Bumble Bee Stripes. The orange glow of a dog's eyes reflecting the moon. The phosphorescence of plankton framing the pool's edges in a shimmering celestial blue. And then colours of magenta, chartreuse, ultramarine, honeydew, neon green. Exploding from the water and skittering across the sky. And not just dazzling our eyes, but igniting the air with a charge, causing our hairs to stand on end, our toes to fizz. In reply, the Jasmine flowers releasing the most beguiling scent. The deer at the edge of the forest galloping side by side, heads held high. The cicadas applauding with rhythmic, pulsating trills. The mountains hum, a deep bassy grumble, like the soothing, hypnotic chant of monks.

Trickles of mercury water appear from the face of the mountainside, once slow moving streams and nursery springs, home to tiny minnows and Water Boatmen, start to run and then gush down the hills. The moss and bracken lying back, bathing in the silvery cascade. Granules of soil and stone climbing on board the ride. The soft stampede joining the waterfalls to create a curtain of colours, revolving, spiraling downwards, flashing and meeting the pool, showering us all with a fine, embracing spray. A delicate kiss on the eyelids. A wordless whisper.

We are Grace. We are Robin. We are all that cross into this realm. And that were here all along.